SPEECHLESS

Unfortunate Souls #1

MADELINE FREEMAN

laurealinde
publishing, llc.

"Now he is certainly sailing above, he on whom my wishes hang, and in whose hand I should like to lay my life's happiness. I will dare everything to win him…"

Chapter One

*E*ven here, thirty meters underwater, Aria couldn't shake the feeling someone was watching her—and for someone to see Aria swimming would be disaster.

The faded shafts of light that penetrated this far down illuminated nothing out of the ordinary among the ruins of Los Angeles. Still, the sense of unease didn't let up as she inhaled a breath of salty ocean water and exhaled through the gill slits on her neck.

Although no person technically owned the submerged remnants of the old city, it hadn't stopped salvage companies from staking informal claims—and defending against perceived incursions. But she and Alonzo had been careful. No one, least of all Cavanaugh and his thugs, knew they were here.

A voice crackled over the comm in her ear. "We should get going or we'll be late for work."

Aria twisted, the current lifting her hair and swirling it around her head like a halo of red tendrils. Alonzo Gonzales floated two meters away, striking the plastic-and-rubber fins on his feet at intervals to keep himself just above the ocean floor. No matter how many times Aria saw Alonzo's face obscured by his scuba gear, she never got over how silly and out of place he looked. But ever since he had come to live with her family a decade earlier, there were few places she went that he didn't follow—even if he had to look ridiculous to do so.

Instead of typing a message on her wrist comm, Aria pointed at the tunnel they were excavating and held up her right hand, fingers splayed. The only draw-back to her not needing a mask to breathe underwater was the limit to her communication.

Alonzo's sigh was so loud that the comm in Aria's ear dropped out for a second. "We've been at this for weeks. Another five minutes won't make a huge differ-ence. Let's go. We promised Melody we'd be on time for once."

Aria stuck her tongue out, the salt water tart on her taste buds. She sucked in a mouthful of the briny liquid and blew a stream in his direction, knowing it would disperse long before reaching him anyway. They still had plenty of time to return to the DuoCraft and make their way to the restaurant before their shift. When Melody had approached them about working tonight, Aria tried to talk her way out of it without giving too much away. She didn't want to get her sister's hopes up if this salvage didn't live up to their expectations. But, if this was all Aria hoped it would be, the credits from tonight's shift would pale in comparison to what they would find.

They were close to a breakthrough; she could feel it. Tingles sparked up her fingers whenever they were close to a discovery. Alonzo called it her "fish sense," but while he made light of it, she'd grown to trust the feeling over her years salvaging the flooded ruins of this once-thriving city.

She swam back into the tunnel, darting through the area they'd been widening for Alonzo and his scuba gear. With one press of a button, the flashlight in her wrist comm illuminated the layers of sea-slick brick. She squinted through crevices into the blackness, hoping to glimpse something—anything—beyond.

Just then, a high buzz reverberated through the water and sent a spike of adrenaline zipping up her spine. The noise was unmistakable.

A motor.

Panic flashed along her arms and legs, gathering like pinpricks in her palms and on the soles of her feet.

In the two weeks they had been working down here, no one had come anywhere close to their location. Tourist season didn't begin for at least another week, and there was only one company who ventured here anyway. Their "Ghosts of Old LA" tour combined special holographic renderings of the sea floor with a guide telling spooky, allegedly true stories. Two summers ago, one of their boats veered off course and came nail-bitingly close to one of Aria's scouting missions. Cover had been thin and if they had moved much closer, they would have seen her.

Unless this wasn't tourists. Were Cavanaugh's men patrolling the area?

Aria's feet slid against the flexible tunnel shielding as she backed her way out. Fingers closed around her ankle and, with Alonzo's help, she lurched the rest of the way out, her heart hammering in her chest. Alonzo floated into view, his wide eyes visible even behind his mask.

Aria peered into the water above them, scanning for any sign of the craft. The buzzing hum suffused the surrounding water, as if the sound were coming from everywhere at once.

"I don't have eyes on," Alonzo said through the comm. "We need to hide."

Clenching her jaw, Aria squinted through the shimmering slants of sunlight. The obvious place was their excavation tunnel, but her father's most important rule was to never hide where you're searching so no one gets suspicious and pokes around to discover your treasures when you're not there.

Actually, that was rule number two. The most important rule was for no one to see Aria in the water.

She and Alonzo typically selected a hiding place when they first arrived at a salvage site, but this part of the old city had been so decimated by the earthquake that there were no good options to choose from. Aria closed her eyes, calling up the routes they had taken on their different excavation runs. They always parked their DuoCraft in positions a kilometer away from the site, so she had entered the area from countless directions. Her mind's eye traveled along the meters and meters of black cord she had stretched along the ocean floor to act as a tether for Alonzo. The currents here were unpredictable and so strong they had threatened to whisk even Aria away on more than one occasion.

She imagined the various routes they had taken to reach this location—through parking lots filled with waterlogged internal combustion automobiles, past heaps of rubble with twisted steel beams stretching upward like skeletal fingers—trying to recall anywhere suitable. An image popped into her head—a seaweed-lined building due south that appeared largely intact. Aria opened her eyes and tugged on Alonzo's arm, beckoning for him to follow.

The persistent hum of the motor haunted them as they propelled themselves toward the building. Aria glanced up at intervals but still saw no signs of a boat. Her only comfort came from the fact that the motor sounded no nearer than it had before. It was quite possible the boat would pass by without coming too close.

As Aria led the way over a high kelp bed, the building came into view. Although at least half of the structure had collapsed, the front appeared unscathed. She kicked her feet behind her, darting toward the front door. It was only half on its hinge, but the opening still wasn't large enough to pass through. The accumulation of more than a hundred years' worth of sea life and sediment drift made it nearly impossible to edge the door open further.

Aria braced her feet against the side of the building and pulled at the door with all her might. Whether it was tourists or Cavanaugh's men drawing near, she couldn't let anyone think there was anything interesting about this particular stretch of ocean floor.

She had managed to open the door several centimeters when Alonzo gripped her shoulder.

"They're gone," he said.

Aria paused, straining her ears. He was right. The motor's buzz had faded until it was an indistinct hum that blended with the muddled sounds of the ocean.

Alonzo hitched his thumb over his shoulder. "We should head back to the Duo."

A measure of the tension coiling Aria's muscles drained. She nodded, but when she began to follow him back the way they came, a flash of light caught her eye. She spun around, peering into the dark interior of the building. Her gaze followed a strip of light filtering in through a small hole in a translucent window. A palm-sized orb glittered blue and red beneath the remnants of a table.

She had wiggled through the small door opening

before Alonzo realized she wasn't following. "I thought we were leaving."

Aria didn't bother glancing back at him. The boat was gone, and she would only be a second.

Her fingers closed around the edge of the table and she pulled herself toward the cracked tile now smeared with sea slime. Trinkets littered the floor—picture frames decorated with seashells, sunglasses, aluminum license plates—but Aria fixed her attention on the glassy ball that caught her eye in the first place. A rusty red color dominated one half, interrupted by the occasional vein of blue and a cap of icy white. The other half was almost entirely opposite—mostly blue with red peeking up in some areas. A tremor passed through her fingers as she reached for it. She had several similar miniatures at home, but each of them represented a different epoch than the one frozen here.

A zing of electricity shot up her arm when her palm touched the sphere. As always, it was as close as she had ever come, yet exactly as far away as she had ever been.

"Aria." Alonzo's tone held a hint of warning.

She tucked the globe inside the mesh bag on her back and swam back toward the door as she swung the pack back over her shoulders.

Alonzo barely waited for her to squeeze through the door gap before seizing her bag and peering through the mesh. He released her and shook his head.

"Another Mars? Don't you have a dozen of those at home?"

She pressed her lips together but didn't type a response. No matter how many times she tried to explain her collection of planet figurines, Alonzo couldn't seem to wrap his head around her obsession.

"We should leave while the coast is clear." Alonzo pointed toward the surface. "If that was Cavanaugh, we want to be long gone in case he doubles back."

Aria nodded and the two of them swam to the salvage site where Alonzo could clip himself to the lead line for safety on the way back to their boat. Instead of swimming ahead, Aria stuck close to her adopted brother, her muscles coiled and ready to react on a moment's notice. Despite straining her ears, she couldn't detect a hint of a motor. Still, she couldn't shake the feeling she was being watched.

Chapter Two

*A*ria's father towered over her in the restaurant's cramped receiving area. Sweat from working in the hot kitchen beaded his brow. But she'd seen this flush in his cheeks too many times to believe it had only to do with standing too close to the cooktop. "Forty-seven minutes late."

Aria cringed at the disappointment in his voice.

"It wasn't her fault," Alonzo said, redirecting their father's attention. To his credit, he didn't flinch under the taller man's gaze—but it wasn't much of a surprise. Too often Alonzo had been in this exact position, standing beside Aria when his adopted father expressed his displeasure. "We would have been on time, but right when we were getting ready to leave, some stupid tourists got lost overhead and it wasn't like we could surface with them—well, you know."

Aria kicked Alonzo's foot, but it was too late—the

damage had been done. Her father's sea-green eyes swiveled back to her, their depths turning stormy. "Tourists? Where were you scavenging?"

Aria bit her lower lip as her mind spun to come up with an answer close enough to the truth that her father wouldn't sniff out the lie. "We anchored the boat on the north side of the usual salvage grounds." She kept to herself the fact she and Alonzo had been considerably west of the boat.

"Dad, we're getting backed up in here!" Harmony, Aria's older sister, called from deeper within the kitchen.

Her father harrumphed, crossing his arms over his chest. "This conversation isn't over. Nothing you can scavenge is worth getting caught. Period."

Alonzo nudged Aria with his elbow, but she ignored him. They agreed when they decided to attempt this salvage they would keep it to themselves. No use getting everyone's hopes up if it turned out to be a bust.

Melody and Harmony had been co-managing Under the Sea, Old LA's top-rated restaurant, for a decade, but they didn't own it. Any time they approached the owner, Enzo, about buying him out, he turned them down. But two months ago, an investor in New LA made Enzo an offer too substantial to refuse. As a courtesy, Enzo gave Melody and Harmony three months to come up with a counter offer. But scrimping, saving, and donating wages earned from shifts at the restaurant—even in a family as large as Aria's—hadn't brought them anywhere near their goal.

But if they found what they hoped they would, not only would they have enough to surpass the investor's offer, Aria and Alonzo could afford a new DuoCraft designed for long-distance voyages. Maybe Aria would never make it to Mars, but she refused to be stuck in Old LA for the rest of her life.

"I won't get caught, Dad," Aria assured him. "I'm careful. Just like you taught me."

The muscle in her father's jaw jumped the way it always did when she referenced the fact that everything she knew, she learned from him. In the years since he transitioned from salvaging for a living to being the head cook at Under the Sea, he had become increasingly leery of the life he left behind. "Times are changing. People... They're more afraid than they used to be. Quicker to jump to conclusions. I see it on the news streams all the time." His lips twitched. "It's safest if you keep to shore until tourist season is over."

Aria gaped. "You can't be serious."

He narrowed his gaze. "Do I look serious?"

She opened her mouth, but before she could mount a defense, Harmony called for their father again. This time, he returned to the kitchen to answer his older daughter's summons.

Aria didn't suck in a full breath until her father disappeared back into the bustling kitchen.

Alonzo raked a hand through his dark brown hair,

the corners of his mouth quirking in an attempted smile. "Well, that could've been worse."

Aria shook her head as she pulled an apron off the wall hook. "Really? How could that have been worse?" She traded the black laces behind her back and looped them into a bow in the front.

Alonzo's brow furrowed. "He didn't lock you in a tower," he suggested after a moment.

"Yet." Aria opened a metal drawer and pulled out two tablets—one from slot seven and the other from slot twelve, which she handed to Alonzo.

He tucked his tablet into the front pocket of his apron. "Do you think he's right?"

The question clashed against Aria's ear drum like a discordant note on a piano. "Are you kidding?"

He didn't meet her eyes. "It all worked out today, but what if that boat came closer? What if someone saw you?"

Aria tugged at the ends of her hair, ensuring it covered her neck. "No one ever has."

"And that means no one ever will?" Alonzo held her gaze. "We should take it easy for a few days. Or if we go back, you could wear gear so if someone—"

Aria wrinkled her nose. "No way. That canned air makes me sick. Besides..." She paused, rubbing her neck, feeling the soft ridges behind her ear. While nearly invisible when she was on dry land, her gill-slits opened of their own volition when she was in the water. If someone got close enough to them when they were submerged, they would see the evidence of her aberration even if she wore full scuba gear.

"We'll figure it out." Alonzo squeezed her upper arm. "I'll hate it as much as you if we can't help Harmy and Mels buy this place, but if it's out of our hands, so be it. And if we have to wait a few months to finish the job to make sure you're safe, I'm all for it. The world will still be there for us to explore."

Aria sighed and nodded, but she couldn't coax a smile her lips. On the one hand, she knew he was right. If they had to delay their plans to explore the world for another month, another six months, another year, it wasn't as if the sights, sounds, and locations would cease to exist. But she felt as if she might. Being cooped up in Old LA, especially with the oppressive presence of out-of-towners and without the outlet of the ocean, made her feel as if she might crawl out of her skin.

She stuck close to Alonzo as they wove their way through the kitchen, dodging dishwashers and other wait staff, but before she reached the swinging door to the dining room, a small hand hooked her elbow.

"Auntie Aria!" squealed Sera, Melody's daughter. She jumped up and down with the joy only a seven-year-old could possess. "When are we going swimming?"

The smile that had eluded her moments ago twisted her lips. "You know that's up to your mom."

Sera was born with the same ability as Aria and her father. But since both Melody and her husband were conforms who lacked any aberration, they had been hesitant to allow Sera out in the ocean.

"But *Auntie.*"

Aria touched the tip of her niece's nose. "I'll talk to her. I know a few secluded beaches north of here where no one ever goes."

Sera darted forward and squeezed Aria around the waist. "Thank you!" With a final happy leap, she streaked back to the small office off the kitchen.

Still smiling, Aria pushed through the door to the main dining room, but the scene that greeted her stopped her short. The restaurant was packed, with at least a dozen people crammed in the small waiting area between the door and the hostess podium. Guilt coiled in her stomach. They weren't usually so busy on a weeknight.

Her sister Cadence waved her over to the front of the room. Her blonde hair was swept up into a messy top knot. She only ever pulled it up when she was frazzled, claiming the hair around her shoulders made it hard for her to think.

"Good, you're here." Cadence spoke with genuine relief, not the irritation that had laced their father's tone. "I already sent Alonzo to his section. I need you on section two. Jamie had to leave and I've been covering her section and mine for way too long."

Aria nodded. "Of course. I'll—"

Cadence squeezed her upper arm. "And avoid Piper as long as possible."

Aria sighed. Like she needed *that* reminder. It was standard procedure for Aria to avoid that particular sister. Although Piper was closest in age to Aria—only seven years older, to Cadence's nine years, Harmony's eleven, and Melody's thirteen—she was the sister Aria got along with least. While Piper didn't hold any position of authority over her at the restaurant—they were both waitresses—she never missed an opportunity to reprimand Aria for the slightest errors.

Pinning a practiced smile to her face, Aria headed to section two to check on her customers. Patrons at most tables seemed surprised when she informed them she'd be taking over for her sister, their expressions making it clear they wouldn't have noticed the switch if she hadn't pointed it out. She wasn't sure how they couldn't notice. Cadence was taller by several inches and her hair was blonde where Aria's was red. Then again, she was certain she could have sat down in the booth with at least a couple groups and they wouldn't have given her a second glance. Their eyes were glued to the screens installed on the wall, and each booth in her section was tuned to a different view of the same stream.

The Colonists.

It wasn't anything new. Since its premiere four years ago, The Colonists had been a must-watch stream. Over time it had expanded from a single view of the first settlers on the terraformed planet to multiple ones that followed different groups, targeted to different ages and interests. It would be difficult to find anyone on Earth who didn't tune in at least a couple of times a week to check up on favorite characters, and with the birth of the first "Martian" baby imminent, people were more obsessed than usual.

But based on the conversations she overheard between taking orders and refilling drinks, the big news tonight was the possibility of the streams going dark for a day or two because of high solar activity. She fought the urge to linger by several tables to find out more about the threatened shutdown, imagining Piper's gaze on her any time she considered it.

By the time Melody and Cadence ushered the last of the night's patrons out the door, Aria was exhausted. Spending twelve straight hours battling strong currents in meters-deep icy water invigorated her, but just a few hours at the restaurant had her running on empty.

She was wiping down tables with long, practiced strokes, when Piper appeared. Her sister leaned up against the side of the booth, arms crossed over her chest, pale blue eyes narrowed in the way she seemed to reserve only for Aria.

"Well?" Piper arched her eyebrows.

Aria finished wiping down the tabletop before turning to face her sister. "Well what?"

"You were late. Again."

Aria brushed past her and began to wipe down the next table. "So?"

Piper's cheeks flushed. "Do you have a reason?"

Aria slapped the rag down on the table. "You're not my boss, Piper. I don't have to explain myself to you."

"It's a good thing I'm not your boss. Because, family or not, I would've fired you a long time ago. You made the night harder for everyone because you can't be bothered to show up on time."

Spinning on her heel, Aria stalked toward the kitchen, desperate to put space between herself and her sister. She was never in the mood for one of Piper's lectures, but her exhaustion made the prospect of dealing with it even less appealing.

Piper didn't take the hint. Seconds after Aria entered the kitchen, her older sister spilled in behind her. "I'm not done talking to you."

"But I'm done listening. I'm sick of hearing you say the same things over and over."

"Then *change*," Piper snapped over the clink and clatter of plates and silverware, the ebb and flow of conversation, and the drone of the dishwasher. "You'll be eighteen next month. It's time to stop acting like a child."

Aria's toes curled in her shoes as she rounded on her sister. "Maybe you should stop treating me like one, then!"

The noise in the room ceased, leaving only the constant hum of the dishwasher. The kitchen door swung open and Harmony rushed in, eyes wide. When she took in the scene, she let out a breath. "Again?"

Aria clenched her jaw but didn't tear her eyes from

Piper. She didn't want to give her sister the satisfaction of being the last to look away.

Harmony glanced passed them at the rest of the staff. "Back to work." She didn't speak again until the cleanup noise swelled once more. "How many times do we have to go through this?"

Piper rolled her eyes as she turned to their older sister. "I don't know. How many times is she going to be an hour late for her shift?"

"Forty-seven minutes," Aria muttered.

Harmony held up a hand to quiet Aria. "I agree that Aria being late is something we need to deal with, but when I say 'we,' I mean me and Melody. You're not Aria's boss. Stop pretending like you are."

Piper opened her mouth, but Harmony talked over her. "Go home, Piper. Aria will clean your section."

Aria dug her nails into her palm, but managed to keep her expression as impassive as possible while Piper smirked with satisfaction.

Harmony waited until Piper was out of earshot before speaking again. "She's got a point, you know."

Aria sighed. "Not now, Harmony, please."

Harmony crossed her arms over her chest. "This isn't your sister talking, it's your boss." She held her younger sister's gaze and Aria blinked first. "I get that waiting tables isn't your calling. The restaurant is my dream, not yours. And I appreciate how much you've been helping out. But you have to think about how your actions affect other people."

Aria's cheeks burned and she kept her eyes glued to the floor. Getting told off by Piper was par for the course, but hearing disappointment in Harmony's voice was more than she cared to deal with. "I should get to work since I've got an extra section to clean up."

Harmony pressed her lips together before nodding.

Aria wiped down the rest of the tables in her section and started on the ones in Piper's, doing her best to clear her mind as she worked. She couldn't be mad at Harmony for what she said. Piper, on the other hand...

Most of the other wait staff had filtered out of the dining room by the time Aria filled up the bucket to mop the floor, so she turned on the main screen and switched to her favorite Colonists stream. As usual for this time of day, most of the teens were at the Hub, the one building large enough to accommodate the island's two-hundred person population. About once a month, the whole community gathered in the building to discuss the Colony's progress, but in the evenings, the teens used the space as a VR gaming spot. Tonight, they were playing human foosball.

As she mopped, Aria scanned the screen until she spied the one figure she sought. Enrique Martinez. Her heart skipped as it always did when she glimpsed his smile.

Since The Colonists premiered, Aria had felt a connection to Enrique. He was always up for an adventure, like hiking through the forests at the base of the volcano that dominated the island, or climbing to the top of the tallest pine tree he and his friends could find. But he also knew his limits, unlike some other guys his age, one of whom broke his arm a few months after the Colonists arrived by trying his luck on a makeshift zipline that snapped before he made it more than two meters.

As she continued to clean the floor, Aria slipped into a familiar fantasy. She's on the Colony with Enrique and they strike off to explore the rest of the Martian frontier together. They set sail in a DuoCraft heading toward the setting sun. As the sky darkens, they watch Phobos and Deimos streak across the sky and pick out the pale blue dot of Earth among the stars. When a comet streaks overhead, Enrique cups her cheek in his hand and leans in to kiss her.

So lost in her daydream was Aria that the special news report alert made her jump. The mop handle slipped from her fingers and clattered to the ground.

She stalked toward the screen to turn it off, grumbling as she went, but three words made her freeze in her tracks.

Aberration detention facility.

The news anchor, a man with a strong jaw and a precise haircut, stared straight at the screen, a glimmer of excitement in his eyes, as he continued his report. "The facility receives its first prisoners tomorrow morning. There are one hundred seventy-six aberrations in prison throughout the country, but experts warn this number reflects only those who used their aberrant abilities while committing their crimes. As there is no reliable test to identify aberrations, there may be more within the prison system who are unknown."

The camera angle changed to a wider shot to show a woman with sleek black hair next to her co-host. "That's right, Magnus. While some believe isolating aberrations in their own facility will ensure the safety of incarcerated conforms, others fear concentrating violent aberrations in one place is dangerous and—"

Aria blinked as the screen went blank. Her father stood by the bar, arms crossed over his chest. "Now do you see?" He gestured to the screen. "Detention facilities. How long before they round up any aberration they find, whether or not they've committed a crime?"

She opened her mouth, but no sound came out.

"Promise me you'll stay out of the water until tourist season is over," he pressed.

Gulping, Aria nodded.

Her father held her gaze for another moment before turning and pushing through the swinging door back into the kitchen.

The door was still swinging when Alonzo came through it. He crossed to Aria, his brow creased with concern. "You okay?"

She glanced over his shoulder to be sure they were alone. "We have to finish the job. Tomorrow."

The corners of his lips twitched. "But you told—"

"If we finish this job, we'll never need to salvage

again. We'll have enough to help Melody and Harmony buy this place. Plus we can go anywhere in the world."

Alonzo rocked on the balls of his feet. "What about... I mean, what if Trent's right about the detention facility? Maybe it's best if we take a break."

She squared her shoulders. They hadn't gotten this far to give up when they were so close to a breakthrough. "I'm doing this, with or without you. Are you in or not?"

He glanced over his shoulder toward the kitchen before taking a half step closer. "You know I am. And I know Trent is a little paranoid about this stuff, but it doesn't mean he's wrong. On the streams they mentioned the capacity of that facility. If there are only one hundred seventy-some known aberrations in prison, why can it hold a thousand?"

The hairs on Aria's arms stood up, but she gritted her teeth, determined to ignore the implications. "No one's ever come close to catching us. One more time out there won't change that. And then we'll have all we need to help Melody and Harmony *and* travel the world."

Alonzo sighed. "You're right."

She forced a smile. She sure hoped she was. If she was wrong and Cavanaugh caught her salvaging, one of the thousand spots at the aberration detention facility would be hers.

*a*s the ball streaked toward him, Enrique Martinez lunged sideways as far as his sliding bar would allow before winding up and kicking with all his might. The bright orange sphere streaked toward the goal until Maria Gould slid in front of it. The ball ricocheted off her legs and Enrique readied himself for another kick, but Ravi Patel glided into position and launched the ball into the black rectangle at the end of the field.

"Goal!" Shira Maddox raised her arms triumphantly before winking out of sight.

One by one, the other players on the foosball field disappeared. Ravi, Maria, Tanis, Oscar. Gone.

Enrique pressed the power button on his VR goggles and the game field dissolved into reality. He and his friends stood in the middle of the Colony's all-purpose meeting house. He had spent more nights here at the Hub than he could count, and he knew every ding in the wall, every worn-down piece of flooring, and every joint in the ceiling as well as he knew the backs of his own hands.

Ravi was still shouting about his game-winning shot. "Did you see that? It was like slow motion." He arced his hand through the air. "Who's up for another round?"

Oscar Davila groaned. "I'm sick of foosball. Can't we do something else?"

Enrique scanned the faces of his friends. Twenty-eight sets of eyes squinted with concentration as they considered the question.

"We haven't done bowling in a while," Maria suggested. "Or—ooh—how about baseball?"

Gabe Tremblay tipped his head back and let out a half sigh, half growl. "All we ever do is play VR games. I'd give anything for a little excitement."

Tanis Vasil cleared her throat and pointed to the ceiling. As the daughter of the Colony's chief communications officer, she was always quick to remind them of the ever-present cameras recording their every movement and beaming the images back to Earth. It was an unspoken rule to limit complaining of all kinds, but especially about boredom.

As if they could forget about the cameras. Although none of them had ever seen the streams broadcast to people back on Earth, they knew about them. Originally pitched as educational, over the years they evolved into entertainment for those back home. Colonists living the most entertaining lives received rewards like an extra treat ration or a reprieve from sanitation duty.

Gabe snorted, waving away Tanis's concern. "You and I both know all the streams are focused on the Tanakas."

Oscar grinned. "You're right. Everyone on Earth's waiting for that baby to drop."

Shira rolled her eyes. "Nice."

"You know what I mean." Oscar rubbed his hands together. "Maybe it's time we hike up the volcano?"

As Oscar and Gabe headed toward the back corner of the Hub to make plans, Enrique dug his fingernails into his palms to keep from joining them and two dozen others who congregated together. While he agreed with Oscar and Gabe about being sick of doing the same things day in and day out, he had already hiked up the volcano as far as he could, until the loose, pebbly soil threatened to send him slipping back down the way he came. He wasn't sure what he wanted to do, but he knew it wasn't that.

Maria sighed as she watched the group in the corner. "Any takers for bowling?"

"Sure," Shira said, while Jade Osborne, Louis Benoit, and Noam Levi put their VR goggles back on.

"Can't," Tanis sighed. "Told my mom I'd pick up her slack on sanitation so she could help get everything ready for the shower."

Ravi blew a raspberry. "Good luck with that."

Tanis snorted. "Yeah, thanks."

"I'll help." The words escaped Enrique's mouth before he weighed them.

A chorus of *oohs* rose among his friends. Tanis rolled her eyes, but Enrique thought he detected a flush in her cheeks. He bit the insides of his cheeks. The last thing he wanted was to give Tanis the wrong impression about his motivations.

"Real mature, guys," Enrique muttered. "Have fun bowling."

Tanis didn't speak until they were on the path outside the Hub. "You don't have to do this. I mean, who's crazy enough to sign up for extra sanitation duty?"

"Besides you, you mean?" Enrique offered a smile.

Despite what Ravi and the others might think, his offer to help wasn't the first step toward couple status with Tanis. In the four years since they'd been on the Colony, nearly everyone his age had been in a pairing —or several—but those kinds of relationships didn't interest Enrique. He didn't want to be with someone for a ratings spike. If he ever dated one of his fellow Colonists, it would be because he was serious about wanting to be with her.

"So," Enrique said as they shuffled down the path, "any news from back home?"

Tanis released a heavy sigh. "I should've known that's why you tagged along."

Enrique's stomach clenched at the disappointment in her tone.

"Sorry to let you down," Tanis said, her voice back to normal. "All my dad's been mentioning for days is the solar flares."

Enrique nodded. When scientists had terraformed Mars, they created an artificial magnetosphere to protect the planet from typical solar ejections, but no one was sure how it would stand up against the prolonged storm caused by the higher-than-usual solar activity.

"But Dad said something today about the possibility of having to shut down the streams," Tanis continued.

Enrique stopped in his tracks. "Shut down the streams? Like, not broadcast our lives every minute of every sol?"

Tanis turned to face him, her nose wrinkled. "Not forever. But for a day or two sometime within the next week. If at all." She gave a soft snort. "How much you want to bet the streams shut down just as Samara goes into labor? People back home would go bonkers."

She continued hypothesizing how viewers would react as she walked down the path. Although Enrique walked beside her, he didn't hear anything she said. His mind spun as the news electrified every neuron in his brain.

The streams didn't simply broadcast their lives. Enrique was sure there were people employed to monitor every camera feed to keep tabs on what every person on the Colony was doing at all times. A few years back, Oscar, Noam, and Gabe planned to take the transport shuttle on a joyride around the island. Even though, according to them, they had hatched their scheme in secret, security officers had stopped them before they got more than fifty meters from the supply depot. Whenever anyone tried to break any of the Colony's rules, someone back on Earth would notify security within about thirty minutes.

But with no one on Earth monitoring them, there was almost no limit to what they could do. Or where they could go.

For the first time in years, excitement electrified his senses. A shadowy plan took form in his mind. Enrique's fingers twitched with the desire to scroll through topographical maps and double-check security rotations. He would finally have his adventure.

Or die trying.

Chapter Four

*A*ria cut the Duo's engine as Alonzo threw the anchor overboard. The first rays of sunlight glittered off the surface of the water, dancing to its unceasing rhythm.

Usually, the sight would fill her with peace. But today, the scope and mystery of the water chilled her more than any submarine current.

They were hundreds of meters from where they'd stopped yesterday, but Aria couldn't shake the feeling someone would spot their craft and figure out what they were doing. The boat yesterday had been a fluke— an overzealous tourist with no idea how to navigate on the water. That was all. It had to be. The alternative— that Cavanaugh knew what they were doing—wasn't an option.

Aria sucked in a deep breath of salty air to shake off the remnants of sleepiness that clung to her.

"Are you sure you had enough to eat?" Alonzo asked around a mouthful of breakfast burrito.

She glanced over her shoulder. Alonzo's dark hair still stuck up in the back, but his eyes were bright and alert the way they always were when he was close to excavating new treasure. He looked more like the nine-year-old boy who had first moved in with her family than the nineteen-year-old he was now. "Yeah, I'm good."

With effort, he swallowed. "A hundred percent?" He held up the last half of his breakfast. "The chorizo is fantastic today."

She snorted. "I'm fine."

He shrugged. "Your loss."

Aria turned back as he took another bite. Would there ever come a time when Alonzo didn't look out for her? Aria's mother died only months before her father took Alonzo in, and although Alonzo had spent years living on the streets of Old LA and fending for himself, he quickly carved out a role of protector in his new family. Since he no longer had to spend his time keeping himself alive, he had redirected his attention to making sure Aria didn't lose herself in grief.

Not a day passed when she wasn't thankful for him, even on the occasions when his brotherly love came in the form of a half-eaten burrito.

She pulled off her tee-shirt and jeans, revealing the second skin of her hydrophobic swimsuit. After she stowed her clothes in the compartment beneath the back bench seat, she swung her mesh bag onto her back and pressed her earpiece in place. Alonzo pushed the green button that opened the Duo's back door. She squeezed past him onto the craft's open-air stern. "I'll go get the lead line. Think you can be ready by the time I get back?"

Alonzo swallowed the last of his breakfast and licked his fingertips. "For sure."

Aria's lips twitched. "So, there's a solid fifty percent chance?"

He wrinkled his nose, and she grinned before stepping onto the gunwale and diving into the water. The sides of her neck prickled as her gill slits opened, ready to begin their work. She passed through the sun-warmed upper layers and slipped into the cooler, darker depths below.

As she descended, the ruins of the old city came into focus. No matter how much time she spent in this submerged, forgotten world, she never lost her sense of wonder as she swam through it. The people who had lived here had been going about their normal lives when one earthquake changed everything.

Only a handful of walls remained upright amid the piles of rubble, jutting up defiantly as if mocking the disaster that wiped out the rest of the area. Sponge clung to them and bright-colored fish darted in and out of empty windows.

Aria swam for a dozen meters before spotting one such wall that resembled a triangle. She dove toward the seafloor and followed a fallen light pole that had been nearly swallowed by a bed of seaweed, stopping when she came to the remnants of an old automobile. A thick black cord twisted around the steering wheel— one of several lead lines Aria had stretched out to help guide Alonzo to their project. The currents weren't bad this far out, but the closer they moved toward the heart of the old city, the more unpredictable the water became. Even with the aid of his flippers, Alonzo was no match for the undertow.

She slipped her pack off and reached in for Alonzo's tether. After clipping it to the lead line, she swam back to the Duo, spooling the rope out behind her.

Her head broke the surface of the water and she took in a deep breath. Her lungs burned, as they always did, from the abrupt change. "You ready?"

Alonzo leaned out of the Duo's open hatch, his wetsuit and oxygen tank in place. He held his mask in his hand. "Yeah. What took you so long?" The nonchalant lilt of his voice was marred by a mild breathlessness that assured Aria he had only just finished.

"You changed out your air supply from yesterday, right?"

The corner of his mouth quirked. "Of course."

Aria lifted an eyebrow. "Really?"

He adjusted his mask and brought it to his head. "Trust me. I've got plenty of air."

"Plenty of hot air," Aria muttered as Alonzo pulled the mask over his face.

Less than a minute later, Alonzo was in the water. "Colder than yesterday."

She splashed him but didn't disagree. She learned years ago that her tolerance for water temperature was much different from his—or even than her sisters'. The only one who seemed as unaffected as her was her father, but it had been years since he'd gone for a swim with her.

Alonzo kicked his way to her, and she clipped the tether to his suit before submerging and following the rope toward the center of the ruins.

She kept track of Alonzo as they moved toward what was once the heart of the city. He wasn't as quick as she was, but she didn't mind. The leisurely pace gave her the opportunity to relax, to slow her breathing and heartbeat to match the rhythm of the ocean.

When they reached the site, Aria slipped into the dark passage, tapping her wrist comm until a stream of light beamed around its edges. It cast a yellow glow in the cramped space around her, causing the shadows to move like specters as she worked.

Time turned fluid as she removed chunk after chunk of debris and passed it back to Alonzo to dispose of. With each chunk of rubble she freed, hoped swelled in her, but each time the path remained blocked.

The small bits gave way to one hunk of concrete as large as her torso. She attacked it from every angle, using her telescopic pry bar to wrest it out of its place. After fifteen minutes, it broke free and she passed it back to Alonzo before reaching for the next obstacle.

Except there was none.

Heart hammering, she slipped into the cavernous opening. She couldn't believe her eyes. The inside looked just as she imagined it would. Glass-topped cases wound through the space like snakes. She spun in a circle before lifting her wrist and tapping out a message to Alonzo. *We're in. Get down here.*

The light from Alonzo's comm bounced down the tunnel, but Aria didn't wait for him to arrive before investigating their discovery. They were here.

Treasures Untold had been Los Angeles' premiere boutique jewelry store before the Big One hit. But the whole area had been submerged in meters of water within moments of the earthquake. Based on anecdotes she had overheard through the years, both from other salvagers her father knew and from people at the market, it had lain untouched since the quake.

Until now.

Alonzo pulled his way through the remainder of the tunnel, his eyes wide behind his mask. "Ultra," he murmured, kicking his legs until he was even with Aria. "This is so beyond what I imagined."

She nodded before striking out toward the closest case. The glass was dulled from its time in the ocean and more translucent than transparent. Her wrist comm's light reflected off it and she swam around to the latch on the back of the case, but it was locked.

"I got it," Alonzo said, unzipping his waist pouch.

As he broke the glass with his specialized tool, she swam on, jiggling each latch as she passed, but not one was open.

Finally, in the back corner of the room, she found a broken case. The swell of happiness in her chest ebbed as she sifted through the display, taking care not to slice her fingers on errant shards of glass. She found nothing but a couple of unremarkable gold chains.

They had scouted the building for a full day before picking a spot for their tunnel. Based on the density of the rubble covering the room they were in now, no other salvagers had beaten them here. But what if there was more to the story she hadn't accounted for?

She bit her lip, the sharp sting chasing the thought from her mind. They'd worked too hard to get this far. There had to be more here somewhere.

Alonzo worked to open case after case, announcing each time he found a ring, bracelet, or necklace. But the excitement injected into his tone wasn't enough to mask the underlying current of disappointment.

She swam on ahead, checking for anything promising, when a hulking shape in a back room caught her eye. Her heart hammered in her chest as she drifted toward it. Although the steel was dulled and crusted over from its time in the water, there was no mistaking what she was looking at. The safe.

She waved her arms to get Alonzo's attention. His

eyes widened behind his goggles as he kicked his way over, and Aria couldn't keep a grin off her face.

Alonzo replaced his glass breaker and pulled two small canisters off his belt. Aria relieved him of one of the laser cutters and got to work on the safe's upper hinge.

She had just cut through when a flashing light on Alonzo's back caught her attention. "Phobos," she muttered as she tugged on his shoulder.

He shut off the torch. "What?"

She tapped out a message on her wrist comm. *I thought you said you changed your air supply?*

He didn't answer, not that she expected him to. She could kick herself for not checking his tank herself. They were so close to breaking through the safe door.

"We've still got time," Alonzo said, as if reading her thoughts.

Based on the seconds between flashes, Alonzo still had fifteen minutes of air. She spun the remaining steps in her head. He might be right. If they ran into any trouble, she could always send Alonzo back to the surface and finish things on her own.

Cutting through the hinges took less than a minute, then she and Alonzo used their pry bars until the door began to open.

"Try that," Alonzo said when the crack was two handbreadths wide.

Aria tried to squeeze through, but the passage was too narrow. Alonzo braced his feet against the wall and attempted to pull the door open further. With a stran-gled grunt that reverberated against Aria's eardrum, he got it to open a few more centimeters but halted when the rubble overhead grumbled. A few small pebbles of concrete floated from the ceiling, settling silently on the slimy floor beneath.

Aria's stomach twisted. That was never a good sign.

Alonzo backed away from the opening and Aria propelled herself toward it. Holding her breath, she wriggled through the slit. Her hip bone banged against the steel frame, but she ignored it and directed the beam of her wrist comm to the dark recesses of the room's interior.

Metal lockboxes lined the far wall. Aria gripped her laser torch and considered whether they would be worth it to cut into. There was no telling which boxes were empty and which held treasure. Instead, she focused on the remnants of two long tables that domi-nated the center of the room. One had toppled over in the quake. The other was upright, but warped from its time in the water.

Aria turned up the intensity on her wrist comm light and scoured the tabletop for anything that glit-tered. She ran her fingers over the soft crevices in the wood, brushing the accumulated aquatic vegetation aside.

She had stowed two rings, a watch, and a necklace in her bag and was scanning the floor when the scraping groan of metal on concrete drew her attention. Alonzo's arms, head, and shoulders appeared through the doorway.

Aria sucked her teeth. Leave it to Alonzo to be impatient. Rolling her eyes, she continued her search, locating several jewel-laden bracelets clustered in one spot on the floor.

"A little help?"

She ignored Alonzo as she scooped up her findings. His soft grunts of effort pinged in her ear as she tucked the pieces into her bag. Her fingers were closing around a ring when Alonzo uttered the worst two syllables to voice while meters upon meters underwater.

"Uh oh."

She turned, ready to shoot him a death glare, but the flashing light by his shoulder made her blood turn cold. The indicator had turned from yellow to red.

In an instant she closed the distance between them and punched him in the shoulder. What was he thinking, trying to squeeze in here? Even without scuba gear, it had been a tight fit for her.

Red was bad. It meant Alonzo was down to five minutes' worth of air. They'd have to leave now if they had any chance of getting him out.

She pointed toward the main room, but Alonzo shook his head. "We're so close. Grab what you can."

"Deimos." Turning, she kicked her way deeper into the vault. She swung her bag off her back and focused on the area beside the toppled table. Anything that reflected light got scooped into her bag.

As she pulled her pack onto her back, the surrounding walls rumbled. Debris fell from the ceiling, thudding as it landed on the floor around her.

"Phobos *and* Deimos," she spat, darting toward the exit as the rumbling continued.

Even Alonzo's face mask couldn't disguise his sheepish look as Aria pushed her way into the store's main room. His attempt to force his way into the safe had disturbed the structure. If they were lucky, the fallen walls would reach equilibrium again soon. If they weren't lucky...

They needed to get out of here.

Alonzo was halfway to the tunnel that would lead them out of the building. The flashing red light picked up speed, now pulsing once a second.

Aria dodged chunks of debris as they floated down from the ceiling. The rumblings of the unsettled ruins shook her to her core as she wound her way toward Alonzo. She was less than a meter from him when a shrill beep pierced the water.

Alonzo turned, his eyes wide behind his mask. Aria closed the remaining distance, her gaze locked on the warning beacon on his air tank. No longer was the indicator light flashing. The red glow was constant, growing steadily brighter with each passing second.

Less than a minute left. They'd never navigate the tunnel and get to the surface in time.

Chapter Five

*A*s soon as Alonzo's tank was empty, he would be on borrowed time.

An idea flashed into her mind. Once, not long after Alonzo moved in, he showed her a few lines in a story he was reading about how a mermaid saved a pirate captain who had been forced to walk the plank. It was before Alonzo had any idea about her ability and she had panicked, insisting such a thing was ridiculous. But now she wondered if there wasn't a lesson to learn from it.

She tapped her lips and mimed pulling off his mask. The terror in Alonzo's eyes didn't abate, but he took a deep breath and did what she directed.

Aria swallowed. If this didn't work, she just wasted Alonzo's last precious seconds of oxygen for nothing.

This would work. It had to.

Slipping her hands around the back of Alonzo's

head, she pulled him to her and closed her mouth over his. He fought for a moment before relaxing. For a split second she almost pulled away, afraid he'd passed out.

Aria took in a measure of briny water through her nose, allowing the liquid to pass through her, to slip over the feathery gills on either side of her neck. She let the oxygen pool in her mouth so Alonzo could take a few big gulps before pulling away.

She blinked when she met his gaze, but he held steady and nodded once before pointing to the tunnel. She gripped his hand and pulled him toward it.

The ascent was painstakingly slow. Although Aria started up head first, Alonzo grabbed her ankle moments later. He couldn't hold his breath as long as she'd hoped. Instead, she had to ease herself through feet-first, keeping her face near his so he could breathe as necessary.

The progress was awkward. Aria's feet slid against the flexible walls of the tunnel reinforcement as she moved backwards. Much of the fear had faded from Alonzo's eyes, but discomfort radiated off him.

Relief flooded her when they made it into open water. They were home free. Under ordinary circumstances, they would swim away from a salvage area before surfacing, but this situation was anything but ordinary. She started upward, but Alonzo's fingers closed around her ankle.

Right. He couldn't breathe just because they were out of the tunnel. She reached for his hand and pulled him to her level. After pushing more oxygen into his mouth, she led the way upward, keeping hold of his hand both in case of an unexpected current and in the event he needed air sooner than she expected.

As the water grew lighter and warmer, Aria scanned the surface for anything out of the ordinary. Although she didn't hear any motors, she didn't want to take any chances that someone had anchored nearby.

When they broke the surface, Alonzo gulped in several deep breaths. He turned, a grin plastered to his face, but Aria punched him in the shoulder before he could say anything. Without the water's resistance, her fist collided with a satisfying force.

"Hey! What's that for?" Alonzo kicked his flippers and put a meter of space between them, rubbing his arm.

"What's that for? You can't be serious." She jabbed a finger at his oxygen tank. "You said you changed it out."

He didn't meet her gaze. "I realized it when we were halfway out here and it was too late to turn back. It would've been enough air if the hose hadn't gotten messed up."

She snorted. "You mean if you hadn't ripped it trying to squeeze somewhere you'd didn't belong."

He held up his hands. "What? Everything worked out, didn't it?"

With a kick of her legs, she launched herself

forward and punched him again. "You could've died. You realize that, right?"

He tilted his head. "You'd never let that happen. You can punch me all you want, but we both know you'd be lost without me."

She made a show of rolling her eyes before striking out toward where their DuoCraft was anchored. Her limbs were shakier than usual as the adrenaline of their escape ebbed from her system. While she didn't agree with Alonzo's assessment, the idea of a world without him unsettled her.

She climbed aboard the Duo and wrung out her hair. "I've got the taste of your breakfast burrito in my mouth."

Alonzo hauled himself over the side of the craft. "You're welcome."

She stuck out her tongue as she toweled herself dry. "Gross."

"What?" He pulled the flippers off his feet. "Everybody likes chorizo."

Aria tossed the towel at Alonzo's head before moving to the Duo's covered area. As she pressed her thumb to the rectangle beside the control panel to turn the craft on, she checked the time. They could still make it to the market before it opened—barely.

After raising the anchor and setting the return coordinates, Aria joined Alonzo at the back of the craft. She swung her bag off her back and pulled it open. Resisting the urge to tip out the contents onto the deck, she fished inside and pulled pieces out one by one. The gold chains Alonzo had found in the display case. The watch and bracelets she found in the vault. By the time Alonzo finished removing his gear, she was organizing the rings.

Alonzo picked up one of them and peered at the dark stone. He squinted as he rubbed at sea slime coating it. "Could be an emerald. I wish we'd brought along some supplies to start cleaning these up."

Aria nodded as she fingered the other pieces, tallying up how many credits Alonzo could get out of each. If it wasn't enough, what then? As much as she wanted her sisters to outbid the New LA buyer for the restaurant, she didn't know if she could give up on her dream of a long-distance DuoCraft so she and Alonzo could explore the world.

She stopped her calculations and replaced the items in her bag. If anyone could get the best prices for the pieces they found, it was Alonzo. She had to trust he would make enough both to help Melody and Harmony and to ensure their escape from Old LA.

Chapter Six

By the time Aria and Alonzo arrived at the market, it was buzzing with vendors. They parked their DuoCraft in the nook of space they reserved in the back corner of their booth. Alonzo made his way to the other side of the curtain, and the telltale screech of metal scraped against Aria's eardrums as the front gate rolled up to open them for business. Aria settled down at the small table opposite the Duo and tipped the jewelry out of her bag. The Martian globe rolled out, and she snatched it before it crashed to the floor and tucked it back into the bag.

She flipped on the screen hanging above her table and made sure the volume was down. Alonzo teased her whenever she turned on The Colonists, but he stopped what he was doing to sit and watch it with her enough that she knew he enjoyed it, too. She didn't consider herself obsessed, but if what she overheard at the restaurant last night was true and the stream could be down for any length of time, she wanted to watch it while she still could.

She tuned into her favorite channel, but the people who took front stage weren't any of the teens who dominated this feed. Instead, a man and woman sat side by side, beaming at the people assembled around them. The woman's belly was the size of a watermelon.

Ren and Samara Tanaka, the soon-to-be parents of the first child born on Mars.

The Agency announced the impending birth of the first "Martian" several months ago, but with the pregnancy drawing to a close, Ren and Samara took up more and more screen time as everyone on Earth waited in anticipation for their child to arrive.

The Colony's two hundred citizens were gathered in the Hub. Today, tables lined the walls. Groups chatted and mingled. Aria scanned the crowd for the one face she always searched for, but Enrique Martinez was nowhere in sight.

Someone else caught her eye instead. The girl hovering by the Hub's main door had the long, sleek muscles of a dancer and thick dark hair that cascaded over her shoulder. Under normal circumstances, her beauty would make her recognizable, but it had been so long since Aria had seen her on the streams that it took a few seconds before she could recall a name.

Zora.

The daughter of Chief Science Officer Rashid

Korbel and Dr. Eliza Korbel, the settlement's head doctor, Zora had faded into obscurity after the first few months on the Colony.

None of the colonists her age tried to engage her in conversation today—not that they were likely to make much headway with her mother standing like a sentry in front of her. And all eyes were on the beaming couple in the center of the room anyway. No one gave Zora a second glance.

Only one figure moved away from the commotion and to the two people standing apart from it. After exchanging a few words with his wife, Rashid turned to his daughter and led her out of the building.

When they were gone, Dr. Eliza wove her way through the crowd toward Ren and Samara. But Aria stared at the door through which Zora and her father disappeared. She hadn't spared a thought for Zora in years, but suddenly her mind teemed with them. Why wasn't Zora ever on screen anymore? How could she get away with not participating in work rotations?

A switch in camera angles interrupted her thoughts. A smile curved Aria's lips. Enrique was front and center, looking effortlessly handsome as he handed Samara and Ren their meal trays. He laughed at something Ren said before returning to the cart and moving to the next table.

"Hey, Ar, have we got—oh, no."

Aria swiped at the screen, but it was too late.

Alonzo poked his head around her curtain and sighed. "Don't you watch this stream enough?"

Aria straightened her back and did her best to ignore the heat blossoming in her cheeks. "Is there something you want?"

He held her gaze for a moment longer before shaking his head. "Didn't we get a blue vase the other day? I can't find it."

Setting down the ring she'd been cleaning, she sprang to her feet and ducked under the curtain Alonzo held back for her. She crouched and reached to the back of the bottom shelf. "You stuck it here with that bronze flower. Said you'd never forget such an obvious place." She pulled the vase out and handed it to him.

He grinned as he relieved her of the object and patted her on the head. "I knew I kept you around for a reason." Winking, he turned his attention to the customer standing on the other side of the table. Aria left him to it. This was where he shined—the salesman, talking with such sincerity and passion that he could sell seawater to a sailor. Aria preferred to stay behind the curtain, bringing out the beauty in the objects they reclaimed from the ocean.

When she returned to her chair and turned The Colonists back on, the scene on her screen had changed. For a moment, she thought she'd accidentally switched the stream, but after a few taps, she confirmed she was tuned to the right channel. Instead of a scene from The Colonists, she was met with a woman whose tight black bun and piercing green eyes looked vaguely familiar. Aria caught her name on the scroll at the bottom of the screen. Agent Mercer of the United Coalition Colonization Agency. Aria wrinkled her nose and brought her finger to the screen, wondering if the Agency woman had taken over every Colonists stream. But before she could swipe to a new channel, a phrase piqued her interest.

New colonists.

The words came from the disembodied voice of a reporter off screen. Agent Mercer's gaze flicked from the person speaking back to the camera. "While I still stand behind our original selection process for the second mission, the Agency has received a tremendous amount of feedback in the two years since that expedition was scrubbed, and I'm here today to tell you we've listened. After much discussion within our own ranks and with leaders around the world, we've decided this selection system is the fairest way to choose the men and women who will inhabit the next Martian colony."

Aria sat frozen, transfixed, as Agent Mercer pointed to a reporter in the front row. Her skin tingled. The Agency hand-selected the original Colonists based on skills needed to perform specialized tasks on the planet. A year after the Colonists landed on the surface, governments around the world pressed the Agency to send more people. Controversy arose six months later when the Agency released the names of the second wave of would-be Martians. Everyone on the list was rich, famous, or both, and countless people accused the Agency of letting people buy their way off the planet. When the mission was delayed and ultimately cancelled, each of the chosen made statements about moving on with their lives and not waiting around for the mission to be given a green light.

The shiny pate of a reporter in the front row swayed at the bottom of the screen. "What details can you give us about this selection system?"

Mercer's lips curled, but not enough to be considered a smile. "First, please know we've reserved some spots for individuals with certain expertise. Doctors, engineers—skills of that nature. People with these qualifications will go through a separate process. But over half of the available spots will be open to individuals, married couples, and families. We're basing selection on criteria including overall health, stamina, mental and physical fitness, and personality. The process itself will take place over several weeks and, given estimates of participation levels, will include multiple rounds."

Aria gripped the edge of her workbench. The Agency hadn't chosen the new wave of colonists yet.

She had a chance.

Longing filled her chest. She and Alonzo had spent countless hours making lists of the sites they wanted to see on their grand adventure, but no matter how much research they did or how many plans they made, something was always missing. The realization took her breath away. All this time, she had been settling on an adventure here on Earth when what she longed for was to experience life on Mars. She simply hadn't allowed herself to consider the dream until now.

Another reporter asked, "Will these new colonists be joining those already living on the planet?"

"No," said Mercer. "We have another site set up for them. It's time for us to explore other parts of Mars, don't you think?"

Disappointment washed over Aria like a wave, followed by a jolt of embarrassment. Sending new colonists would have to mean setting up a new colony. The original colonists lived on an island. There was a finite amount of space to expand into. But that didn't keep her mind from jumping into a fantasy wherein not only was she chosen for the new mission, but she and Enrique Martinez could be together.

She shook her head to dispel the images that gathered in her mind's eye. How many times had she and Alonzo made fun of girls convinced they were destined to fall in love with one of the Colonists? And here Aria was, caught up in a daydream of her own.

"There are ten selection centers," Agent Mercer said, drawing Aria's attention. "Two for families, two for married couples without children, and four for individuals. The Agency has outlined age restrictions for each of these groups. For example, hopefuls as young as sixteen may enter the individual camps, provided they have the authority to enter contracts—typically given when a parent signs over UBI control to their child. All hopefuls should go to the appropriate center within their geographic zone—as outlined on the maps on the Agency's site."

Mercer pointed at someone else in the crowd and another off-camera voice rose up. "When do the centers open?"

The agent's too-red lips twitched and a shadow flitted across her sharp features. But Aria blinked and Mercer's reserved expression returned. "I'm pleased to report things are up and running ahead of schedule. They open in three days."

Giddiness swelled in Aria's chest. Jumping from her chair, she rushed past the curtain to the front of the booth.

Alonzo stood at the table, calling out to passersby with his usual charm, but Aria couldn't focus on what he was saying. She grabbed his arm and spun him around. "I'm going to Mars."

His eyebrows hiked upward as he pushed her hand away. "You're doing what now?"

"Mars." Saying it out loud sent a shiver down her spine. "They're setting up selection camps to choose the next group of Colonists, and I'm going."

Alonzo patted her hand, which still hung in the air between them. "Are you feeling okay?"

She grabbed his fingers and squeezed. "I can feel it, Lonz. When the center opens, I'll go and they'll pick me for the mission. You'll come, too—and they'll pick both of us."

"So, both of us are going to Mars?" He crossed his arms over his chest as he turned back to the people streaming past the booth. "Talk to me when you're back from fantasy land."

Aria rankled at his dismissal, but before she could reason with him, shouts from across the footpath drew her attention. A tall man with dark hair stood outside Gary's booth. Aria sighed. Since Gary had moved into the booth diagonal from them, such scenes happened at least once a month. The older man sold a variety of tonics and tinctures and made grand claims about the benefits one could reap by ingesting them. Frequently, people returned when the products didn't live up to the hype.

Alonzo groaned, lifting his wrist and tapping his comm. "I'll ping security."

The enraged customer's voice rose above the general commotion of the market. "You're sorry? I'll make you sorry!"

A white light erupted from Gary's booth and Aria raised her hand to shield her eyes.

"Get down!" Alonzo yanked on her arm and pulled her under the table as an explosion rocked the ground beneath them.

Aria pressed her hands to her ringing ears. The acrid tang of burning chemicals filled her lungs and smoke burned her eyes. She shifted, but Alonzo kept a firm hold on her, shielding her body with his. Her mind spun as she tried to make sense of what was happening.

The ringing in her ears faded, replaced by screams and the thuds of running footsteps.

Alonzo crouched and moved toward the far wall, but Aria grabbed his hand to keep him close.

He wriggled his fingers out of her grip. "I'll be right back. I need to..." Stretching out an arm, he pressed the yellow button nestled between two shelving units and the metal door facing the footpath clanged and clattered closed.

A bang and click sealed them off from the outside, leaving them bathed in the pale yellow glow from the lamp swinging over Aria's cleaning table. Alonzo offered his hand to Aria and she clasped it.

"What... What was that?"

He shook his head. "I'm not sure. But we need to get out of here. The market guards will call the police, and it's better if we're gone by the time they arrive. The last thing I want is to get hauled down to the station and questioned for hours on end."

Aria nodded, although she was sure Alonzo's concern had less to do with time wasted and more to do with the fact that more than a few of the items in their booth had been taken from the homes of wealthy families in New LA. Aria didn't approve of him stealing, but she couldn't stop him. No matter what argument she presented, he defaulted back to the position that the people he stole from had so many possessions they never missed the trinkets he lifted. It was likely true, judging by the items he procured—an elephant carved from quartz, a wooden puzzle box, a glittering sun catcher. Still, Alonzo made it a point to avoid law enforcement of any kind.

He led them toward the back of their booth. Aria scooped up their salvaged jewels and stowed them in her pack. As Alonzo rolled up the back door, Aria climbed into the DuoCraft and pressed her thumb to the control panel.

Nothing happened.

She tapped the instrument panel to check the solar battery's charge, but everything was blank.

"What's wrong?" Alonzo called.

Aria exited the Duo and closed the door behind her. "It's dead. No readouts at all."

Alonzo's eyebrows drew together. "We'll worry about it later. We have to get out of here."

They kept their heads down as they joined the chaos outside. People ran in every direction, many shouting for friends as they went. Just outside the market, people shoved each other out of the way to climb into the transports that shuttled groups from this market to others in adjacent neighborhoods.

Alonzo kept a firm grip on Aria's hand as he led them through the undulating swarms. Bodies pressed in close on all sides, threatening to sweep them away, but Alonzo kept his course. She had no idea where he was taking her. They were passing every transport and the rail station was in a different direction. This wasn't the usual way home.

Chapter Seven

When Aria and Alonzo arrived home half an hour later, Trent yanked them inside and slammed the door closed behind them.

"Where have you two been?" His forehead glistened with sweat and his whole hand trembled as he pointed at the screen hanging on the wall in the main room. "I see this on the news streams and neither of you answer your comms. I lost track of how many pings I sent."

Aria glanced down at her wrist. Her comm screen was blank. She tapped it, but nothing happened. "It's dead."

Alonzo's eyebrows scrunched. "It can't be. As long as you're wearing it, the kinetic battery should..." He stopped short, tapping the screen of his own comm. "Huh."

"That's all you have to say?" Aria's father strode

toward the screen and jabbed his finger at the lower portion. "Isn't this your booth? Right across from the explosion?"

Aria rubbed the back of her neck. "We weren't *right* across from it."

"We're fine, Trent," Alonzo said, crossing the room and clapping a hand on the older man's shoulder. "Gary's a jerk and he got what's coming to him. He swindled the wrong guy, and that guy taught him a lesson."

Alonzo's would-be comforting voice was more stilted than usual. They had spoken little on the walk home and she figured he was in the same position of trying to figure out what had happened. She agreed that Gary's dubious claims about his products were bound to get him in trouble eventually, but she couldn't imagine what broken promises would have made that customer retaliate with an explosion.

Her father shook his head. "I've been watching the news since it happened. It wasn't just an explosion. All electronics within fifty meters stopped working when it went off. Name me an explosive that can do that."

An icy sensation crept up the back of Aria's neck as the words *explosion* and *electronics* echoed through her head. She recalled a story her father shared years ago when explaining why no one outside their family could know about her gills. Two decades earlier, an explosion ripped through an annual War's End celebration in Italy. Besides killing twenty-three people and injuring dozens more, the explosion had knocked out all the electronic devices in the vicinity. It was the first documented attack perpetrated by an aberration. "You don't think..."

Her dad nodded. "I do. And so do the reporters." He touched the side of the screen, raising his finger along the edge. The subtitles disappeared as the volume increased.

"Police have yet to identify the perpetrator of this bombing, which has left seven people injured, including two in intensive care," a woman with springy black curls and a crisp white shirt said into the camera. "Witnesses at the scene have given conflicting reports about the identity of the assailant, but many have strong opinions about who the perpetrator may be."

The scene cut to a man in a baseball hat standing on a street corner a block from the market. "It was an aberration. No doubt in my mind. Mark my words, when you find this sicko, you'll get more than you bargain for. He'll probably shoot lasers out of his eyes or zap you with lightning from his fingertips."

Alonzo snorted. "Laser eyes. Sounds like this guy spends too much time at the V-arcades."

Aria couldn't shake off the witness's ludicrous statement so easily. An invisible weight pressed on her chest, making it difficult to breathe.

The newscaster's face returned to the screen, her serene expression in stark contrast to the red-faced witness. "Several petitions are circulating online calling, once more, for a registry for these so-called aberrations. Similar proposals have been raised dozens of times since the Firenze Massacre twenty-three years ago. It is unclear what—if anything—will come from this new wave of concern. But the activist organization Aberration Rights United has issued a statement saying they will continue to support the rights of law-abiding aberrations."

Aria's father jabbed at the screen and the picture blinked out, revealing the soft brown paint on the wall behind it. "We've taken a step closer today—mark my words."

Aria and Alonzo exchanged glances. For as long as she could remember, Aria's father insisted that the day was nigh when the world's governments would round up aberrations.

But what she, and her father and Sera, could do wasn't dangerous. There was no reason for anyone to come for them. Her father was being paranoid.

Typically, this was the part of the conversation where she would tune out, but something clicked in her mind. While she didn't believe in her father's theories, now might be a good time to pretend like she did.

"You know, Dad, you're right," she began.

Alonzo raised quizzical eyebrow, but her father's gaze remained serious.

She swallowed. "Every time an aberration uses his abilities to harm someone, it makes things more dangerous for the rest of us."

Her father stood a little taller. "Would you look at that? Seems you're getting some sense into that head of yours."

Aria ignored the dig. "I guess being right there for the attack changed the way I look at things. It made me realize that soon there might be no safe place for me here."

She felt Alonzo's eyes on her but fought the urge to turn.

Her father's brow twitched and an agonizingly long time passed before he nodded. "I've been thinking the same thing myself. All it takes is one country—one *city* taking actions against aberrations before things go crazy and governments start passing laws left and right. In that case, there's only one thing we can do to keep you safe."

Aria nodded, fighting to keep a grin from splitting her face. "I can't agree more, Dad. It's a matter of time before there's no safe corner of the world left. And if Earth becomes too dangerous for me, there's only one place left to go. Mars."

Her father stiffened. "Mars? What madness is this?"

Aria took a step backward. "I, um..." She glanced at Alonzo for help, but he stood aloof, his arms crossed over his chest. "I saw on the news today the Agency is selecting the next group of colonists and—"

"I know that," her dad grumbled. "Did you catch the things they plan to do to narrow down the volunteer pool? *Overall health.* Physical fitness. You know what that's code for, don't you? A blood test, Aria."

She threw her hands up. "Ooh, a blood test. I'm not afraid of needles, Dad."

"You should be." He shook his head. "No, the answer is for you to stop going on salvage runs."

Heat creeped up the back of her neck. If he found out she and Alonzo had gone on a run this morning, he would shout until he was red in the face. "We had this conversation already, Dad."

He shook his head. "No. Not just till the end of tourist season. I don't want you going back out at all. It's a miracle no one's discovered you out there already. You need to stay out of the water for good. If no one sees you swimming, they'll have no idea what you can do. You'll be safe."

A weight settled in the pit of her stomach. Before she could mount a response, her dad spun toward the kitchen. Aria watched his retreating back, her mouth hanging open. Stop salvaging? That was his answer? Of course it would be. It was a surprise he'd allowed it to go on as long as he had.

But did he really mean to stay out of the water forever? She didn't know if she could live with that.

She locked eyes with Alonzo and raised her brows. His face scrunched and she pointed at her dad. For years, the two had been able to communicate with glances and gestures, but today the ability seemed to irritate Alonzo.

He swallowed and took a few steps toward the counter separating the dining room from the kitchen. "You know, Trenton, it can't hurt to let her go to the selection center. I mean, let's face it—the odds aren't exactly in her favor."

Aria glared at her brother, but he ignored her.

Her father turned and pressed his palms into the edge of the counter. His shoulders slumped. "What is it you two aren't understanding? What part of *blood test* are you missing?"

Aria bit her lower lip. "All of it, I guess, Dad. It makes sense they'd want a blood test to make sure potential colonists are healthy."

"Or they're using the selection process to get your blood on file so they can put you on some secret registry." Her father's eyes burned with the fever she associated with his railings against the government.

"Dad." Her tone was sharper than she intended and she took a breath before trying again. "You know they haven't been able to figure out a way to identify aberrations with a blood test. That's why the last bill about a registry got shot down."

"Or maybe that's what they want you to think."

Aria sighed, pressing her hand to her forehead. There was no use trying to reason with her father when he got like this. She'd tried to change his way of thinking more times than she could count, but he was too convinced he was right to see any other angle.

"Put this nonsense out of your mind," he said as he

pulled a frying pan out of a low cupboard. "You need to keep your head down and stay safe." He pointed at Alonzo as he crossed to the refrigerator. "It's time to consider giving up your market booth. You two were lucky today. You need to understand that. What if the explosion was at the booth next to yours instead of across from it?"

Alonzo shifted, glancing at Aria out of the corner of his eye. They hadn't told him about their planned adventures abroad, so he had no way of knowing they had put off signing another one-year commitment to the market.

But Trent didn't notice the glance his children exchanged as he laid vegetables out on the counter and selected his best cutting knife. "Your sisters would be happy to give you both more shifts at the restaurant. You'll work there, you'll live here, and you'll be safe."

As he spoke, Aria saw the course of her life unfolding before her. Twelve-hour shifts at the restaurant and crashing from exhaustion as soon as she got home. Her precious downtime spent at V-arcades playing immersive games that gave the illusion of experiences instead of actually having them.

She stepped toward the counter separating her from her dad. "Don't I get a say in this?"

He didn't glance up from the zucchini he was slicing. "Not when your head is full of daydreams and you think reality is a game. It's about time you grew up, Aria."

Something inside Aria broke. She slammed her fist onto the countertop. "Then stop treating me like a child. I'm almost eighteen. It's about time you stop trying to decide for me." She straightened her back as she tried to regain her composure. "Besides, I don't need your permission if I want to sign up for selection. You gave me control over my UBI last year. The woman from the Agency said that was enough to let someone as young as sixteen sign up."

Her father laid the knife down beside the cutting board, his face reddening. "If I thought you'd put your life at risk for some fantasy, I never would have signed over control."

She folded her arms over her chest, ignoring his dig about her wanting to live a fantasy. "But you did. If I want to go, you can't stop me."

"You're not eighteen yet. I can reassert a claim on your UBI." He began chopping the zucchini again. "I could apply for Order Eighty-Two while I'm at it."

A tremor coursed through Aria's body. Order Eighty-Two allowed a parent to retain legal control over their child for an extended period. In extreme cases, a person could be under her parent's control until she was twenty-five. The idea was to ensure these young adults transitioned successfully into adulthood where they contributed instead of squandering their income and becoming a drain on their parents and the government. "You wouldn't do that."

Her father raised his eyebrows. "I'll do whatever it takes to make sure you're safe."

Aria threw up her hands. "For the last time—the selection center isn't a front for an aberration registry!"

"Are you willing to risk it?" He held her gaze. "Willing to risk not just your life, but mine and Sera's too?"

The fight went out of Aria like wind from a sail. She would never do anything to hurt her niece or her father, as much as he annoyed her. The visions of being part of the selection, of arriving at a new Martian colony, of exploring a new world untouched by human hands faded from her mind, replaced by the repetitive drudgery of waiting tables, mopping floors, and staring longingly at the glittering ocean in the distance.

"Don't bother making enough food for me. I'm not hungry." Shoulders stooped, she started down the hall toward her room.

Alonzo followed her. "Wait, let's talk about this."

She placed her hand on her door, not looking at him. "Talking won't change anything. I may as well get used to this: My new life as a prisoner."

She closed the door behind her before he could respond. She was being dramatic, but it didn't make her words any less true.

Aria stood in the center of her bedroom, staring up at the salvaged blown-glass celestial models she had collected over the years. Some depicted spiral galaxies, others colorful nebulae. She had three models of the solar system, one that included several dwarf planets.

Lined up on her dresser were several representations of Mars. On the left were three that depicted a barren red desert. On the right were two that showed the lush blue-and-green landscape of today. She pulled the pack off her back and reached in to retrieve the orb she found the other day, the one that showed Mars mid-terraforming. When she placed it on the dresser in front of the others, the tears that had been brimming in her eyes spilled over.

Despite her moment of hope, nothing had changed. This was her life. She would never get to Mars. She would never even explore her home planet. Old LA was the cage that would trap her forever.

Chapter Eight

*I*t was afternoon when a familiar rhythm tapped against Aria's door. She ignored it, pulling her pillow more firmly over her head. A few seconds later, the knock repeated, louder this time.

"Go away, Alonzo," she muttered.

The latch clicked and Aria groaned. By the time she dug herself out from beneath layers of bedding, Alonzo was in her room, closing the door behind him.

"I said go away."

"Really? Because I heard, 'Come in, Alonzo.'" He held up her wrist comm like some kind of prize. "Look what I fixed." When she didn't respond, he perched on the edge of her bed. "Come on, Ar. It's been two days. When are you going to come out?"

She sat up and drew her knees to her chest. She could feel her hair sticking up at an odd angle but didn't bother trying to tame it. "Why bother? Besides,

I'm sure Dad likes me in here just fine. No chance of anyone figuring out what I am if I'm stuck at home forever."

Alonzo sighed. "You know that's not what he wants."

She tilted her head. "Do I? Because that's how it feels. You know, I could understand him not wanting me to sign up for the selection if it was about him missing me if they chose me for the mission. But it's not —it's all about him being right about some conspiracy against people like us, and about making me the bad guy—like I want someone to find out about me and him and Sera."

Alonzo closed his fingers around her ankle and squeezed it. "You know it's more than that. He loves you. He wants to make sure you're safe."

Aria pressed her lips together. It was always touchy discussing parents with Alonzo. He was an orphan who lived on the streets before her family took him in. And while her father had always treated Alonzo like the son he'd never had, she knew it wasn't the same as having his biological father. More than once, she'd been on the receiving end of an at-least-your-dad-is-still-around speech from Alonzo, and she wasn't in the mood for one today.

"I feel trapped, Lonz."

He set her comm down on her nightstand and scooted closer. "But you're not. You've spent your whole life here in Old LA, but there's a bigger world out there. You don't have to go all the way to Mars for an adventure. I thought you knew that. In case you forgot, we made it into Treasures Untold. Sure, maybe we didn't get the haul we hoped for, but the pieces we found will be more than enough to help buy the restaurant. We'll have plenty left over to buy the new Duo, and then we can leave this place and explore the world."

The knot that had wound around her shoulders and twisted in her stomach for the last two days finally loosened a bit and she took in her first deep breath in what felt like forever. "You're right. There's plenty on Earth we haven't seen yet."

He squeezed her shoulder. "See? You should listen to me more often. I'm usually right about things."

She snorted. "I wouldn't go that far."

He picked up her pillow and bopped her on the head with it. "Are you done with your pity party now? Because I got a ping from Dom over at the market. The police gave us the all clear, so we can go check on the booth and help clean up. Dom wants to reopen as soon as possible."

Aria snatched the pillow from Alonzo. The urge to pull it over her head and block out the world swelled up in her, but she pushed it back. If she stayed hidden in her room now, it wasn't her father's fault—it was hers.

She sat up and swung her legs over the edge of the bed. "Okay, I'm in."

———

It was late afternoon by the time they finished up at the market. Aria's muscles ached when she and Alonzo left. "I should've stayed home," she grumbled, working out a kink in her shoulder.

Alonzo grimaced. "Come on. It wasn't that bad."

He was only partly right. The metal walls of their booth sustained minor damage, and only a few items in their stock were broken beyond repair. The booths across the footpath were another matter. She and Alonzo had helped other booth owners sort through the wreckage and haul loads to the rented recycle truck. Even after scrubbing her hands for ten minutes with the special pumice soap Dom gave her, Aria's fingers were stained black with soot.

She kicked at a tuft of grass growing in a crack in the sidewalk. "I wish the Duo was working."

Alonzo sighed. "I told you already. I couldn't check what part got fried in the explosion until they let us back into the market. I'll have it running tomorrow. Today you'll have to slum it and take the rail."

Another complaint bubbled in Aria's throat, but she swallowed it. Despite how tired and achy she was from the cleanup, the walk to the rail station wouldn't take long.

But the street that led to the station was blocked off. Two bored police officers stood on either side of a laser barricade barring vehicles and pedestrians from crossing. Behind the officers, a mass of people filled the street, all marching in the same direction. Some held signs. The murmur of their voices floated down to Aria, but she couldn't make out what they were saying.

"What do you think that's all about?" Aria asked.

Alonzo ran his hand through his hair. "Phobos. I didn't think they were coming this way."

Aria tilted her head. "Didn't think who was coming what way? What is this?"

"Maybe we should ping a transport," Alonzo said, tapping at his wrist comm. "With all the credits that jewelry will bring in, we can spring for a private one with a personal screen. What do you say?"

She ignored him, stepping toward the marchers. If he knew what was going on, why wouldn't he tell her?

But the answer came as she drew nearer. The indistinct murmur of voices grew clearer by the second. Hundreds of voices shouted as one, "Registration now!" Marching up the street was a group carrying a banner screen that stretched from one curb to the other. "Registration = Safety."

Aria's blood ran cold. Her dad was right. People were finally uniting against aberrations—against people like her.

"You joining?"

Aria jumped at the officer's voice. He moved one side of the barricade to allow passage.

"They're going all the way to City Hall, if you're interested." The officer's tone held no emotion. He simply relayed the information. But somehow his detachment from the situation was unnerving. If he weren't on duty, would he be joining them?

"Uh, yeah. We're joining," Alonzo said.

Aria's eyes widened, but she stayed at Alonzo's heels as he passed the barricade.

He didn't speak until they were several meters from the officers. "It's the fastest way to get home. Just stay close. Follow my lead."

Before she could react, he closed his hand around hers and pulled her into the crowd. They joined in with the marchers. Aria kept her head down and tugged her hair to make sure it covered her neck. Although no one could see her gill slits, something about being around all these angry people made her feel exposed.

She stuck close to Alonzo as he wove his way through the crowd while somehow appearing to be part of the march. No one paid them a passing glance as they edged around small cliques that formed within the mass's ranks. He didn't slow until they reached a line of people with linked arms.

"Just about half a kilometer before we can split off," he murmured, bending toward her ear. "Until then, just try to act natural."

A giggle clawed its way up her throat and she swallowed to smother it. Act natural? There was nothing natural about her being here among people who had assembled to shout their displeasure at her existence.

Alonzo squeezed her hand. At least he was with her.

The chanting grew louder with each step they took, reverberating through her skull, echoing through every corner of her mind. *Registration now. Registration now.*

Hands collided with Aria's back, shoving her forward. Alonzo caught her before she hit the ground, but panic flooded her system. Someone had figured out what she was. She needed to run, but where could she go? There were so many marchers—one of them was bound to grab her before she got far. Still, she had to try.

She scrambled to get her feet under her, but Alonzo kept a firm grip on her upper arms.

"Oh, wow, I'm sorry." A man in his mid-twenties with a close-cropped beard crouched beside Aria. He turned his gaze on Alonzo. "Is she hurt?"

"I think she'll live." Alonzo pulled Aria to her feet. She was glad when he didn't release her. The adrenaline was spiking in her system and she might fall to the ground again at any minute.

The guy offered an apologetic smile. "Sorry. I guess we got a little worked up. I didn't mean to knock into you."

"Maybe you should chill yourself," one of his friends called from a nearby group. A half-dozen people, all in their mid- to late twenties stood still, forming a small blockade around which the rest of the march flowed. As Alonzo urged Aria to continue forward, the small group followed.

"I can't help it if I'm amped," the bearded guy said from his spot near Aria. "This is the time. I can feel it. The government can't keep ignoring the threat these aberrations pose."

Aria squeezed Alonzo's hand. He returned pressure.

"I was at the market the other day, you know," the same guy said, casting a meaningful glance at Aria and Alonzo. "During the attack."

Alonzo made a noncommittal noise in the back of his throat.

It was all the encouragement their new companion needed. "There I was, minding my business, then *bam*! There's an explosion and everyone's running. How can we feel safe anywhere as long as these people are walking around? Anyone could be an aberration and there's no way we'd know it."

"Yeah," Alonzo agreed. "Unacceptable."

Aria bit the inside of her cheek. Alonzo was saying it only to keep their cover, but she still didn't like the sound of it coming from him.

"They need to be registered," called one girl from the group. "We need to know who they are, where they are, and what they can do."

The man beside Aria shook his head. "You're not thinking big enough. What does it matter if you know Bob from down the street can throw fireballs at will?

People like that are a threat to us all. What, are we supposed to give these people whatever they want and hope for the best? I don't think so."

Bile rose in Aria's throat. She was too afraid to ask what his proposed solution would be. Did he think they should lock all the aberrations away, regardless of ability or indicators of violence? Or did he support a more permanent solution to the problem?

"It's too bad there's no way to tell who's one and who isn't," said a girl with dark, glossy hair. "I mean, pass all the laws in the world, but unless you can tell who's one of us and who's not, it doesn't matter."

Aria's legs trembled with the suppressed desire to run, to put as much distance between herself and these people as possible. "Alonzo."

"Uh, yeah—let's check your ankle," he said, his voice louder than necessary. "Maybe we'll catch up with you guys," he added as he led Aria to the edge of the mob.

The bearded guy and his friends waved before continuing up the street, joining in with the ongoing chants about registration. Alonzo led her past a group of older women on the sidewalk who offered bottles of water to passersby, thanking them for doing "the Lord's work." Aria pretended to limp until they were out of sight.

Alonzo squeezed his eyes closed. "I'm so sorry. I didn't think—"

She shook her head. "Let's go home."

Alonzo draped an arm over her shoulders and squeezed her upper arm. "It'll all die down. It always does, right? Remember a few years back when there was a petition in New LA to block aberrations from living there? That got shut down pretty quickly."

Aria didn't respond. Their father had railed about the petition, spouting doom and gloom and insisting that if the measure passed into law in New LA, it would be only a matter of time before it reached them. Aria had shrugged it off. The threat was too nebulous to worry about. Besides, she had no interest in living in New LA.

But now she couldn't share Alonzo's rosy optimism that things would get back to normal. The petition to keep aberrations from living in New LA was a snub based in discrimination, and the people who lived there also looked down their noses at anyone who lived solely on their UBI. Things were different this time. The aberration-only prison was open. And today's march was based on something deeper than a general dislike —it was visceral fear that burned in the marchers' eyes. When enough people were afraid, they were dangerous.

Even if she gave up salvaging for the rest of her life, if people's fears got the better of them, it wouldn't be enough. There was no test to determine if a person was an aberration—yet. But if one were developed, the government could mandate everyone be tested. And then what? Registration might be just a first step. The slightest spark could ignite a fire the led to every aberration being rounded up and imprisoned—or worse.

Her father was right—he had seen this coming. He knew fear would eventually win over rational thought.

But he was wrong about one thing. Hiding wasn't the best thing to do. She had to escape the panic before it was too late.

No matter what, she had to get to Mars.

Chapter Nine

The transport from the hyperloop station was packed past capacity. Aria stood as still as possible and gripped the overhead rail as tightly as she could, but it didn't matter. With each bump and sway of the shuttle, some part of her body brushed against someone crammed around her. The air was hot and stale, and her only sanity came from watching the progress meter along the transport's wall. She would climb out of her skin if they didn't reach their stop soon.

She had expected Alonzo to discover her sneaking out of the house late last night. Or maybe she hoped he would. Even now, she wasn't convinced she made the right decision by leaving him behind.

But if she had told him, she risked him talking her out of it. Or, worse, telling her father.

She glanced at her wrist comm, but no notifications

blazed on the screen. Guilt swooped through her stomach. It was noon now—her father and Alonzo had probably known for hours she wasn't in the house. Her note wouldn't be enough to appease them, so she muted incoming notifications. If she answered even one ping, the conversation would escalate into an argument that she didn't want to deal with. Nothing she could say would convince them this was the right move, and nothing they could say would convince her to come home.

The transport decelerated and the lanky twenty-something guy behind her pressed into her back as if the energy to keep himself stationary was beyond him. She gritted her teeth. The ride was almost over.

The wheels finally ground to a stop and with a hiss of air, all three sets of doors on either side of the shuttle slid open. Aria followed the flow of people around her, shuffling forward at an achingly slow pace.

The oppressive heat hit her before she exited the transport. The sun, no longer tempered by UV tinted glass, glared overhead, and Aria shielded her eyes as she tried to take in her surroundings.

Ruddy mountains loomed in the distance against a hazy blue sky. But the space was dominated by what looked like a walled city that was entirely out of place amid the saguaro cacti.

Three tones rang out through the air and Aria spun around to identify the source, but none was apparent. The murmuring of the crowd died down as a holographic display three meters high flickered to life in the air above them.

A woman with short-cropped white hair loomed over them, her curving smile doing little to make her appear less intimidating. "Hello, hopefuls. I'm Dr. Uma Withers, and I am the head of the Agency's Selection Commission. While I'm sure you're all excited to venture into the center, it's important you understand some rules before moving forward."

A girl with a long, blonde braid knotted down her back snorted. "Get on with it."

The girl's dark-haired companion tittered while a third friend with short blonde hair kept her eyes fixed on the doctor's image.

"Choosing our next colonists is a process," Dr. Withers continued. "In your time at the center, you will undergo various tests and complete different assignments. Take these seriously, as they will form the core of our decision making."

Aria straightened her back and immediately felt silly. It wasn't as if this projection could see her.

"If you have questions during your time here, direct them to an overseer in a blue shirt." Withers indicated her own collared shirt. "Failure to comply with commands issued by overseers could cause expulsion from the center. Fighting will result in immediate dismissal. You are free to leave, but once you exit this center—for any reason—you may not apply for a spot in any colony ever again."

Aria tried to swallow, but her throat was too dry. On the one hand, it was comforting to know the Agency was already thinking about planting additional colonies. But it seemed extreme that if a person failed to make the cut now, their chance to get to Mars was ruined forever.

"In a moment, the overseers will divide you into groups and perform a routine health scan. If you pass the scan, you'll continue into the center. If you don't, we at the Agency thank you for your time and interest."

Withers nodded once, and the holoscreen disappeared, leaving the glare of the afternoon sky in its place. Murmurs broke out among the hopefuls, but a handful of voices rose above the din.

"Thirty to thirty-four!"

"Fifty-five to fifty-nine!"

Aria strained her ears, but the bustling crowd drowned out the voices as people divided themselves into the appropriate age groups.

Sets of green numbers quickly appeared in the air a few meters above the heads of even the tallest hopefuls. Aria peered at each holographic signal until she found the one she was looking for—ages sixteen to nineteen.

Weaving through the crowd, Aria made her way toward the employee beneath her age range. At least two dozen people had bunched in a group nearby, many whom she recognized from her transport. She stood on her toes to get a better look at the overseer at the front. The man in the blue shirt wasn't much older than she was. His dark blond hair was styled as impeccably as the socialites from New LA, but there was a seriousness to his honey-colored eyes. She couldn't shake the feeling that he'd been through a lot in his life.

"Listen up." He surveyed each of them with a disinterested gaze. "In a minute, we'll head into the lab for the blood test. From there, some of you will move on. But, if statistics bear out, at least five of you will be on your way home before dinner." He glanced to the left and right at the other age groups. "If anyone isn't here by now, too bad for them. Let's get a move on."

A wave of nausea crested in Aria's stomach as the overseer turned and led them toward a sleek, white-walled building in the distance.

The girl with the braid cleared her throat as the group started after him. "Excuse me. I didn't catch your name."

The overseer glanced over his shoulder. "Very observant."

"Well," the girl continued, "what are we supposed to call you?"

He stopped in his tracks and Aria and the rest of her group froze in place. As the overseer turned, several people cast sidelong glances at the girl with the braid.

"*Sir*," said the overseer.

When their leader turned and led the way again, the group released a collective breath.

After a few steps, the girl murmured, "Wow. That guy hates this job."

"I would, too," said her companion with short blonde hair. "Out here in the sun all day, saying the same things over and over. Nothing to do but walk people back and forth from the transport to the lab. Boring."

The first girl snorted. "Like you're the authority on what's boring. Last week you said if there was a stream of Enrique Martinez sleeping, you'd stay up to watch it. Honestly, Izzy."

Aria's stomach twisted. These girls hadn't formed their connection on the transport or in the hours spent at the rail station. They were friends. She did her best to ignore the pang of longing stabbing through her chest. She wished Alonzo were here.

"That's not what I meant, and you know it, Lourdes," muttered Izzy. "Shannan, tell her."

"I'm staying out of this," said the one with wavy brown hair.

Giggles gurgled up among the girls and Aria bit the insides of her cheeks. If Alonzo were here, they would be guessing what tasks awaited them—Alonzo's suggestions growing outlandish. Their poorly stifled laughter would earn them a stern look from their overseer.

But Alonzo wasn't here. There was no use imagining what it would be like if he were. In fact, if they selected Aria for this mission, she would have to get used to doing things without her best friend.

When they neared the structure, their overseer

pointed to a spot a meter from where Aria stood. "Line up."

Before she could take even a step forward, someone knocked into Aria from behind. She staggered to keep from falling. By the time she regained her balance, Lourdes, Izzy, and Shannan stood at the front of the line, followed by a handful of others. Aria shuffled into place behind a guy with a slim build and shaggy blond hair.

"There's no prize for going first, so there's no need to rush." The overseer surveyed the line, his gaze lingering on the three girls at the front. While Shannan and Izzy stared at the ground, Lourdes didn't flinch.

A beat passed before he turned to the building. He pressed his thumb to a pad beneath the door's handle and the red light flashed green. The door slid open with a pneumatic hiss.

Glancing over his shoulder, he gestured for Lourdes to follow him into the room.

Minutes ticked by with agonizing slowness. The door opened again and again, each time accepting a new person from the line. No one ever exited. Did that mean everyone so far had moved onto the next phase of selection? She glanced down the line, trying to do a quick calculation. The overseer said statistically five of them wouldn't make the cut. What did that mean for her chances?

When the door opened again, Aria got her best look yet as the guy in front of her walked in. The inside wall was gleaming white and sterile, like the medical bay on a spaceship in one of those old science-fiction movies Alonzo used to obsess over.

Aria's throat went dry. She sucked in a breath and released it slowly. There was nothing to worry about. She was expecting a blood test. But her father's voice echoed in the back of her mind. *Register people against their will.* What if he was right? Every report she'd seen reiterated that no test could identify an aberration, but the reports could be wrong. Reporters didn't know everything. If the government really had a reliable test, would they want people knowing about it?

She shook herself. She refused to let her father's paranoia infect her. He'd seen firsthand the anti-aberration response whenever a single person used their abilities to harm others. But in a colony of a couple hundred individuals, Aria had to believe even if people learned about her ability, they would know *her* well enough to be sure she wasn't a threat to them. She would be safe there, even if things on Earth spun out of control.

It made sense to do a blood draw before admitting people into the selection process. If anything stood out about a person's health, it would be prudent to send them home before allowing them to go any further. By degrees, her heart stopped pounding and returned to its usual rhythm.

The door before her slid open and she crossed the

threshold. It closed so quickly it rustled her hair. She took a hasty step forward.

The room was small—large enough for a long table on the wall across from a glistening stainless steel exam gurney. The overseer, now wearing a white lab coat over his blue shirt, stood with his back to her, facing a screen on the wall.

"Sit down."

Aria complied, doing her best not to allow his clipped tone to unnerve her. If the walk over to this building was any indication, his brusque manner had nothing to do with her.

She sat on the stainless steel exam table and willed her body to relax as the overseer turned toward the opposite wall and busied himself opening a new blood collection kit.

"I'm going to draw your blood. There are certain medical conditions that would make living on Mars difficult or impossible." He spoke in the monotonous drone of someone who had repeated the same sentences countless times. "If this test shows any of those conditions, someone will escort you off the premises. This will not be the only physical test you'll undergo during your time here. Do you understand?"

She nodded. "Yes. Of course."

He picked up a tablet from his workspace and turned to her. He was closer now than he had been on the walk here and the rectangular tag pinned to his shirt caught her eye. *C. Reed. Level 2 Overseer.* "I'll need your thumb print as verification."

Aria blinked before pressing her thumb to the rectangle at the bottom of the screen. A green bar flashed from the top of the rectangle to the bottom and text flashed across the screen.

Terms Accepted by Ayers, Aria Chelan.

She swallowed as Reed pulled the tablet away and set it back on his work bench. He picked up the silver blood collector before turning back to her. "Give me your arm."

Aria's stomach swooped as she complied. Reed cupped her elbow with one hand before bringing the silver cylinder to the inside of her elbow.

She held still through the pinch, staring at the blank screen on the wall. In a matter of moments, Reed pulled the device away and turned to a machine under the screen. With the press of a button, a small glass vial dropped from the cylinder into a corresponding hole. A green light flashed and a quiet whir filled the room.

Aria held her breath.

The screen flickered to life as a set of data filled it. Words, letters, and numbers formed rows of information incomprehensible to Aria.

Reed studied the screen for a moment before turning to her. "Everything looks good. Just one last thing." He reached into the pocket of his lab coat and pulled out a handheld scanner. "I need your wrist comm."

Aria held out her arm. "What for?"

He passed the scanner over her comm and a series of flashes passed between the two devices. "While you're here, you'll receive pings from the organizers. I'm adding your information into our list. And you won't be able to send or receive pings from outside the selection center."

A shiver passed down Aria's neck. "Why not?"

The corner of Reed's mouth twitched. "To keep you from being distracted. Plus it's good practice. It's not like you'll get pings from home if you're on Mars."

"I guess not." Aria glanced at her wrist comm as Reed tucked the scanner back into his pocket. That was it, then. Even if she wanted to, she couldn't contact Alonzo or her father or sisters now. Her stomach clenched.

Reed tapped on his wrist comm and a door slid open across the room from where she'd entered.

Aria swallowed and turned toward the open door. Reed's voice followed her as she stepped over the threshold.

"Good luck," he said in the same deadpan tone. "I have a feeling you're just the kind of person we're looking for."

The door closed before she could react. She should thank C. Reed for his encouragement, but it was too late. Maybe she would have another opportunity.

She inhaled deeply as she turned toward the inside of the center. She had made it through the blood test without setting off any red flags. One hurdle down. One step closer to Mars.

Unfortunately, the blood test was the simple part. She didn't know what awaited her, and the next challenge probably wouldn't be so easy.

Chapter Ten

*A*ria barely had a moment to take a deep breath of dry, desert air before a smiling overseer met Aria on the other side of the door. She expected the woman to give her a tour of the walled city she found herself in or to show her to where she would be staying. Instead, the woman gave Aria a tangy drink and led her to a broad, squat building across the narrow road.

Two hours later, the psych evaluation was over and Aria's stomach was growling and her brain felt like mush. The overseer had started by asking Aria to identify what she saw in dark blobs of ink, and by the end she was zooming in on why Aria believed Piper didn't like her.

As she exited the evaluation building, Aria blinked against the harsh sunlight. Dozens of people walked along the street. A few of them were her age, but most were much older. All of them seemed to know where they were going.

Her overseer hadn't given her further instructions, and Aria hadn't thought to ask for them. She turned back to the building to poke her head in to ask for help, but there was no doorknob on her side.

"Deimos."

She made it two steps before her wrist comm vibrated with an incoming message.

Ayers, Aria Chelan. Barracks G27. No transfers. See attached.

Aria tapped on the clip icon—a relic from a time when communications were actually distributed on stacks of paper—and a schematic hologram display hovered over her comm. A red dot showed where she stood while a white star noted the location of barracks G27. The center was huge. A readout indicated it would take her fifteen minutes to walk to her room.

"What I wouldn't give for my Duo." Aria started up the street. She walked faster than nearly anyone else, but no one paid any attention to her. Everyone was lost in their own head. More than a few people she passed wore expressions verging on disbelief, as if it were just dawning on them the enormity of what they were doing here. She wondered if any of them would choose to leave before the process was over.

Would she?

Aria shoved the question down as soon as it surfaced. Of course she wouldn't drop out.

Keeping her head down, Aria picked up her pace, consulting the schematic on her wrist comm at intervals until she found her way to the barracks quadrant.

At least two dozen long buildings stretched out in orderly rows. Aria located the G aisle quickly. The doorknob to number twenty-seven twisted under her hand and she pushed her way inside.

Three girls looked up from their spots in front of a screen hanging on the wall. She barely had time to register their familiar faces before the one with blonde braid planted her hands on her hips and rounded on Aria.

"Excuse me. Don't you knock?"

Aria's mind spun as it worked to put a name to the girl's face. Lourdes. She blinked and gave herself a shake before tapping on the numerals on the door. "G twenty-seven, right?"

The girl with short blonde hair settled a hand on Lourdes's shoulder. "I bet this is Aria." She offered a smile. "I recognize you from our group when we got here. I'm Izzy, and that's Shannan." She removed her hand from her friend's shoulder. "This is Lourdes."

Shannan beckoned for Aria to follow. "Your bed's over here." She led the way into the main part of the room where four beds were arranged. A miniscreen hung above each with a name on it. Aria's was in the corner of the room furthest from the door.

"It's the one I would've chosen," Lourdes

murmured, her voice sending a shiver down Aria's back.

She opened her mouth to suggest they switch before thinking better of it. If the overseers had wanted them to pick their own bunks, they wouldn't have bothered with the screens.

She shifted under the weight of Lourdes's gaze a moment longer before pointing to a door on the wall behind her. "Is that a bathroom?"

Before anyone responded, Aria was on her way to it. While Izzy and Shannan made a path, Lourdes didn't step aside until Aria came to a stop in front of her.

As soon as Aria entered the room, she closed and locked the door behind her. The automatic light clicked on to reveal a tiny bathroom with toilet squashed between a small square sink and a cramped shower stall. Four bath towels lay folded on the shelf above the sink.

Aria stripped off her sweaty clothes before she could change her mind. Not only would a shower be amazing after hours upon hours spent in transports, on rail cars, and crammed on hard station floors waiting to come to the selection center, but it would give her some time away from Lourdes's calculating gaze.

As she turned on the water and stepped into the stall, she tried to see things from Lourdes's point of view. To her, Aria must seem like an interloper. But

Lourdes would have to get used to being around new people if she wanted to go to Mars.

Aria decided to do her best to put up with Lourdes —to be kind, even. Getting along with people was an important skill to have in a setting like the Colony. Lourdes's opinion of her didn't matter. She had to do her best to prove herself to the overseers.

At least one of them already had a positive opinion of her. Reed had said she was the kind of person they were looking for. That had to count for something.

Aria took as much time as she dared in the shower before climbing out and toweling dry. When she emerged from the bathroom, she ignored Lourdes's reproachful stare as she crossed to her bed. Her stomach growled as she sat down. "Has anyone seen a schedule? It should be about dinnertime now, shouldn't it?"

Izzy pointed to the room's main screen. "A message came through while you were in the bathroom."

Aria stood and crossed to the screen. A text box floated above the day's schedule. *Dinner begins at 18:00 in Conference Room A. To curb your hunger, follow your heart. Don't be a square and let the others leaf you behind. Attendance mandatory. Don't be late.*

Aria blinked and checked the text box for an attachment, but there was none. She pulled up the map that had led her to the barracks, but a quick scan revealed nothing labeled as Conference Room A. She checked the time. Only ten minutes until dinner. "That's odd."

"Right?" Izzy's eyebrows scrunched as she joined Aria. "Why are they so concerned about us being there on time? What does it matter if we're a few minutes late?"

Aria shook her head. "Not that. Do you have any idea where Conference Room A is?"

Lourdes groaned. "Why do you think we're still here? Some overseer must have messed up. We're waiting for another ping to come through with a map."

Aria bit the inside of her cheek. Wouldn't someone have noticed the error and corrected it by now? "What if they don't plan on sending a map?"

Lourdes clucked her tongue. "All the more reason to stay here."

"But it says attendance is mandatory," Aria said.

Lourdes stood, folding her arms over her chest. "How are they going to know who's there and who isn't? There's got to be a couple thousand people here."

Aria reread the message. "If they didn't care whether people showed up, they wouldn't say attendance is mandatory—and that we shouldn't be late. They've planned out everything so far. They grouped us at the hyperloop station, and they even assigned our bunks."

"I don't think everything is as seamless as you're making it out to be," Lourdes said. "Don't let the others *leaf* you behind? That's a pretty glaring mistake."

Aria had caught the error, too. It was a sizable one for the scope of the operation. It could be explained away as a transcription or dictation inaccuracy. But something tugged at the back of Aria's consciousness. "Unless it's not a mistake."

With another groan, Lourdes flopped back onto her bunk. "What else could it be?"

Depending on the location of Conference Room A, it could take at least ten minutes to walk there, and that was all the time she had. "Stay here if you want. I'm going."

She strode toward the door, ignoring a nagging tendril of guilt. She was sure she was right, but she couldn't waste time trying to convince the others. Besides, what was the worst that could happen if they stayed here?

The street outside the barracks was deserted. Those who had struck out to find Conference Room A had probably left soon after receiving the ping.

Aria recited the message to herself. *To curb your hunger, follow your heart.* Somehow, those words were supposed to lead her to Conference Room A.

She brought her wrist comm close to her chest, but it didn't buzz or beep with a new notification. Next, she scanned the vicinity for something heart shaped. Perhaps if she got near a certain location, she'd receive another clue.

The door behind her opened and closed, and foot-steps scraped across the pavement.

"Okay, girl with the plan. Where to?" Lourdes asked, studying her nails like she was already bored.

Shannan and Izzy, on the other hand, looked to Aria with wide eyes.

Aria swallowed around the lump in her throat. "I, um... I think the message is a clue."

Izzy nodded, leaning forward like she expected Aria to divulge a secret. Lourdes planted her hands on her hips and Shannan toed at the ground.

Aria stifled an irritated growl. They weren't here to help. They had decided she was right—that they needed to make it to dinner—but they had no idea where to go.

Less than eight minutes to get to the conference room. Even though she didn't have a clear idea where to go, Aria reasoned heading out of the barracks quadrant was a good start. She took off at a brisk pace, not glancing back to see if Lourdes and the others were keeping up.

She was turning onto the street beyond the barracks when a hand grabbed her upper arm, yanking her backward with such force she slammed down on her behind. "What in the galaxy?"

Lourdes towered above her. "Slow down."

Aria took a deep breath, fighting the urge to jump to her feet and shove Lourdes onto her own rear end. As she stood, something on the nearby curb caught her eye. A shape stamped into the concrete.

"Follow your heart." The heart wasn't straight up

and down, but tilted a few degrees to the left. It had to mean something. She took off at a run. "This way!" She kept her eyes glued to the curb as she ran up the street.

"Slow down!" Shannan called. "I'm going to have a heart attack."

Aria didn't slow. They had less than five minutes to make it to Conference Room A, and she had no way of knowing how much farther they had to go.

"Are we even going the right way?" Lourdes panted.

Two more hearts urged Aria on. But when she reached an open plaza filled with tables, she slowed and spun in a circle. The plaza was flat. There were no more curbs to guide her way.

Lourdes came to a stop beside her. "This doesn't look like a conference room."

"What's wrong?" Izzy asked.

Aria ran a hand through her hair, gathering a fistful and tugging it. "It doesn't make sense. It said to follow your heart. That's what I did."

Lourdes rolled her eyes. "Great. I knew I should've stayed in the room. Shannan, you remember how to get back, right?"

But Shannan's eyes were fixed on her wrist comm. "*Don't be a square and let the others leaf you behind.* What's that mean?"

"Of course," Aria muttered. There was more to the riddle. She looked around the plaza. Buildings boxed it in on three sides and a large pool glittered along the fourth. The plaza was a square.

They were in the right place after all.

"We need to find a leaf."

Lourdes hiked an eyebrow. "A leaf? If you hadn't noticed, we're kind of in the desert."

Aria ignored her as she dashed deeper into the plaza, darting around and between tables. The hearts had been stamped into the cement. Maybe the leaf would be, too.

Lourdes remained on the edge of the square, but Izzy and Shannan joined Aria amid the tables.

Two minutes.

"Here!" Izzy shouted. "I mean, I think!"

Aria dodged jutting bench seats as she streaked to Izzy's side. It looked like the imprint of a dogwood leaf. The narrow point of the tip lined up with an alley on the other side of the plaza.

Aria sped toward it, not bothering to see if the others were following. Her footsteps echoed off the walls of the buildings on either side of her as she ran through the narrow passage. A trickle of people filtered into a building at the far end of another plaza. The holographic lettering above the doors cycled between a set of numbers and a set of words. The time, 17:59, and the words *Conference Room A*.

Pride swelled in Aria as she ran toward the building. She did it.

Blue-shirted overseers flanked each set of doors,

scanning the wrist comms of a few stragglers as they entered.

A stitch in her side made Aria's breath catch, but she pressed on. Ten meters to go. Eight. Six. Five.

An ascending tone resounded through the plaza. Aria skidded to a stop and pressed her hands to her ears to block out the noise, which seemed to make every atom of her body vibrate.

A holoscreen flickered to life above the conference building and in a flash, Dr. Withers appeared. The corners of her lips curled, sending a shiver down Aria's spine.

Lourdes, Shannan, and Izzy skidded to a stop behind Aria, their labored breathing harsh in Aria's ears.

"It is now eighteen hundred hours," the doctor said. "One skill necessary for life on a Martian colony is critical thinking—and the ability to follow directions. This exercise tested both. This is far from the only time you will be asked to display these qualities—unless you did not make it to your designated meal location within the allotted time. For those of you seated at a table, enjoy your meal. For those of you who haven't yet reached your destination, your time here is over. Do not resist as our employees lead you out of the center."

The holoscreen blinked out and Aria's mind whirred to a stop.

It wasn't until overseers left their posts at the doors that the meaning of Withers' words sank in.

Dread curled her stomach. She didn't make it.

Chapter Eleven

*O*verseers in blue shirts moved closer by the second, and Aria's muscles coiled as she readied herself—but for what course of action she wasn't sure.

Dr. Withers couldn't be serious. Aria couldn't be out—not over being a few seconds late for dinner. She hadn't been able to show them how well she would do on a colony. She hadn't been able to prove herself yet.

Half a dozen overseers drifted into the plaza, and the bulges at their hips drew Aria's eye—a warning to those who refused to go quietly.

"No way! That's not fair!" Lourdes pushed past Aria and streaked toward the conference room, zig-zagging around two overseers. Three of the doors were shuttered tight, but one remained cracked. An overseer with perfectly styled blond hair stood with one foot inside the building and one out, watching the scene unfold. "We made it—we're here!" Lourdes shouted. "Let us in."

Aria didn't hear the employee's response, but there was something familiar about him. Three overseers made a wide circle around Aria, Shannan, and Izzy, boxing them in. But Aria's attention was on Lourdes. If the overseer would let her in, Aria should be there, too. If she got escorted off the premises, she'd never have another chance to get to Mars.

"It's not even my fault I'm late," Lourdes pressed. She spun and pointed at Aria. "It's *her* fault. She held me back. I was trying to be a team player and help someone in my barracks. You shouldn't penalize me for that!"

The lie hit Aria like a slap across the face. "*I* held *you* back? You're kidding, right?" She took a few steps forward. When none of the overseers made a move on her, she continued toward Lourdes. "You didn't even want to come to dinner. And you didn't help figure out the clues at all. You never would've gotten this far without me."

The employee guarding the door crossed his arms over his chest. "Interesting."

Aria saw up close for the first time and a shock of recognition shot through her. *C. Reed. Level Two Overseer.* "I know you. You took my blood earlier. You said I'm exactly the kind of person you're looking for on the mission."

His face showed no flicker of recognition, and

Aria's cheeks heated. He probably said the same thing to countless hopefuls. Maybe it was something they had instructed all employees to say. She was foolish to think he'd meant there was something special about her.

Lourdes shoved her way between Aria and Reed. "Believe me, the last thing you want on Mars is someone like *her*. She's a liar who's just out to make herself look good."

The accusation stunned Aria so much she couldn't form words. Lourdes was the one lying, not her. She was trying to take credit for everything Aria had done to get them this far.

A man's voice rose up behind Aria. "Do you want us to haul them out of here?" Shuffling drew her attention. The man stood less than a meter behind her and two female employees now gripped Izzy and Shannan by their upper arms.

"Take *them* if you want, but I'm getting in that conference room." Lourdes charged toward Reed, but when his fingers grazed the bulge at his side, Aria grabbed the girl's wrist and pulled her back.

Lourdes slapped Aria across the face, sending a shockwave through her whole body. Her eyes watered and her grip loosened enough to allow Lourdes to wrench herself away.

When Aria recovered from the blow, her fingers curled. She pulled her arm back and clenched her fist the way Alonzo taught her, but Reed moved between them, his motions swift and catlike. He grabbed Aria's wrist and pressed it down to her side.

"Enough of this," said the man behind Aria. "It doesn't matter how close you got to the building. Besides, fighting is an automatic ejection. I'm going to—"

A tremor passed over Reed's face as he released Aria's wrist. The other employee's footsteps were closing in when Reed held up his hand. "No, I've got this. Leave her—and the other three. Do a perimeter sweep, then check the barracks."

"But—"

"Did I stutter, Brandon? Do it."

Aria's heart hammered in her chest and she held her breath, waiting for something—anything—to happen. The seconds stretched on and each of Aria's nerve endings tingled.

Brandon gritted his teeth. "You heard him. Let's go."

Reed didn't move until Brandon and the others had made it halfway across the plaza.

His shoulders finally relaxed and he swept a hand toward the door he'd stood in earlier. "You four had better get in there. If anyone asks, you were in the bathroom and Calix Reed sent you along."

Lourdes grabbed the door's handle and launched herself inside as soon as Reed finished speaking. Izzy and Shannan shuffled through next, but Aria didn't follow until Calix turned his back and started across the square.

"Phobos, I thought we were done for." Izzy released a shaky breath as they started down the hall toward a low murmur of voices.

Shannan fell into step beside Lourdes. "You were joking, right? You weren't going to just let them throw us out, were you?"

Lourdes drew back her shoulders, but she didn't respond immediately. "We're in this together. Until we aren't."

Shannan tittered, the sound high and brittle. "Good thing we're still in it together, then."

Lourdes made a noncommittal noise in the back of her throat as she led the way through an open door and into the conference room. Dozens of circular tables had been crammed inside. Aria slipped into a chair at the first empty table she came to, even though there were a few tables with extra spaces further in. Despite Reed having allowed them in, she didn't want to use his cover story unless she had to.

Izzy slid into the seat beside Aria. "I'm just glad we're still here."

Aria nodded. But despite her relief, she couldn't shake the feeling that there was more going on here than she realized.

Why had Reed let them stay? His coworker had been ready to escort them all out. What had changed

Reed's mind—and done so enough that he would tie his own name to their fate?

While blue-shirted overseers brought plates of food to the tables, the familiar tritone sounded and a screen lit up the front of the room.

"I hope you're enjoying your meal," Dr. Withers said, the peculiar smile curving her lips. "Congratulations on making it this far. By now, anyone who didn't make it to dinner on time has been escorted off the premises."

Aria's ears burned and she kept her head down. No one so much as glanced in her direction.

"For some of you, this round of eliminations may have been unsettling, but I assure you they were necessary. Life in the Colony won't always be predictable. Sometimes the ability to think quickly and follow directions will be all that stands between you living and dying." A steely glint flickered in Dr. Withers' gray eyes. "However, I assure you there will be no more surprise eliminations. From now on, elimination will occur nightly based on individual rankings. We have a desired number of people for each age group; therefore, each of you has been sorted into a leader board according to your age."

For the first time, Aria took a good look at the other hopefuls in the room. They were all her age. The older applicant groups must be eating somewhere else.

Withers continued speaking. "We will update ranks throughout the day, but final rankings will be revealed at the end of dinner each night. The bottom ten in each age group will be cut."

A murmur rose up around the room. Aria's stomach twisted. She knew there would be competition within the center, but cutting people every night seemed extreme.

"This may sound harsh. Some of you may be thinking, isn't a person allowed to have an off day? Should your suitability for this mission depend on your performance for a single day? In short, yes. We require excellence. Not only that, the untamed environments on Mars demand our smartest, strongest, most resourceful individuals."

Aria sat up straighter.

"In the next few moments, you'll each receive a ping showing your current placement on the leader board. So you don't have to search through hundreds of names, your portion of the list contains only twenty. Some of you will find you're in the red zone. If this were a normal day, being red would get you cut, so consider this a warning. There's an entire day ahead of you before the next round of eliminations. Plenty of time to rise up in the rankings."

Dr. Withers' face blinked away and a series of chimes and buzzes chorused through the room as each wrist comm received a ping. Aria's fingers trembled as she tapped on the icon to load the leader board.

Her section of names popped up and her stomach twisted. Half of them were yellow while the other half were red. Aria scanned for her name, but all the letters ran together into nonsense.

She squeezed her eyes closed before trying again, starting at the bottom.

A relieved sigh escaped her lips. Hers wasn't among the red names.

But a sharp intake of breath from Shannan drew her attention. She looked at the list again, afraid she'd missed her own name, but it only took a few moments to understand Shannan's distress.

The name at the top of the red zone was Shannan Cline.

Izzy placed a hand on Shannan's shoulder. "It's okay. You've got all day tomorrow to pull yourself up the rankings. All you need is to do better than one person... Deimos."

Aria looked at the names above Shannan's and her breath caught. Coming in just above Shannan was Izzy, followed by Lourdes and Aria.

She wasn't as safe as she thought.

Chapter Twelve

*C*alix Reed jogged through the selection center toward his personal quarters. While still on duty, this was too important to wait. Guarding the door to the conference hall was a low priority next to his primary directive.

He turned the corner to the employee quadrant and ducked his head to avoid being seen by a knot of blue-shirted overseers standing near the employee lodge. Just ten meters to his room.

"You mind telling me what that was about?"

Calix groaned at the sound of Brandon Garrison's voice. The selection centers had proven more difficult to staff than Dr. Withers anticipated and they'd had to bring on outside help to make sure they were operational in time. But outside staff had several drawbacks —not least of which being people like Brandon who never stopped looking for ways to get a leg up on those around him.

Calix glanced over his shoulder but didn't slow his pace. Brandon had split off from the others and was following him. "I don't have time for this, Brandon."

"Aren't you supposed to be at your post? Tricia said—"

"Since when do I care what Tricia has to say?" Calix snapped. His quarters were in view. This news couldn't wait and Brandon was chafing his last nerve. "Aren't you supposed to be on patrol?"

Brandon snorted. "You can't get on me for not being on duty when you're not either. Some of us have been wondering if you're going rogue. During training, Dr. Withers made it very clear that the rules are in place to ensure we choose the best, most resourceful people for the next colony. How's she going to feel when she finds out you're letting people stay whenever the mood strikes you?"

Calix rubbed his thumb along the tips of his fingers, wishing he had the strength to punch Brandon and his smug face into next week. But no—that kind of power wasn't his to wield at the moment, and that fact was the reason he needed to get back to his room. "If you want to file a report on me, go ahead. Now, if you'll excuse me, I have my own report to file."

Brandon's eyebrows hiked upward. "What kind of report?"

"Phobos." He turned his back and continued

toward his room. "I'd get back to my duties if I were you, Brandon. You've been working here for, what? A week? I've been working with Withers for years. Who do you think she'll listen to?"

Brandon's face twisted with anger, but Calix didn't slow his pace to enjoy it. He was sure Brandon would head to his own room to type up the fastest report he could, but it wouldn't matter. There was nothing someone like Brandon could say that would make Withers fire Calix. Brandon—all the new employees— were a means to an end.

And Calix may have discovered that end.

He punched in the passcode and the door to his quarters slid open. "Screen on. Ping Uma Withers."

The wall screen across from his bed blazed to life and a green wheel spun in the upper right corner. He paced, tapping his thumbs against his fingertips as he went. All their time searching and Calix had finally found the one they were looking for. Not a minute too soon, either. When he thought of what would happen if they hadn't found a suitable person... He pushed the idea from his head. It didn't matter now.

The spinning wheel stopped and blinked three times before the blank screen was replaced with the scowling image of a woman with short white hair and an angular chin. "Calix. This is unexpected."

He did his best to ignore the iciness in her tone. "I know my check-in isn't for a few more hours, but I didn't think you'd want to wait to hear this. Can we talk?"

Uma sighed. Her image shook as she shifted her miniscreen from one hand to the other and pulled something from the side. She pressed a small earpiece into her ear. "Go ahead."

"I found her." He pressed his lips together as he waited for a response, but Uma's face remained blank. He opened his mouth to repeat himself, worried her earpiece was malfunctioning.

"Are you positive?" Her lips barely moved as she spoke, and her gray eyes flicked up as if she were checking her surroundings. The walls behind her shifted as she walked out of the room she was in.

"I haven't done any tests yet. Her blood work was promising, and I've had only brief contact with her so far, but if she is what I think—"

"Don't think, Calix. I don't pay you to think." Uma pursed her lips, staring at a spot just above her screen. "You're at the Phoenix center, right? I can be there by tomorrow afternoon. I trust that's enough time for you to make a final determination."

Calix fought to keep his expression neutral. The challenges for tomorrow were already set, and none of them would highlight what he needed. It would take some finagling, and changing things in such a short amount of time would raise suspicions with some new employees, but it would be worth it if this girl was what he believed her to be. "No problem at all."

The corners of Uma's mouth curled. "That's what I like to hear. Now, for your sake, I hope this girl lives up to your expectations."

The screen blinked out and Calix exhaled the breath he hadn't realized he'd been holding. He also hoped this girl was what he thought she was, but not for his sake. He hadn't thrown in with Uma Withers because he believed in her cause or because he thought only she could solve the world's biggest problems. She had many acolytes who followed her for those reasons, but his was at once both simpler and, perhaps, more foolhardy.

And he'd never been closer to his goal than today.

Chapter Thirteen

*A*ria sat with her elbows pressed against a stainless steel tabletop as she chewed the dry, tasteless energy bar the overseer had given her. She wanted nothing more than to press her forehead to the metal surface and snag a few minutes of rest, but she didn't dare. She couldn't show weakness if she wanted to avoid being cut.

So far today, Aria had run on a treadmill for so long she was sure her feet would have blisters, and she completed screen-based aptitude and reasoning exams that made her brain feel like mush.

It wasn't even noon yet.

Every time she felt the urge to complain or ask for a break, her standings from last night flashed in her mind's eye and she gritted her teeth and pushed through. She needed to give this her all or risk being cut tonight at dinner.

A pneumatic hiss sliced through the air as the testing room door slid open to reveal Aria's overseer of the day. Bindi offered Aria a kind smile as she approached, the skin around her eyes crinkling. "Good, you're almost done with your snack. It's time for the next phase."

Aria's stomach twisted, and she fought to keep her expression neutral. How could these people expect anyone to do their best work under these kinds of conditions? She understood the reasoning—that life on Mars required strength and resourcefulness. But she had watched The Colonists long enough to know this was nothing like what those people experienced.

She gritted her teeth as she pushed herself to her feet but quickly twisted her lips into a smile. The last thing she wanted was for Bindi to knock her down the leader board for having a bad attitude.

Her legs ached in protest as she followed Bindi out of the room and down a long, white-walled hallway.

"The next task is also a physical one. But you get lunch when you're done. Followed by a rest period." Bindi winked like the two were sharing an inside joke.

Aria was about to ask what the afternoon task was but thought decided against it. It was better not to know, otherwise she might focus on it instead of the current test.

Bindi stopped at a door at the end of the hall. "Your task is to shelve boxes. Thrilling, I know." She smiled.

Aria attempted to reciprocate, but she feared it came out as a grimace.

"You're row K. When you've finished the boxes there, exit through the door on the other side of the room. I'll be keeping an eye on you." Bindi tapped the tablet cradled in the crook of her arm. "Questions?"

Aria shook her head. Her only questions were the ones she shouldn't ask. Why did she have to shelve boxes? How would this task help them determine whether she moved up or down in ranking?

Bindi pressed her thumb to the rectangular panel beside the door. The light above it flashed from red to green and the door slid open. The room beyond was only twenty meters across, but it was wide and lined with shelves. Rows A-E were to her left, but F-Z stretched out to her right.

She swallowed. At least she only had one aisle to shelve.

Rows F and G were empty, but a short blonde girl was busy moving boxes in row H. Aria's step faltered for a second, but she kept going without saying hello. It shouldn't surprise her she wasn't the only person in the room. Everyone at the center was probably engaged in some kind of testing or another.

No one worked in row I, but a guy of around nineteen lounged in row J. He jumped to his feet as Aria passed before letting out a shaky laugh.

"I thought you were an overseer," he said, pushing a lock of brown hair off his forehead.

Aria shook her head. "No. Just on my way to row K." She gave a small wave before continuing on. Bindi said she would be watching, and Aria didn't want the overseer thinking she was wasting time chatting when she had a task to do. If Bindi was timing the test, Aria couldn't waste precious seconds making small talk with a stranger.

Row K was set up the same as the other rows she had passed, with boxes of varying sizes stacked in the center of the aisle and empty metal shelves lining each side.

She picked up the first box, relieved that it wasn't much heavier than a stack of plates. When she placed it on the shelf, she glimpsed flashes of the brown-haired guy between boxes he already stowed. He whistled as he worked. For a few seconds, she tried to pick out the tune, but as he lifted another box, she shook herself. She needed to focus. He was around her age, which meant they were vying for the same spots. If all she did was stand around watching him work, his ranking would increase while hers sank lower.

The second and third boxes were the same weight as the first, but the fourth box was more like a chunk of concrete. Staggering, she made her way to the shelf and managed—barely—to push it on.

She wiped her brow with the back of her hand. As long as there were no boxes heavier than that one, she should be okay.

She had filled one shelf and was well onto the next

when she tried to lift a box that wouldn't budge. No matter how she approached it, she couldn't get it even a centimeter off the ground.

Sweat blossomed on her brow and she swiped at it before attempting to push the box toward the shelving unit. With an almighty grunt, she shoved it incrementally along. Straightening, she stared at the box. She could leave it there. There were plenty more boxes. But what would it say of her work ethic if she gave up on a job just because it was difficult? Sucking in a breath, she crouched down again. She braced her feet against the opposite shelving unit and pushed against the box with her shoulder. A strangled scream escaped her lips when it barely moved.

"Hey, you okay?"

The brunette guy stood at the end of her aisle, his thick eyebrows raised.

Aria pushed herself to her feet and gestured to the box. "It's too heavy. I can't move it."

He took a step forward. "I'm happy to help, if you like."

She pressed her lips together, weighing her options. Bindi said her task was to shelve the boxes in her row. She didn't specify she had to do everything alone.

If Alonzo were here, he'd chide her for being so stubborn. There was only one choice. "Sure, I'd appreciate it."

The guy flashed a dazzling smile before sauntering down the aisle. He squatted on one side of the box and

Aria copied his posture on the other side. She counted to three and the two of them lifted. Even throwing all her power behind it, the box barely rose—but it was enough to start moving.

They staggered a few shuffling steps to the side before Aria's tenuous grasp slipped. "I'm losing it."

The guy lowered his side of the box just in time. Aria stood and stretched out her fingers. Her companion swiped the back of his hand across his forehead. "What do you think they've got in there? Lead?"

Aria shrugged. "It doesn't matter, does it?"

The box was about as long as Aria's whole arm and as wide as her forearm, but it wasn't deep. But for its weight, it was no more interesting than any of the other boxes.

Her companion poked at it with his toe before crouching down and running his fingers along the edge of the packing tape. "Could be nothing, I suppose. But maybe it's something interesting. Or valuable."

She knocked his hand away. "Our assignment was to move the boxes, not to investigate what's in them."

Instead of looking at all chastised, the guy offered another of his carefree grins. "Fair enough. Should we try again?"

In response, Aria took up her position on her side of the box. They lifted and shuffled to the side again. Aria's fingers ached, but she refused to let go until this thing was in its place. She slipped her end onto the edge of the bottom shelf and helped her companion shove it the rest of the way on.

"Woo!" The guy ran a hand through his hair and leaned against the shelving. "I thought we lost it for a second there. I'm Declan, by the way."

Aria stared at the hand he held out to her. After a beat, she took it, squeezing it the way her father had taught her. "Aria."

He grinned as he returned pressure in her hand. She waited for him to continue, but he merely stared at her, his hazel eyes not breaking contact with hers, like he was waiting for something to happen. The moment stretched out until it felt forced and unnatural. She dropped his hand and went back to her stack for something to do. The next box she lifted was a lighter one she could handle on her own. She hoped Declan would get the hint and go back to his aisle, but he folded his arms over his chest and leaned against the rack again, studying her.

She shelved one box, then another. Didn't he have a task to complete, too? She couldn't figure out why he was hanging around. He offered help, she took it, now their interaction was complete. It wasn't until she pushed the third box onto the shelf that her manners caught up with her. "Uh, thank you. I couldn't have moved that box without you."

Declan flashed a smile. "Always happy to help a damsel in distress."

Aria narrowed her eyes and Declan held up his

hands.

"Anyone. Anyone in distress. And, for the record, you don't look particularly damsel-y. Very strong and in-charge. In fact, I'm sure you would've moved that box by yourself eventually."

The corners of her mouth quirked. It was the kind of thing Alonzo would say—except Alonzo would be much smoother about it. He had a knack for sensing what people wanted to hear and how to put them at ease. It was part of what made him a good salesman. And a good friend.

Declan tilted his head. "Look, I understand where this is coming from. Really, I do. But you shouldn't go falling in love with me. At least, not before we make it to Mars."

Aria froze halfway to the shelf. "Come again?"

He held his hands up. "You're not the first to succumb to my charm. But we're in competition, and I wouldn't want you to risk your chances by focusing on your intense attraction to me."

A grin stretched across her face before she realized he wasn't joking. She schooled her features before continuing on her course. "It's not that. You remind me of someone. His name's Alonzo."

Declan nodded as he crossed to her pile of boxes and scooped one up. "Ah. And he's the one you're in love with."

Aria snorted. "No. He's my brother. I mean, he's adopted, but we might as well be blood related."

Declan lifted an eyebrow, and he glanced up and down the aisle. "Is he here somewhere? Are you guys in an all-or-nothing pact?"

She dropped her gaze, grabbing another box. "No. He... He's not here." She forced a smile. "Maybe he'll come up on the next wave."

Aria swallowed around the lump clogging her throat. Leaving her family behind wasn't a new concept. For years she had planned to travel the world and see all the sights it had to offer. But in those daydreams, Alonzo was always by her side. She had never considered going on an adventure—especially not one as big as going to Mars—without him.

"He's still back at home, I take it?" Declan's tone was light, but careful. "Where are you from?"

"Old LA," she said, grateful for the gentle shift in topic. "You?"

He shrugged. "I'm kind of a nomad. I've seen most every corner of this world worth seeing, so I figured why not check out another planet?"

They shelved more boxes in companionable silence before Declan started whistling the same song as before. He went through it several times until the melody was familiar and she found herself humming along.

With each new box placed on the shelves, available space dwindled. She wondered what she was supposed to do if she ran out of room to place the remaining items.

Except when she turned around, no boxes remained.

She brushed her palms against her pants. "Wow. I can't believe we're done." She squinted toward the far wall. "I think the exit's over there."

Declan nodded. "I think you're right. I wonder what fresh torture you'll find on the other side."

She squinted. "You mean we?"

The corner of his mouth quirked. "I've got a little more work to do. But I'll see you on the other side, yeah?"

"Yeah, sure," she murmured, but Declan was on his way back toward his own aisle. The whole time he'd been here helping her, she'd assumed he was finished with his own project. Her stomach knotted. It wasn't her fault he'd chosen to help her. She hadn't sought him out. Helping was his idea. Her eyes strayed to the exit. Bindi had said she'd be watching on her tablet. Or had she said timing? Aria couldn't recall. But even if she were keeping track of how long the task took her, Aria was finished with the boxes in her aisle. Maybe staying late to assist Declan wouldn't count against her.

Grunts floated over from the next row. She recognized the strain. Declan must have a heavy box like the one she'd had. There was no way he could move it on his own—he'd barely been able to lift it with her help.

"Phobos and Deimos," she muttered, striking off in his direction. When she arrived in his aisle, he was prone on the floor, bracing his feet against one set of shelves and pressing his shoulder into the offending box. "Need help?"

His eyes popped open, and he scrambled to his feet. "I mean, if you're offering, I won't offend you by turning you down. But as you can see, I've got things under control."

"Uh huh." She positioned herself on one side of the box and the two worked together as they'd done before to shift it into its new place on a shelf.

Once they stowed it, Declan rested against the shelving unit, sweat glistening on his forehead. "Thanks for the assist. I assume you're on your way out now?"

Aria's eyes strayed to the door. There had only been one exceptionally heavy box in her pile, but what if there was another hiding somewhere in Declan's group? And even if there wasn't, Declan hadn't needed to stay and help her with her task, yet he had. The least she could do was repay his courtesy. "What do you call a male damsel in distress?"

Declan flashed a grin.

There were less than half a dozen boxes remaining when the familiar sounds of struggle rose up in another corner of the room.

"How much you want to bet each row has one impossible-to-move box?" Declan asked.

"Only one way to find out." Leaving Declan to finish his last boxes on his own, Aria headed down to row H where the short blonde was straining to budge the last box in her aisle. "Need help?"

The girl glanced up. Her face was beet red and sweat plastered her bangs against her forehead. "No. I've got it."

Aria crossed her arms over her chest. "I'm guessing you don't. Me and the guy a couple rows over both had a box like that. It took both of us to move them. Let me help—then you'll be done."

The blonde's lips puckered as she considered the offer. Aria wondered if she'd looked this distrustful when Declan extended a helping hand.

"Okay," she said finally.

Within a minute, Aria and the blonde stowed the box. The girl leaned against the shelves and swiped her forehead. "How can they expect a single person to lift something so heavy?"

"Maybe they're looking for super strong people," Declan suggested as he turned down the aisle.

The hairs on the back of Aria's neck rose. Did he mean aberration strong? She dismissed the thought. More of her father's paranoia rearing its head. The explanation could be so much simpler. "What if this task isn't about speed or strength? What if it's about this?" She circled her finger to connect the three of them. "About helping each other?"

The blonde pushed off from her shelf. "Then we should go see if there's anyone else still working and help them before we leave."

For a split second, Aria regretted sharing her theory with the others. If offering assistance was the object of this test, it might help her ranking if she alone went around helping others. But it was Declan who reached out to her in the first place, and she longed to leave this room and have lunch and a rest period.

Aria followed Declan and the blonde out of the aisle. The blonde went right, toward rows A through E while Declan and Aria took the latter part of the alphabet. Declan found a guy in row N and Aria helped another guy in row Q. The girl in row T was so thrilled by the offer of assistance that she kissed both Declan and Aria on the cheek.

When she made it to row X, Aria stifled a groan.

Lourdes.

She sat on the concrete floor and shoved at the single remaining box with her feet, but it didn't budge.

For an instant, Aria considered walking away. Lourdes hadn't spotted her yet, and it was possible someone else would come along to assist. But if the overseers were watching, walking away would look bad.

Smiling the practiced smile she used when waiting tables, Aria approached Lourdes. "Need some help?"

Lourdes leapt to her feet and spun to face her. "What? No. I've got this."

Aria took a step closer. "I can guarantee you don't. The overseers put one ridiculously heavy box in every row. I think they want us to help each other."

Crossing her arms over her chest, Lourdes glowered. "I don't care what you think."

Declan stepped into the aisle opposite where Aria

stood. "Good news. I think she's the last one in here."

Lourdes scowled. "So you two just went around helping everyone?"

Declan tilted his head. "Yeah. Didn't Aria explain?" He took a step forward, reaching for the box.

Lourdes put out her hand to stop him. "If no one else has done this on their own, I'll be the first. They'll see I'm the strongest competitor."

Aria sighed, shifting on the balls of her feet. "But that's not the point of this exercise."

"You want to make me look bad," Lourdes snapped. "First you tried to get me kicked out at dinner. Now this?"

Aria gaped. How could Lourdes rewrite history like that? Aria had been the one to figure out the riddle. If she hadn't allowed Lourdes and the others to follow her, they would be out already. She opened her mouth, intending to point that out, but Declan cut her off.

"I guess that's it, then." He beckoned for Aria to follow. "Let's go. You can't force help on somebody."

After a beat, Aria passed Lourdes and headed toward the exit with Declan. He was right. Lourdes wasn't her responsibility. If she wanted to get herself cut, so be it.

But as she walked toward the door, uneasiness coiled in her stomach like a snake. Lourdes lied last night when they made it to Conference Room A, and she lied again today. How long before one of her fabrications got Aria in trouble?

Chapter Fourteen

*W*hen Aria's wrist comm vibrated with an incoming message, she jolted awake, her heart pounding as she tried to decipher her surroundings.

The barracks at the selection center. After lunch, she'd come back to her quarters and fallen asleep.

The room was dim, quiet, and empty. Aria's panic didn't fade as she tried to remember where she was supposed to be. Had she missed a test?

No. The schedule for the sixteen-to-nineteen age group had been clear until dinner. She glanced at her wrist comm to check the time, but a notification from the overseers dominated the screen.

Dinner tonight will take place in the plaza marked on the attached map. Attendance is mandatory. Don't be late.

After checking her reflection in the bathroom mirror and running her fingers through her hair to comb out some snarls, she headed out of the room. On her way to the plaza, she wondered if Lourdes was still in row X, struggling with her final box.

She shook off the lingering guilt for not sticking around to convince Lourdes to accept help. It wasn't her fault Lourdes insisted she could do it herself.

The hum of voices reached Aria before the plaza came into view. A knot of people clogged the street ahead, and she turned to find another way in.

Two more streets led into the plaza, each as crowded as the last. Aria was about to turn back when she saw an alley along the far wall. It was empty, and she followed it into the square, coming in beside the pool.

It was larger than she realized last night. Sunlight shimmered against the motionless water. Aria's fingers itched with the desire to slip her hands through the cool liquid, to feel it envelop her body. But even if she wasn't on her way to the mandatory meal time, she couldn't risk taking a swim. If she wet more than her hands, her gills would unseal and anyone with an unobstructed view of her neck would see her for what she was.

She turned from the glistening surface toward the sea of people packing the plaza. Hopefuls filled many of the round tables. After last night's surprise elimination, it seemed those remaining didn't want to risk tardiness. And like last night, everyone she saw was around her age. She wondered where the older age groups were eating tonight.

Declan sat at a table on her right. A handful of guys joined him, but there were still empty seats. Aria fought the urge to ask if she could sit with him. She had enjoyed his company during the last challenge, but she shouldn't let herself get attached. This was a competition. And if it came down to the two of them on opposite sides of a challenge, she didn't want any friendly feelings to keep her from claiming her spot in the new colony.

She caught sight of Lourdes, Shannan, and Izzy seated at a table on her left, deep in conversation with two broad-shouldered guys. She decided against joining her roommates. Listening to Lourdes make baseless accusations about how Aria was trying to make her fail didn't sound like a pleasant way to spend dinner.

Instead, Aria asked if she could sit in an open seat at a table full of people she didn't recognize. The girl nearest to her shrugged, which was enough for Aria. The other people at the table barely glanced in her direction.

Overseers moved between tables, pushing carts laden with plated meals. Aria's stomach growled, and she dug into her corn, black bean, and rice casserole as soon as the overseer set it in front of her.

The familiar chimes reverberated through the air as Aria chewed the last bite of her meal. A hologram of Dr. Withers blinked into focus above them and humming voices silenced.

"Good evening. I hope you all took advantage of

the rest time in today's schedule. You deserved it after this morning's tests." She paused, her eyes roaming from side to side as if examining the crowd. Aria's stomach lurched, even though this pre-recorded message couldn't see any of them. "Living on another planet, it will be important to work at your personal best at all times. Giving less than that could cause failure on the mission. However, as today's test showed, sometimes you can't complete a job alone. Future colonists should be responsible enough to do their assigned work but wise enough to accept help where necessary because we are stronger together."

Eyes prickled the back of Aria's neck and she turned to see Lourdes glaring at her. Aria pressed her lips together and turned back to Dr. Withers' image. Lourdes could be mad if she wanted, but Aria had tried to do the right thing. It was Lourdes's own stubbornness that kept her from accepting assistance.

Dr. Withers offered one of her tight-lipped smiles, but as she opened her mouth to continue, her image blinked out and was replaced with a larger-than-life version of Calix Reed. His expression was animated, for once, and Aria couldn't help wondering what had him so excited.

"Before we share the updated rankings, I have a special announcement. This evening, we've selected your age group for an optional challenge."

Murmuring voices rose like a wave around Aria.

Her curiosity crested, but her aching muscles clung like a barnacle to the word *optional.*

"Some of you may wonder why you should risk participating in another challenge when you don't know your current standings," Reed continued. "After all, if you're in the danger zone, why would you want to risk lowering your rank? And if you're in the green, why not rest after a day full of exhausting tasks?" He paused, smiling. The size of his projection made it feel like he was looking Aria right in the eye. "This challenge can only help your rankings. And if you win, you get one reprieve—so if you ever find yourself in the red zone, you can use your reprieve to keep from being cut."

Murmurs rose again and Aria sat straighter. Her muscles weren't *that* sore.

"There's only one catch. Since today's main task highlighted the need to accept help, this challenge will also require you work as a group."

Aria's stomach twisted with dread.

"Everyone in your barracks must compete as a team, or no one from your room can compete. You have five minutes to organize before I give you further details." Reed's face blinked out of view.

Aria sat still as a statue as a chill raced down her back. Everyone around her sprang into motion. Her table emptied as the others left to locate their roommates.

"We're doing this." Lourdes crossed her arms over

her chest as she took up residence in the space to Aria's left. Not bothering to sit, she towered over Aria, glaring.

Retorts spun through Aria's mind. The vindictive part of her wanted to refuse. Given Lourdes's ranking last night and her performance at the shelving task earlier, Aria guessed Lourdes would get cut today. After Dr. Withers' confirmation that she'd done the right thing by helping others in the challenge, Aria felt confident she was safe—at least for now.

But the part of her brain that calculated water currents and routes that wouldn't make people suspicious when she went salvaging weighed all the options. Sure, she felt confident about her performance today, but she couldn't say the same for tomorrow, or the day after. Having a reprieve could come in handy—even if it meant Lourdes would get one too.

"You owe me," Lourdes snarled.

Aria blinked, baffled. After a second she sputtered, "What?"

Lourdes flicked her braid over her shoulder. "You tricked me during the challenge today, and you know it."

Aria stared at her, unsure how to respond. She looked to Shannan and Izzy, hoping to share her bewilderment, but she was met with stony expressions. "What are you talking about?"

"You manipulated me!" Lourdes planted her hands on her hips. "You could've told me it was a teamwork challenge, but no. You came in trying to show off. You and your friend were going to move that box and leave me standing there like an idiot."

Aria gaped. "That's not at all what happened. Declan wasn't even there when I offered to help." She looked from Lourdes to her other roommates. While Izzy wouldn't meet her eyes, Shannan's expression was every bit as hard as Lourdes's.

Aria blew out a breath. "You know what? Fine. Believe whatever you want." She stood, scowling. "I'm doing this for me, not for you."

The chimes sounded again, but this time no face in the sky accompanied them. Instead, Reed's voice boomed over the crowd. "If you'll all make your way to the pool at the south side of the plaza, I'll give further directions."

Aria's throat went dry as everyone around her lurched forward. The pool? Her knees threatened to buckle beneath her. If they were meeting there, did it mean the challenge had something to do with water?

If so, Aria was screwed.

Chapter Fifteen

*A*ria fell into step beside Izzy, but her movements were mechanical. Her mind spun with possibilities. Perhaps the pool was just a starting point. The challenge might be unrelated.

Still, Aria's heartbeat pounded in her ears.

As the last stragglers slowed to a stop at the back of the group, a series of lights shone down from the tops of two surrounding buildings, illuminating Calix Reed, who stood on a small skiff in the center of the pool.

"Your task is simple," Calix said, his voice still amplified. "Each barracks will take a position by one of the poles surrounding the pool. Attached to each pole is a rope. Follow the rope to the boat under water, and do whatever you can to raise that boat to the surface. The first team who completes the challenge is the winner."

Aria's breathing shallowed. Under water. They had to go under water. She couldn't. There was no way someone wouldn't notice her gills. She couldn't trust Lourdes or the other to keep her secret—and what then? Being an aberration wasn't against the rules, but if Lourdes made up another lie, Calix Reed and the other overseers might believe her. She could get carted off to an aberration detention facility.

"Teams, take your positions."

Aria froze.

"Come on," Lourdes said.

Aria tried to shake her head, but her muscles wouldn't respond.

Izzy cupped a hand on Aria's shoulder. "Come on. It won't be that bad."

"I... I can't," Aria murmured.

"What do you mean, you can't?" Lourdes sneered. "You have to."

Aria shook her head. "I... I can't swim," she blurted.

Shannan rolled her eyes. "It's not swimming. It's the opposite. We have to get to the bottom of the pool." She reached for Aria's hand and tugged her forward.

Aria wrenched her arm away. "I'm afraid of water." It wasn't a lie. At this moment, there was nothing more terrifying than the idea of submerging herself. "I can't do this. I'm sorry."

"You *have* to," Lourdes repeated. "I need this reprieve, and I can't do the challenge unless you get in the water."

Aria took a step backward. "I'm sorry, but—"

Lourdes lunged toward her and grabbed both her wrists. When Aria tried to pull away, Shannan circled her and shoved between her shoulder blades.

"I'm not going home because of you. Take her hands, Izzy."

Aria tried to twist away, but between trying to keep her balance with Shannan shoving her from behind and her limbs trembling with adrenaline and fear, she only knocked herself off kilter. As Izzy gripped Aria's wrists, Lourdes yanked Aria's feet out from under her. With Shannan supporting Aria's middle, the three half-carried, half-dragged Aria toward the pool.

"Stop!" Aria shouted, writhing against their grip. "I can't go in the water! I can't!"

But no matter how she struggled, the water came nearer. They would throw her in against her will, and then everyone would know her secret.

She twisted her hands. "Izzy! Izzy, please! Don't do this!"

Izzy glanced down, her resolve wavering.

"Don't you dare let go, Iz," Lourdes snapped.

Izzy shifted her gaze to the water and stared forward, her jaw clenched. Her grip on Aria's wrists tightened.

The pool's edge was three meters away. Aria shrieked, hoping someone—anyone—would intervene. But the other groups were too busy staking claims around the pool, dozens of people splashing in ankle-deep water already.

Two meters.

She had always been so careful, making sure no one outside her family saw her for what she was. Now these girls would expose her in front of hundreds.

One meter.

Would they register her? Ship her to an aberration facility? Make an example of her? Or worse—would they go back to Old LA, to her family, and test them for the same aberrant ability? They could haul away her father and Sera, too.

She bucked against the girls with renewed force as shouts rose up through the crowd. Shannan stumbled and cried out, her hold on Aria's middle loosening. Using all her might, Aria bent her knees as close to her chest as she could before propelling both legs straight, hoping to shake Lourdes's grip. But before the effort had any effect, arms clamped around her stomach again.

And yanked her backward, away from the water.

"Let her go!"

The male voice threw Aria off guard. It was familiar, like one she'd heard a million times before. But it couldn't be...

"I said let go of her!" Strong arms pulled her back once more with such force that Izzy's grip broke and Lourdes stumbled and dropped to her knees. Aria's back pressed against the torso of her rescuer and she craned her neck to glimpse his face.

"Alonzo?"

"Teams ready?" boomed Calix Reed's voice over the loudspeaker. "On your mark. Get set. Go!"

Whoops and shouts rent the air as hundreds of feet splashed into the water.

Alonzo loosened his grip, but only enough for Aria to twist around within the protective circle of his arms. His usual easy smile curved his lips, but Aria detected another emotion beneath the thin veneer of normalcy. Fear.

She drew back her fist and punched his shoulder. It was as solid as the rest of him. She wasn't hallucinating. "What are you doing here?"

"Saving you, apparently." He shot a pointed glare over her head and Aria imagined Lourdes seething back. When he looked at her again, his expression sobered. "Come on. Did you think you could get rid of me that easily?" The corners of his mouth quirked. "I figured you'd be lost without me, so here I am."

Tears prickled Aria's eyes, and she threw her arms around Alonzo, squeezing him with all her might. She was ecstatic to have him here—and not just because he saved her from the water. He was her best friend—a part of her. And while she would never admit it, she agreed with him. No matter how much she wanted to get to Mars, if she got there without him, part of her would always be lost.

"And it appears we have a winner," announced Reed. "Return to the shore and have your wrist comms scanned by the nearest overseer."

Aria turned toward the water as all the participants sloshed their way back to shore.

Lourdes glared. "This is your fault. We could have a reprieve now if it wasn't for you." Balling her hand into a fist, she stalked forward.

Alonzo put himself between her and Aria. "I seem to remember fighting being cause for automatic ejection. You're lucky they haven't dragged you out for trying to haul Aria into the water."

Shannan and Izzy averted their gaze. While Lourdes's step faltered and her arm dropped to her side, her eyes blazed with hate.

Three tones chimed and Aria glanced skyward for whatever holographic image they were about to project, but nothing flickered to life.

"In a few moments, you will experience your first scheduled cut," said the familiar voice of Dr. Withers.

Alonzo nudged Aria and raised his chin toward the water. Standing on a raised platform on the far side was a woman with cropped white hair and an angular chin. Although she was too far away to make out the rest of her features, Aria recognized her. Dr. Withers was here, in person.

"I understand that this can be an emotional moment. And to those of you who haven't made today's cut, I—we—wish you well, and believe you will go on to make incredible contributions to this planet. For those whose names appear in red, please meet the overseers on the east side of the water. We expect you to leave willingly, but every overseer has been trained to remove anyone who makes a scene."

Aria shivered as she remembered the bulges on the hips of the overseers.

"You will receive your updated rankings... now."

Aria's wrist comm buzzed, as did those of everyone surrounding her. This was it. She was either in... or she was out.

Chapter Sixteen

*A*ria lifted the screen but didn't open the attachment. Instead, she watched as Alonzo opened his and sighed with relief to see his name in the green zone.

Yellow flashed in her periphery as Shannan and Izzy opened their portion of the list. Both were safe —for now.

Aria tapped her comm screen and her list loaded.

Green.

She was safe.

She blew out a breath, but before she could close her list, another name a few spaces above hers caught her eye. Declan Perth. The corners of her mouth twitched. He deserved it.

"No."

The syllable was barely more than a whisper, but it made the hair on the back of Aria's neck stand on end.

Lourdes swiped at the screen of her wrist comm, but the display didn't evaporate fast enough to conceal the glare of red. She stepped toward the water as if in a trance, her eyes fixed on the figure still standing on the raised platform on the opposite side of the pool. "Just give me one more day!" she shouted. "I can prove myself—I promise! I just need—"

Lourdes's words were cut off as a half dozen overseers circled her. She attempted to dart through their ranks, but two women caught her around the waist and a man touched her shoulder. The fight went out of Lourdes.

Her eyes found Aria in the crowd and remained locked on her as the overseers led Lourdes away.

Shannan and Izzy trailed behind their friend, like puppies not sure what to do when left alone for the first time. Murmurs rose in the crowd as those listed in green or yellow averted their attention from those being ejected from the center.

"Let's get out of here." Alonzo placed his hand between Aria's shoulder blades and pressed her away from the water and out of the plaza.

The question that had pinged around in Aria's brain since she processed Alonzo's appearance tumbled out of her mouth as soon as the crowds around them thinned. "Is Dad mad?"

"That you came here even though it's a front for registering people against their will?" The corner of

Alonzo's mouth quirked. "I don't know. I didn't tell him."

Aria's jaw dropped. "You left without saying anything? How could you do that?"

Alonzo snorted. "Don't act all high and mighty like you didn't do the same thing."

Aria opened her mouth to defend herself, but Alonzo spoke over her.

"I lied to him. Told him the march spooked you so much you convinced me we should head inland for a while. Figured that way, if you didn't make the cut here, you'd still have a home to go to. And if you did— well, then he'd have to accept that this whole thing isn't some elaborate ruse to find..." He glanced around. There were other people on the street, taking advantage of the time remaining before curfew, but none were within earshot. "...aberrations."

Aria's stomach clenched, but the knot of fear dissolved quickly. "They've already done the blood test. It didn't set off any alarms, and no one's carted me off to a black site yet, so I think it's safe to say Dad was being paranoid."

"It was still a risk," Alonzo murmured.

Aria snorted. "You were at that march, too. Me being alive is a risk."

Neither of them spoke as they turned down a street that led toward the barracks quadrant. She still couldn't believe he was here. It was a sign—it had to be. Her one reservation about being here had been leaving

Alonzo behind, but now she wouldn't have to. They would help each other, like they always did, and they would both make it to the end of the selection process.

Feet shuffled on the street behind them, but Aria didn't think much of the sound until a voice cut through the night air.

"Is that her?"

Aria's skin prickled. She fought the urge to look over her shoulder and kept her pace steady as she and Alonzo continued down the street.

It wasn't until a familiar voice reached her ears that she froze.

"Stop. It's okay—really." Izzy's voice was higher than usual.

"How can you say that?" Shannan asked.

Aria stopped and turned toward the girls' voices. Shannan and Izzy stood on the other side of the street, flanked by the broad-shouldered guys they were sitting with at dinner.

"Is that her?" the guy on the right asked again.

Izzy gripped her friend's arm. "Shannan, don't."

But Shannan glared at Aria. "Yeah, it's her."

Alonzo tugged on Aria's wrist enough to get her moving. "Let's get out of here."

She and Alonzo took off at the quickest pace they could without breaking into a jog. They were too exposed out here. But where could they go? For once, there were no blue-shirted overseers in sight.

"Hey! Hey, where you going?" the guy called, his

voice still just as loud. Aria didn't have to turn to know they were being followed.

"Stay calm," Alonzo whispered. "They'll lose interest."

"He asked you a question!" called the other guy. "You too good to answer a question?"

"Nah," said the first one. "I bet her and her boyfriend are too busy plotting who they're gonna get sent home next."

Is that the tale the girls were spinning? Heat flared through Aria's body at the audacity of the lie. She stopped and spun to face the guys, ignoring Alonzo's persistent tug on her wrist. "The only person to blame for Lourdes getting cut is Lourdes. I tried to help her during the shelving challenge, but she insisted she could do it herself. Don't try to blame me for her crappy performance."

Aria turned her attention to Shannan and Izzy as they fell into line beside the guys. "I know she was your friend, and I get that you're upset she got cut. But maybe it's a good thing. I got the feeling she would've trampled over the two of you if you stood in her way. The overseers must have seen that, too. That's why she got ranked red."

The flashes of pain in Shannan and Izzy's eyes gave Aria no pleasure as she spun around to continue in the direction she and Alonzo had been heading. She didn't even want to think about how tense things would be once she got back to the barracks. Sometimes the truth hurt, but maybe Shannan and Izzy needed to hear it before they could accept it.

Fingers clamped like a vise around Aria's wrist. "Hey, I'm not done with you." The first guy whirled Aria around, yanking her so close she could feel heat radiating off his body.

"Get your hands off her." Alonzo grabbed the guy's shoulder in an attempt to shake him off.

"You stay out of this," said the second guy.

Alonzo dropped his hand and turned his attention to the person speaking. "Just leave us alone. We don't want a fight."

The words had barely left Alonzo's mouth when the second guy landed a punch to Alonzo's stomach. Izzy yelped with surprise and Aria leapt toward the attacker, but the other man kept a firm grip on her wrist, tethering her to the spot.

Alonzo held up his hands. "Look, man," he wheezed. "They'll kick you out for fighting. I don't know about you, but I don't want to go home for something stupid."

"You calling me stupid?" Snarling, the guy punched Alonzo again.

Aria lashed out with her leg, connecting with the guy's upper thigh. Sneering, he backhanded her.

Stars popped in Aria's vision. As she blinked to clear them, Alonzo landed a punch on the guy's sternum.

"Stop!" Aria twisted against her captor. "Alonzo, he's not worth it!"

Her words fell on deaf ears. Alonzo bobbed and shuffled as he tried to avoid the other guy's fists. A small crowd gathered, forming a ring around the fighters, a subset cheering when the broad-shouldered guy landed punch after punch.

Alonzo managed a couple of jabs, each one twisting Aria's gut. This was her fault. He was only here because of her, and now he would get kicked out defending her.

"Is that all you got?" the guy asked, a grin spreading across his face. "You hit like a child." He wound up to strike Alonzo again, but his step faltered.

Concerned murmurs rose around the circle, followed by gasps as the man staggered forward.

"Make a path! Everyone clear out of here!" Calix Reed led a group of overseers past the onlookers and into the center of the circle as the guy who had been fighting Alonzo dropped to his knees.

Aria remained rooted to the spot, barely registering when the pressure around her wrist disappeared and vaguely noting Shannan's voice urging Izzy to leave.

Overseers kneeled on either side of the fallen fighter and rolled him onto his back. Aria's mind spun as she tried to make sense of what she saw. Two spots on the man's abdomen—on the left side of his stomach and on his right, below his heart—were white and frosty, with steam-like wisps curling upward and dissipating into the night air.

"What on Eris?" Alonzo took a step forward, his eyes fixed on his opponent.

"Oh, no you don't," Reed said, getting between the men. He raised his chin and two male overseers flanked Alonzo. "Take him."

As the employees grabbed Alonzo's upper arms, time caught up with Aria. "No, wait! It wasn't his fault! He was defending me!"

Reed rounded on her. "You know him?"

The other overseers led a bewildered Alonzo away. Aria took a step to follow, but Reed stepped in her path. "Do you know him?"

When it was clear he wouldn't let her pass, she focused on his face. "Yes. Yes, he's my brother. One of my roommates got cut today, and that guy was giving me a hard time about it."

"So, what? Your brother figured he'd freeze the guy?"

As if to punctuate the point, the other fighter groaned as the employees prodded his torso.

Aria's head spun as she played back the events in her mind. Nothing made sense. "No. I don't know what happened. That guy punched Alonzo, then he slapped me. That's when Alonzo hit him back. But I don't know how *that* happened to him." She gestured to the icy spots. "Alonzo's not... He's not..."

"An aberration?" Reed raised his eyebrows. "Evidence to the contrary."

Her heart thundered in her chest. "But he's not. I swear he's not. I would know!"

"If he's your brother, why should I believe you? You'd say anything to keep him out of the detention facility."

Aria's blood ran cold. "No. You wouldn't. You *can't*."

"It's the law," Reed said. "Any aberration who uses his powers to harm another person goes to the facility until a judge can review the case."

"But he's *not* an aberration." Aria's eyes burned as tears sprang into them. "Once they realize he's not one of them, they'll kill him. I've seen it on the news streams. That's why they made the facilities to isolate the aberration prisoners—they kill conforms!"

"I'm sorry," Reed said, even though he didn't look it. "My hands are tied." He turned, but Aria grabbed his hand and sank to her knees.

"Please, please do something." Tears spilled over her cheeks. Her mind spun, grasping for anything that could help. "I have credits. Alonzo and I have been saving for years. I'll give it to you—all of it." She thought of the jewelry they found at Treasures Untold. The credits from those items were supposed to go to help Melody and Harmony buy the restaurant, but it meant nothing next to Alonzo's life. "And if it's not enough, I can get more."

"I'm not interested in your credits." Reed extricated his hand from her grip.

Aria sucked in a shuttering breath. "If not credits, then what? I'll give you anything. I'll do *anything*. Just, please... Please..."

Reed took hold of her elbows to help her to her feet.

"Now, 'anything' is something I can work with."

Chapter Seventeen

*A*ria sat in the white-walled room where Calix Reed had deposited her, drumming her fingers on the arm of the cold metal chair she sat in. How much time had passed? Five minutes? Fifteen? Or perhaps he had closed the door only seconds ago. In her distracted state, it was impossible to determine.

She would give anything to know where Alonzo was. Were they keeping him in a room like this, or was he on his way to the hyperloop station to be transported to the detention facility? Not for the first time, she wished she had a useful aberration, like telepathy or X-ray vision. Her gills were of no use on land.

The door slid open. Reed entered, followed by the last person she expected to see.

Dr. Withers pressed her thumb to the panel beside the door, which hissed closed. She folded her arms across her chest and stood at the back of the room while Reed moved forward and took a seat in the chair facing Aria.

Aria jumped to her feet. "Where's Alonzo?" Her gaze slid to Dr. Withers but quickly found Reed's face again. Although Withers was the one in charge of the selection centers, Aria wasn't sure she should address the woman directly.

"In a holding cell." Reed tilted his head. "What? No wondering how the guy he froze is doing?"

"I already told you, Alonzo didn't do that. He's not an aberration."

Reed opened his mouth, but when Withers placed a hand on his shoulder, he fell silent.

"Oh, we know," she said.

Aria's jaw fell slack. "You... you know?" Relief crested over her like a wave. "Good. You can let him go and—"

"Why would we let him go?" Withers asked.

"You said you knew—"

"Of course we do. The man your brother fought has worked for me for three years." Withers patted Reed's shoulder. "I'll admit, when Calix asked me to bring him from one of our other facilities, I was dubious. But the plan worked better than I expected."

Aria blinked as she tried to process what Withers was saying. "So, the other guy—your employee—*he's* the aberration?"

Withers chuckled. "You sound surprised. I would

think you'd understand better than most that people aren't always what they seem."

The hairs on the back of Aria's neck stood at attention. Was Withers saying she knew what Aria was? There was no way. "If you know the other guy is the aberration, why not let Alonzo go?"

Dr. Withers tilted her head. "Leverage. Mr. Gonzales may not be an aberration, but you are."

Aria felt like she had just plunged head-first into icy water. They knew. But how could they? She tugged at the ends of her hair, covering her neck. "N-no, I'm not."

Withers' lips twisted into a smile that made Aria's stomach clench. "Deny it if you want, but we know the truth. You may as well be honest."

"Even if it were true—and I'm not saying it is—why would I tell you?" Aria's mind spun as she tried to figure out their angle, but nothing made sense. Maybe all her father's rantings hadn't been as far off base as she believed. "So you can ship me off to a detention facility?"

"We have a job for you," Reed said, standing. "Something specialized that requires a specific gift to accomplish."

That was it, then. They wanted to use her. But what would happen when they were done with her? If they were willing to lie and claim Alonzo was an aberration, she couldn't trust them not to tell her secret. And if their job was something criminal and she got caught using her aberration to commit it, she would end up at the detention facility anyway.

"I can't help you," she said, pleased her voice was steady.

"Really?" Reed took a step closer, his brow knitting. "I could've sworn you told me you'd do *anything* to save your brother." He strode toward her slowly, methodically, not taking his eyes off her. Brushing his shoulder against hers, he circled her like a predator. "Now I'm wondering if that *anything* didn't come with a limit." He trailed his finger up her spine, making goosebumps break out on her arms. "What's your line, Ayers, Aria Chelan?"

Aria panted through parted lips. How far *would* she go? If they asked her to commit a crime without using her abilities, would she do it? What would she give up to save her best friend?

Since joining her family, Alonzo had made it his mission to protect Aria and keep her safe. Now it was her turn.

"If I agree to do this, you'll let Alonzo go?"

Dr. Withers chuckled. "Of course not."

Aria gaped as Reed put distance between the two of them. "But you said—"

"Agreeing to help isn't enough," Withers said. "We'll let your brother go if you're successful." Her lips stretched in an unnerving smile. "Do we have a deal?"

Aria gulped. If she ever hoped to face her own reflection again, there was only one answer. "Yes."

Withers clasped her hands. "Excellent. Time is of the essence. I'll leave Calix to get you up to speed while I make preparations for your mission."

Aria looked at Reed as Withers exited the room, closing the door behind her. "What do you need me to do? Break in somewhere? Steal something? Kill someone?" She said the last part as a joke but regretted it as soon as the words passed her lips. She had no idea what these people wanted and had no desire to put ideas into their heads.

The corners of Reed's mouth quirked. "No murder on the agenda at the moment. And *technically* no on the other two." He reclaimed the chair he'd sat in when he arrived and motioned for Aria to sit as well. After a beat, she complied. "Your job is to get inside somewhere inaccessible to, well, to someone without your ability. You'll pass undetected through the area, copy some data, and leave. Easy."

The mission formed in Aria's mind. Where could they send her that would require her gills? Had a shuttle crashed or a boat sank? And if that was the case, wouldn't it be easier to send a submersible to retrieve the information? "If it's so easy, why am I the only person who can do it? You have heard of scuba gear, haven't you?"

Reed raised his eyebrows. "Of course. But for this to work, we can't have someone hauling gear like that around, and we can't risk them stashing it somewhere in case someone else finds it."

His words made her thoughts grind to a halt. "The job's not underwater?"

He shook his head. "Not all of it."

She opened her mouth to ask what he meant, but he held up a hand to silence her.

"We have a limited window to act, but as long as we get there quickly, time shouldn't be an issue. The mission is straightforward." He tapped on his wrist comm until a holographic image of a white orb floated above it. "Latest reports put solar activity hitting its peak tomorrow evening. All the news streams are saying the satellites will go into shielded mode just before the peak hits and stay that way for about twenty-four hours. The blackout will give us the cover we need."

She wrinkled her nose. "I thought only satellites around Mars had to go into shielded mode. That won't affect comms on Earth. How does that blackout have anything to do with us?"

Reed blew out a breath. "I don't have time to ease you into this, so I'm just going to tell you. Those people aren't on Mars; they're here on Earth. Everything you know about the Martian Colony is a lie."

Chapter Eighteen

The Colony was a lie.

The sentence spun like a whirlpool through Aria's mind.

How could that be? The Colonists had been live-streamed for more than four years. How could the Agency keep up a deception for that long?

"Why?"

Aria wasn't aware she'd spoken until Reed stopped, mid-sentence, to stare at her.

"What?"

"Why would the Agency lie?" Aria scratched at her cheek. "Wait—don't you and Dr. Withers work for the Agency? These are their selection centers, right?"

He pressed his lips together as if irritated by her interruption. "Technically. Although most of us work for Uma. We're loyal to her."

Aria tilted her head. "Uma? You mean Dr. Withers?"

Reed nodded. "She doesn't believe the Agency has the best interests at heart for the future of humanity. But working for them gives her access she wouldn't otherwise have."

"Access to what?"

He sighed. "People. Information. See, even within the Agency itself, not many people know the truth about the Colony."

"That it's on Earth." Saying the words out loud made Aria feel ridiculous. "If that's true, why shut down the streams at all? None of Earth's satellites are going into shielded mode."

"They have to keep up appearances," Reed said. "Agency scientists track solar activity. If they say the satellites around Mars need to go into shielded mode or they'll get fried, there's no way the stream can stay online without people asking serious questions. *All* information flow to and from the Colony has to go dark. Wouldn't want some hacker to pick up on a data stream when they're supposed to be down."

Aria shook her head. "You realize you sound crazy, right?"

"You'll see." Reed shrugged.

She stared at him for a long moment. "I still don't see why you need me."

Reed stood and crossed to the wall. With a few taps, a screen blazed to life. He pulled up a map of

Earth and zoomed in on an area in the north Pacific ocean. "The Colony is located here, in a satellite blind spot and away from standard flight paths. Our information says the island itself is housed inside a dome." He tapped the screen and the image changed to display a sketch of a semicircle resting on top of choppy waters. "The only way to get inside is through an underwater hatch. It's too deep to free dive, but even if it weren't, we couldn't risk sending in a normal swimmer because someone could see them while they were swimming to the island. Like I said before, scuba gear is out of the question because if a Colonist found it, there'd be panic. They all believe they're on Mars. We have to make sure they keep believing that."

"Let's say you're right," Aria said. "And I'm not convinced you are, but... Why would the Agency lie about it? Why spend generations terraforming Mars to make it habitable just to lie about people living there?"

Reed's wrist comm buzzed before he could answer. "That's a question for another time. They're ready for you."

Panic surged in her veins. "Ready for me to do what?"

Ignoring her question, he led the way out of the small, white room, back through the long hallway they'd entered through less than an hour earlier. But instead of taking the hall all the way to the exit, Reed turned to a door on the right and pressed his thumb to the entry pad. The door slid open and he motioned for her to enter before him.

Standing at the far end of the room beside an odd-looking chair with a large, round opening in the back rest was Dr. Withers. She typed something onto a screen hanging on the wall. But when Aria was no more than a few steps inside, another figure caught her attention. It took a moment for her to register she recognized him.

"Declan?"

He held up a finger as he strode toward her. "Before you say anything, let me say I'm sure this will work. Like eighty-seven percent." He pressed his lips together, squinting. "A solid eighty-four. Eighty-one and a quarter."

Aria tipped her head to the side. "What are you talking about?"

Declan glanced over her head. "You didn't tell her?"

Aria followed his gaze to Reed, who shrugged. She turned her attention back to Declan. "Wait. You're one of them?"

Declan held up both hands at shoulder level, miming fireworks sparkling through the air. "Surprise."

She ran her hands through her hair as she sucked in a breath. "You weren't a contestant. So, what? Shelving one row over was a setup? A way to gain my trust?" She rubbed her forehead.

"Intel gathering," Reed corrected. "We needed to

know your pressure point. Would you help us for money? Would some kind of status motivate you? Turns out, you'll do anything for your brother. Lucky for us, we didn't need to go to Old LA to find him." He swept his hand toward the chair. "Now, if you don't mind, we're kind of on a clock."

Aria took cautious steps forward but didn't sit. "What are you going to do?"

"The Colony streams will be down," Declan said, breezing past her and joining Withers at the screen. "But the Colonists will still be there. They believe they're on Mars. So we can't have a redheaded stranger show up out of nowhere. They have to think you belong there."

Aria glanced at Reed, but his face gave away nothing. "How are you going to do that?"

Dr. Withers turned, holding a silvery device the size of the last knuckle on her little finger. "The military developed this tech during the War Years to allow soldiers to infiltrate ranks of rival armies undetected. This is the only working prototype remaining."

"*Working* might be overstating things," Declan said. "I mean, it'll function—but with the heavy demand, it won't last more than thirty-six hours, max. All the test data is promising, but so far as how it'll perform in the real world..." He shrugged. "As long as you're in control of your limbs, you should be good."

Aria gaped. "You want to put some experimental

tech in my head? No way. I'm not going to let you fry my brain."

Withers tapped her wrist comm and the screen behind her changed from graphs and data points to a live feed of Alonzo sitting on a thin mattress in a featureless gray cell. His knees were pulled to his chest and the tight expression on his face reminded her of the scared boy who came to live with her all those years ago. "Shall I go ahead with the transport to the detention facility, then?"

Aria's stomach dropped. They had her pinned and they knew it. Whatever they demanded, she would comply. She hung her head. "What do I have to do?"

Declan patted the round part of the odd chair. "Sit down and rest your face here. The doctor and I will handle the rest."

Although his tone was light, it did nothing to calm Aria's nerves. She swallowed and did as instructed, flinching when Declan's fingers grazed the back of her neck as he gathered her hair to one side.

"Deep breath in," Withers instructed.

No sooner had Aria complied than a sharp pinch twisted the center of her neck, followed by a prickling heat. She clenched her fists and bit her lower lip, not out of pain, but fear.

Declan's feet appeared before her. He ducked down until they could lock eyes. "You're doing great."

She wanted to ask how he could know, but the words wouldn't come. It took all of her willpower to keep from jumping out of the chair. She conjured the image of Alonzo in a cell, vulnerable. At Withers' mercy to ship off to an aberration detention facility the moment Aria stepped out of line.

She had to do this. For him.

There was pressure at the base of her neck, but no pain. The thundering of her heartbeat quieted and Declan nodded. This wasn't so bad. She could handle this.

But then a jolt of electricity shot through her body. Her muscles seized and white light flashed across her vision.

Dr. Withers shouted something, but Aria couldn't make out the words. Hands gripped her shoulders as her body continued to shake and twitch. Every millimeter of her flesh felt like it was burning. She opened her mouth, but the scream caught in her throat.

Blackness enveloped her.

Chapter Nineteen

*A*ria jerked awake. She tried to sit up, but something kept her tethered to the table. She opened her eyes, searching for Declan—for anything familiar—but all she could see was a gleaming expanse of silvery white.

The chip had blinded her. Her breath came in short pants as she attempted to swallow. How was she supposed to complete her mission if she couldn't see?

"She's up."

Aria turned toward the sound of Declan's voice. Her panic ebbed as the scene before her changed. The silvery-white wasn't the only thing in the universe—just the only thing she could see. She was stashed in a cubby designed for sleeping. Declan approached from her left, his easy smile not quite disguising the tightness around his eyes.

She tried to sit up again, but something stayed her progress.

Declan held out his hand. "Wait a second. I've got to undo these straps." He busied himself near her feet before moving up toward her hips. She only realized there had been pressure across those points as it was released. Finally, he undid the belt across her shoulders and offered a hand to help her up.

Aria placed her hand in his and froze. She wiggled the fingers. They moved at her command, but it didn't change the fact that the fingers she was seeing weren't hers. Where her skin was freckled and pink from the time she spent in the sun, this flesh was darker and richer, the fingers more slender and tapered than hers.

Declan squeezed the hand, and Aria's skin tingled with the gentle pressure. "Want to take a look?" The corner of his mouth quirked and he pulled a miniscreen from his belt holster. After tapping it, he held it up to her face.

The image that greeted her in the camera's display was at once unsettling and familiar.

Unsettling because it wasn't *her* face, even though she was in control of it. She wrinkled her nose and raised her eyebrows, and the person staring back at her mirrored the motions.

Familiar because she recognized the girl the experimental tech had turned her into. She had seen the dark hair, smooth skin, and wide eyes on the streams just the other day. They had turned her into the perfect person to infiltrate the Colony: the reclusive Zora Korbel.

Aria handed the miniscreen back to Declan and opened her mouth to thank him, but no words came out. She swallowed to moisten her throat, but when she tried to speak again, she couldn't.

Declan tilted his head as he watched her struggle. "Deimos. I told Withers this was a possibility."

Aria tried to ask what, but the words still wouldn't come. Her heart pounded in her chest. She couldn't speak. She pressed her hands to her throat as if there was a way to feel the problem, to coax sound to emerge.

Declan stretched his fingers and reached for the back of her neck before hesitating. "May I?"

She covered the spot with both hands, her eyebrows drawing together.

He clapped his palm to his forehead. "Everything happened so fast, I doubt Calix mentioned it... I'm an aberration, too. Although I prefer the term *anomaly*." He offered a smile as he wiggled his fingers. "I have a gift with technology. If you let me, I can check that device in your head and see if I can get it working any better. I promise it won't hurt."

Aria stared in disbelief. Declan had abilities? Outside her father and Sera, she'd never met another aberration. But since her time at the selection center, she had encountered two. She had always assumed people with abilities were few and far between. There might be families here or there with a tendency to develop powers, but it couldn't be a common occurrence. Maybe she was wrong.

Her hands drifted to her sides, and Declan pressed his fingertips to the back of her neck. He probed the skin at the base of her skull for a few seconds before pressing flat against her upper vertebrae. She winced at the pressure on the tender spot but remained as still as she could.

She counted the seconds to keep herself calm. At almost a minute, he removed his hand and blew out a breath.

"Sorry, there's nothing I can do. I can see why the military abandoned this technology. There are too many moving parts for them all to work properly." He shrugged, holding his hand out to her. "At least you look the part. Let's get you above deck. We've got to be getting close now. You've been out for about a day."

Deck? Aria pressed her palms to the edges of her thin mattress. Now that he mentioned it, she was surprised she hadn't noticed already. The rhythmic moving of her surroundings was a dead giveaway for being out on the water. She supposed since she spent so much time on the ocean herself, the fact that they were no longer on land hadn't registered as odd.

Ignoring Declan's hand, she slid off the edge of the bed. But no sooner had her feet hit the ground than stabbing sensations raced through her legs, starting in her feet and ricocheting upward to her knees. She stumbled and reached for Declan, who grabbed her arms before she crashed to the floor.

"What's wrong?" He pulled her to her feet and peered at her, waiting for a response, before shaking his head. "What am I thinking?" He eased her back to the mattress and pulled the miniscreen from his belt holster.

"Let me..." He tapped at the screen a few times before grinning and holding it out to her. "Type it. What's wrong?"

Aria grabbed the screen and tapped out a single word: *pain*.

"Phobos," he murmured, pressing his fingers to the back of her neck again. "Seems Zora's taller than you by about five centimeters. Adding the extra height is messing with the nerves in your legs." He pressed his lips together. "Can you walk?"

Bile threatened to rise at the idea of putting pressure on her feet again, but Aria sucked in a breath. She had to do this. Withers had made it very clear—if she wanted Alonzo to go free, she had to complete the mission. She locked eyes with Declan and nodded, hoping she could hold up her end of things.

When he offered his hands this time, she took them. The knife-like pain shot through her heels and up into her calves again, and she was glad her voice couldn't betray her. She clenched her teeth and did her best to keep her breathing even. Still, if the look on Declan's face was any indication, she was doing a poor job of hiding the pain.

He helped her across the small room. With every step, she reminded herself that she could endure the discomfort. She would have to if she wanted to help Alonzo.

They were nearly to the stairs when Reed's voice floated down. "We're almost there."

"We'll be right up," Declan called. He offered Aria a strained smile. "Up for some stairs?"

It took three times as long as it should have to climb the short flight to the boat's main deck, but Declan didn't press her to go faster than she could.

Reed, on the other hand, called for them twice more, impatience lacing his voice.

By the time Declan helped Aria settle on a bench and made his way to the cockpit, the boat had slowed to a stop.

Aria craned her head in all directions, searching for what they could have reached. As far as she could see, only pitch dark ocean reflected the light of the moon overhead.

As a salvager, she'd spent lots of time on open water. And while she typically weighed anchor after land had disappeared from view, there was a sense of isolation here that she'd never experienced before. Declan said she was out for a day. Had they been on the sea that whole time?

"Calix, be a pal and drop the anchor, would you?"

Reed glared at Declan for a long moment before striding to the stern to comply.

Declan moved to the bow and leaned forward, stretching out his hand. Aria opened her mouth to ask what he was doing, only to remember she had no voice.

After a few seconds, Declan turned, grinning. "Deimos, this is some next level stuff." He motioned for her to join him.

Aria stared at the area beyond the boat's bow, but it looked no different than the rest of the black night around them. But this whole thing couldn't be an intricate setup to get her out to the middle of nowhere, so she gritted her teeth and forced herself to her feet. Her movements were still slower than usual, but she made it to Declan without a problem.

He stood at the edge, staring out over open water, when she reached him. She tapped on his shoulder and held out upturned palms to ask what he wanted.

His grin was that of a little boy receiving the best gift he could imagine. He lifted his hand and held it out into the air in front of them. When she didn't follow suit, he nodded encouragingly. "Go on."

She raised an eyebrow but did as he requested, pushing out her hand, unsure what she was supposed to be reaching for. When she hit something solid, she almost pulled her hand away again.

She turned to him, eyebrows drawn together as she tapped on the firm surface before them. To say it was like glass would be incorrect. At least with glass, there was a sense of looking through something. This was like an invisible wall.

"Ultra, right?" Declan pressed his other palm to the surface and leaned in toward it. "It's refractive technology. They're bending the light so that the dome is invisible. From this side, at least. On the inside, you'd see whatever the Agency needs to you see. A sol on Mars is a little longer than an Earth day, so they'd have to account for that. Plus the sun would be smaller in the sky and the stars a little different based on position in space, but..." He shook his head. "They covered all their bases."

The science of it all was beyond Aria's understanding, but it didn't matter. All that was important was that she got inside. She pulled off her shirt to reveal the moisture-wicking suit she always wore. Tapping on Declan's shoulder, she pointed at the water.

But Declan raised his chin toward Reed, who was making his way back from the stern. "Check with him. It's how I let him think he's the boss."

Reed crossed his arms over his chest. "Out here, I *am* the boss."

Declan nodded as he turned back to the invisible dome. "Sure you are."

A muscle in Reed's jaw jumped. "Just find a point of ingress, will you?" He held up a slim pack. "Wear this around your waist. Inside is everything you'll need to complete the mission: A change of clothes, a couple ration pods, but most importantly..." He unzipped the compartment and pulled out two small devices. One was flat, black, and smaller than Aria's little finger. The other was a silver cylinder a little longer than her middle finger. He held up the black device. "This is the data transfer chip. Once you get to land, you'll make your way to the supply depot at the base of the volcano. They store the transport shuttle in the depot's courtyard. Board it, and Declan will fly you into the caldera where the spaceship is. He'll tell you where to plug it in and how to transfer the data."

Declan glanced over his shoulder and grinned. "See? I'm the boss."

Reed ignored him as he held up the silver cylinder. "This is a tool of last resort. Your objective is to get in and out without being seen. We made you look like..." He clenched his teeth and took in a breath. "You look the way you do so that if someone glimpses you, they'll see someone familiar, not a complete stranger. But if something goes wrong and someone figures out you don't belong there, use this."

Aria took the device from him and studied it. The top half of one side was made from a different material and appeared more milky white than the rest. Opposite the odd material was a depression that fit the pad of Aria's thumb.

"This device disrupts memory formation. If you press that button until it vibrates once, you can wipe a person's memory going back about six hours. If you keep holding until it vibrates twice, it disrupts for twelve hours. Three times is twenty-four hours, and that's the absolute limit. After you charge it, release the button, hold it as close to the person's eyes as you can, and push the button one more time. You can leave the person like that and in a few minutes they'll come to and go about their business. Or, if you need to, you can feed them a story to overwrite something they saw. They'll be very open to suggestion for about thirty seconds." He tucked the first device back into the pouch and reached for the one she held.

Aria handed it over and tapped on Declan's shoulder, gesturing toward his miniscreen. Although his eyebrows drew together, Declan handed it over. With tech like this device, maybe she didn't need to look like Zora.

She typed out a message and handed the screen to Reed, who scanned it and shook his head. "No, we can't take the tech out of your head. This thing will work on one person. Maybe two, if you're not trying to disrupt memories for a long period. And you would have to do each person separately. If a whole group saw you as you, there would be no fixing that."

She exhaled through her nostrils. She would have to deal with this chip after all.

As she handed the cylinder back to Reed, Declan turned and held out a tiny earpiece like the one she wore when salvaging with Alonzo. Her stomach twisted as she put it in place. She had to focus on the mission now, not her brother.

"Can you hear me?"

Declan's whispered voice came through the ear comm loud and clear and Aria nodded. Declan grinned and pointed starboard. "About twenty meters north, and fifty meters down, there's an access panel that leads to a maintenance tunnel. The passcode is four-nine-two-nine-zero."

Aria nodded as Declan placed his hand on her wrist comm to tweak the settings and ensure they could communicate once she was inside. She wiped her damp palms on the thighs of her suit as he instructed her how to get through the maintenance tunnel. As Reed helped her strap the pack around her waist, she took in calming breaths.

"There aren't any cameras in the tunnel—for obvious reasons—but it's just as dangerous for you to be there as in the Colony itself," Declan said. "Someone at the Agency monitors the doors. They won't notice anything now, since the data streams are down, but you have to get out before they start up again or they'll realize you're in there and the mission is blown."

Aria nodded, but her minds spun with terrible possibilities. What if the chip in her head interfered with her aberration? If she couldn't breathe under water, what would happen? She'd never had to hold her breath while swimming, so she had no concept of whether fifty meters down would take too long to reach. Declan hadn't been able to detect all the malfunctions with the chip the first time he'd interfaced with it. There could still be more issues they hadn't discovered. Any number of them could lead to her drowning in the dark ocean.

She closed her eyes, willing herself to remain calm. She could do this. It was no different than any other salvage run. Catching Declan's eye, she nodded before turning toward the boat's gunwale.

Reed's hand circled her wrist, firm and insistent. When she turned, his lips were set in a tight line, his gaze intense.

She opened her mouth to ask what he was doing, but no words came out. She was about to pull away when a small shudder passed over him and he released her on his own.

For a moment she stared at him, not sure what that could have been about. Perhaps she'd misread him and he was concerned about her safety, but she somehow doubted that.

Declan pressed his hand to the invisible boundary again and a series of blue lights appeared twenty meters to the north, disappearing down into the black ocean.

Gripping the bag in her hand, Aria stepped up onto the bench and dove into the water.

Chapter Twenty

*E*nrique Martinez stared out over the water as the first evening stars blinked into view on the darkening eastern horizon.

According to his father, the live stream that had broadcasted every second of his life since they'd touched down on Martian soil almost four years ago should be off by now.

He never thought he'd be thankful for a solar storm, but many things about life on Mars had been unexpected.

When his dad first told him the Agency selected them to go, he imagined they were about to become pioneers who tamed the Martian wilderness. Instead, the ship had landed on an island full of prefabricated housing materials and pre-packaged foods. He'd begged his dad over and over to take him on an adventure, to go with him and explore the rest of the surface, but his dad's answer was always the same.

Later, son.

Enrique wondered if his father wouldn't have been more inclined to go along with his plans if it hadn't been for Phoebe, Enrique's stepmother. The two had married a year before word came down that they'd been selected to travel to Mars. They would be part of the first colony to live on the formerly red planet without being limited to the confines of glass domes, like the first scientist settlers who had helped in the terraforming process. In his recollections, his father had been much more fun before Phoebe came along, but maybe that was wishful thinking.

Checking his surroundings once more, Enrique pulled the compressed raft up on its end and reread the inflation instructions for what felt like the millionth time.

If his father wouldn't take him on an adventure, it was high time he go on one by himself. He was eighteen now. On Earth, that would mean something. He'd be considered an adult there—able to move out of his family home, to choose his career path. Those things didn't apply here on Mars, but Enrique longed for his age to mean something. He wanted to have an adventure. He wanted to escape.

Escape wasn't the right word—although part of him wished it were. He wanted to explore the areas of Mars that people had yet to step foot on. But soon into his planning, he realized there was no way he could haul enough provisions for a long journey without drawing attention to himself. So he had to settle for the next best thing.

According to the map and his calculations, it should take about eight hours to paddle across the water to the nearest shore. It would be faster if he could use one of the motorized haulers, but they wouldn't start up without the proper passcode, which he didn't have. But even with the travel time, he could explore for about six hours and return before the cameras started up again. It wasn't perfect, but he'd take it.

Enrique laid the compressed raft down at the water's edge and pressed the red tab in the corner. As it inflated, he tamped down guilt that roiled in his stomach. The rafts weren't for recreational use. They were included in their supplies in case of emergency—if they ever needed to leave the island due to unstoppable wildfire or some other unforeseen natural disaster. He comforted himself with the fact that he was taking one of the smaller rafts—one meant to haul supplies. Besides, when he got back, he could return it. No harm done.

The raft popped into its final shape and the hissing stopped. With one last glance to be sure no one was watching, Enrique kicked off his shoes and tossed them, along with a paddle and a satchel of supplies, into the raft before pushing it into the water and clambering in over the side.

As he dug the paddle into the silty sea floor and pushed away from shore, he couldn't help glancing back at the row of pines shielding the access path from view. He'd chosen this spot because of its seclusion, but part of him expected someone to show up and stop him before he even began.

He shook off the feeling and turned toward the watery horizon. It didn't matter. Even if someone arrived now, they couldn't stop him.

He sliced his paddle through the water. This was really happening. When he returned, Enrique would be in more trouble than he could imagine, but no amount of punishment could take away the memories of his experiences.

Still, guilt twanged within him with each meter he put between himself and the Colony. He hoped Ravi wouldn't be too mad at him. While Enrique was sure the adults would do their best to downplay his little vacation, he had a feeling the stream's producers would end up rewarding him with more screen time after the exploit. But that wasn't why he was doing this. Unlike Ravi and the others, Enrique didn't spend hours each week orchestrating drama or planning elaborate stunts to interest viewers and receive one of the few coveted luxuries. Enrique was going on this adventure for himself. If he had told Ravi, there was a possibility his friend would have let word slip and his trip would have been over before it started.

Enrique shivered as night fell. It was cooler out here on the water than it had been on land, but it wasn't the temperature that concerned him, it was the darkness. There was a lamp in his satchel, but if he turned it on too soon, he could draw unwanted attention to himself.

When he imagined his grand adventure, he always skipped right from jumping onto the raft to arriving on a distant shore. He hadn't thought about what it would be like paddling alone through the black night.

In the first days after arriving at the Colony, his stepmother had trained groups how to use the rafts in case of emergency. He had snickered with Ravi and the other guys his age when Phoebe demonstrated how to affix the safety strap around a volunteer's ankle. Securing themselves to the vessel seemed unnecessary. But now, with nothing but open water surrounding him, Enrique was grateful for the tether. If a large wave hit and knocked him out of the craft, at least he wouldn't be left adrift on the sea.

He paused paddling for a moment to peer up into the sky as it populated with stars. He hadn't spent much time looking up when he lived back on Earth—not that there would have been much to see in his Madrid suburb. But now, staring up never ceased to fill him with wonder. He scanned the sky for a few moments before locating a pale blue dot amid pinpricks of white light. Earth.

It was funny—when he was still on Earth, he couldn't wait to get to Mars. Now that he'd lived on Mars, he wanted little more than to know what things were like back on Earth.

Sighing, he turned his attention back to paddling. He shifted his feet to steady his footing, but a quiet splash drew his attention. There was water in the raft. He ran through everything that had happened since he'd climbed in, trying to determine whether he could have splashed in so much on his own, but even as he considered all the possibilities, more water pooled around his shoes.

A leak.

His fingers trembled against the oar as he spun to the seat at the bow and paddled back toward shore, but with each stroke the raft lost pressure. After ten minutes of paddling, he knew he was out far over his head. The other side of the craft lifted out of the water as his side sank under his weight.

He needed to get back to shore, but what was he supposed to do with the raft? He couldn't leave it out here. Besides being a laughingstock for his botched adventure, he'd be in serious trouble for losing emergency supplies. He'd have to haul it back to shore.

"Phobos," he muttered.

The raft sank further by the moment. Water soaked his shins, and the gunwale of the craft was close to being even with the water line. He pressed himself to standing, but the shift of his weight tilted the little boat and he dropped back down. As the raft settled, the paddle rocked over the too-low gunwale and drifted away. Enrique reached for it, but the pressure on the side of the raft was too much. The sinking craft rebelled against the sudden motion and threw him face-first into the frigid water.

The impact stung his exposed skin. He beat at the sea to breach the surface. With his head above water, he gulped down a lungful of air. He could do this. He just had to get himself and the raft to shore.

He swam toward the craft and reached for the rope that circled it. Only the top edge was still above the water. His muscles already protested the movement in the icy sea, but he fought to keep moving.

The tether around his ankle tightened as the last bit of the raft disappeared under the surface. He grabbed for it, but his fingers wouldn't obey his order to close around the rubber handle. The strap cinched further and he turned his attention to it, but he couldn't find the hook and loop closure. As the raft sank, it tugged at his body, pulling at him.

Enrique kicked against the water with all his might. "Help!" He splashed and flailed his arms. "Help! Someone! I'm in the water!"

He grabbed at the rope tethering him to the raft and tried to yank it back up, but it was no use. Its pull was too much.

With all his strength, he fought to keep his head

above the surface. He kicked his free foot at the ankle strap, hoping to loosen it enough to free himself. But the tug on his leg only increased until the sinking raft pulled him down with it.

Chapter Twenty-One

*G*uided by the ghostly blue lights, Aria found her way to the maintenance hatch. Salt water had eaten away much of the black paint that had once filled the etched numbers on the keypad, but the three-by-four grid was so familiar Aria could pick out the digits without a problem. She typed in the code Declan had given her—four-nine-two-nine-zero—and the red light above the keypad flashed green as a loud thud echoed through the water.

Aria pulled on the metal handle, but nothing happened. She braced her feet against the side of the structure and tried again. Centimeter by centimeter, the door creaked open far enough to allow her entry. She slid into the water-filled compartment, closed the door behind her, and pulled the inside handle into the lock position. A buzzer reverberated through the enclosed space.

The chamber filled with a mechanical hum and a white light flickered on above her head. By degrees, a gap of air appeared at the top of the room as the water drained out the bottom.

Aria scanned the surroundings. The airlock was large enough to accommodate four divers in scuba gear. She stood on a metal grate painted the same drab gray as the rounded walls and waited until the water was to her knees before moving toward the second door. There was no keypad, only a rectangle that glowed red. When the water had drained, the light flashed green and the door clicked. She twisted the handle and pushed, glad when the door swung easily.

"You in?"

Aria jumped at the sound of Declan's voice in her ear. She'd forgotten about the communicator he'd given her. She opened her mouth to respond before remembering her voice didn't work.

"Aria?"

She closed the door behind her and peered at her surroundings. The rounded walls made her feel like she was passing through a tube. An oppressive hum filled her ears. Metal conduits overhead and panels of controls with flashing lights indicated this structure's purpose: to maintain and control a complex system. But the intermittent emergency lighting and oppressive stillness made it clear the place was empty. The Colony was self-sufficient, not to requiring a team to monitor it at all times.

"Aria, please re—" Declan stopped short, laughing. "Oh, right. Um, tap once on the comm if you can hear me."

She rolled her eyes as she complied with his request.

"Oh, good. Now that you're in, it should be easy to get you through to the other side. Follow the hallway to the left for about ten meters."

Aria did as he said. As strange as it was having his voice in her ear, it was also comforting. She definitely didn't trust Declan after his deception at the selection center, but it was nice knowing she wasn't alone on the mission. With his help, she could sneak through the camp, get the information Withers wanted, and be back home by tomorrow. Alonzo would be safe. And if they played their cards right, her father might never know she had disobeyed his wishes and gone to the selection center.

Once she'd gone ten meters, she tapped the comm again.

"There should be a hallway to your right. Follow it."

She kept walking. Fifteen meters ahead was a junction and she limped toward it as fast as her aching legs would allow. The drone of the machinery that kept the dome functioning reverberated through her bones and she feared she might turn to jelly if forced to stay in here too much longer.

Every step sent shocks of pain up her legs, but she did her best to ignore it. The sooner she got through this structure, the sooner she would be back in the water where her legs didn't hurt.

She was only a few meters from the intersection when a figure appeared on her left. Her hand flew to her heart as she stumbled backward.

She bumped against the concave wall behind her, her eyes glued to the figure. Her heart thudded in her chest despite her deep breaths meant to calm it. There was no one there—no lone employee patrolling the facility. It was only a wall-sized poster of an astronaut from the Common Era. She took a shaking step forward and brushed her fingers down the glossy page. Paper posters like these hadn't been made since before the war years. She'd come across a few in flooded houses, but the sea had mostly degraded what was left of them.

"Are you at the junction yet?"

Declan's voice snapped her back to the present. She shook herself. She didn't have time to waste inspecting the poster. Ignoring the throb in her feet, she hurried to the end of the hall and tapped her comm again.

"Go left about ten meters, then right again, and you should reach an exit hatch."

Aria hobbled forward as fast as she could, the promise of being back in the water too tempting to allow herself to get distracted again. She reached the exit hatch within minutes. The door groaned on its hinges as she swung it open, but the noise was a welcome reprieve from the monotonous drone of the system's hum. She tapped the comm when she was inside the airlock.

She crossed to the keypad by the opposite door.

"Wait—wait. It's a different code."

Aria's finger froze centimeters from the four button. Of course the code would be different. The Agency wouldn't take a chance that a maintenance person might use his access code to move into the Colony. Employees could be trusted to get this far, but no farther.

She bit her lower lip as she waited for Declan to speak again. The seconds ticked by and Aria tried to determine whether shifting her weight or staying still made the pain in her legs less severe. By the time he spoke, she hadn't decided.

"Try six-seven-one-five-two."

Her finger hovered over the first number. *Try?* But Declan had been correct about everything so far. She may as well trust him now, even if what he had given her was only a best guess.

She typed in the code and held her breath. After an agonizingly long pause, the red light above the panel turned green and the overhead light flickered as water filled the compartment.

The coolness of the water was a reprieve to her aching legs even before she could float. The promise of being weightless was enough to dull the pain as the compartment flooded.

When the water reached her shoulders, Aria dipped

her head underneath and lifted her feet off the grates. But as she took her first liquid breath, her nose wrinkled. This wasn't the same water she'd swum through to get here. She couldn't put her finger on what was different, but she had tasted seawater enough times to know this wasn't it.

The Agency pulled out all the stops to make this place seem like a different planet.

A buzzer sounded and the lock clicked. Aria pushed open the door and swung it closed behind her. The light on the panel above the keypad flashed red.

She tapped the comm as she swam away from the barrier. Her body felt heavier in the water, her movements more sluggish.

"Hope you're up for a swim. I finally hacked into the system and pulled up schematics of this place. It's even more massive than Withers thought. My best guess is the island is about ten kilometers from the wall."

Although Declan sounded apologetic, Aria looked forward to the swim. It was harder to move through this water than she was used to, but it was still easier than walking.

Declan fell silent, for which Aria was thankful. The weight of the water pressed in around her, reminding her of countless hours spent on salvage runs when she would get lost in the task at hand—moving bricks or winding through long-forgotten hallways.

At intervals, Declan checked in, asking her to

surface and check her surroundings. When she dipped under again, she typed out a message to him on her wrist comm. During the most recent survey, Aria detected a faint glow in the distance. The light of the Colony.

On the fourth check, Declan urged her to be careful. Aria rolled her eyes, despite the fact he couldn't see her. When Withers selected Aria for her ability, the doctor hadn't realized Aria's help also came with her expertise. If there was one thing she excelled at, it was keeping out of sight while swimming.

When she was less than a meter from the surface, a disturbance reverberated through the water. She froze, floating in place.

Who would be out this far this late? She couldn't recall any footage from The Colonists where swimmers had struck out anywhere beyond the main beach, and that didn't extend more than ten meters into the water. She was too far out to be anywhere near to it, unless Declan's calculations were way off.

Maybe it was a fish. She wracked her memory for any information about marine life on "Mars." Scientists imported genetically modified fish decades ago, but she didn't think any were large enough to make such a racket.

Then she heard the voice.

It was indistinct, but there was a person nearby shouting.

Someone was in trouble.

"Aria, I'm hearing interference on your end. What's going on?"

Aria tapped on her comm, although she wasn't sure what meaning Declan would take from it. She was fine —someone else was in danger.

The mission was simple. She was supposed to get in and out without interacting with anyone. Zora's reclusive status made her the perfect disguise because it wasn't as if she had a group of friends who would expect her to be with them or notice if she was acting strange.

But she couldn't let someone drown. A disappearance like that wouldn't go unnoticed for long in the Colony, and if there was some kind of investigation, she could get caught up in it. There was no way someone would miss two Zoras if they were interviewing potential witnesses—and Aria wouldn't even be able to talk her way out of things.

She struck out toward the noises, which were fading by the second.

"Aria, what's going on? Deimos, it'd make things a whole lot easier if you could talk. Aria?"

She ignored Declan's voice as best she could, focusing instead on the sounds of hands breaking the surface of the water.

She swiped the screen of her wrist comm, turning on the light she had used hundreds of times before on salvage runs. A bulky inflatable raft was sinking toward the ocean floor, the weight of the water fighting to press out the remaining air keeping it buoyant. Aria darted toward it.

Where there was a boat, there were people.

A figure strained to swim toward the surface. Aria spotted the rope tethering the guy to the sinking craft and grabbed it. What she wouldn't give for a knife.

She pulled at the tether, trying to help the swimmer haul the raft upward, but the weight was too much to overcome. He broke the surface again, but he wasn't up long enough to call out. His leg struck out against the water, and Aria barely avoided being kicked in the head.

She followed the rope down to the collapsed raft, searching for the connection point. Her father had spent countless hours impressing on her the importance of being able to identify different knots. If this person had tied the line to the boat, she could get it undone.

Except what she found was a prefabricated connection, the end of the line secured to itself with a metal band. No matter how she and the swimmer struggled against it, this connection wouldn't break loose.

Only he wasn't struggling anymore. The guy floated limply just below the water's surface. Aria lunged upward, grabbing for his ankle. Her fingers fumbled against the hook-and-loop strap as the raft continued to tug the guy downward, but after a few tries she gained enough purchase to rip it apart. As soon as he was free, she looped her hands under his armpits and pulled his head above the water.

She had to get him to shore. She focused all her energy on swimming toward the faint glow in the distance. The Colony. They were close. She could only hope they were close enough.

Aria recognized the change in the water's temperature as they neared the shore. She swam the guy as close to shore as she could before dragging him onto dry land.

She tipped his head back, following what she remembered from the VR water safety course her father had made her take before he allowed Alonzo to accompany Aria in the water. The skills flooded her mind as she took in a lungful of air and covered the swimmer's mouth with hers.

On the forth forced breath, his body convulsed. Aria tilted him on his side as he sputtered and coughed. The adrenaline ebbed from her system, replaced by a wave of relief—and another of confusion. Why was someone out in a raft? Who would be foolish enough to take off alone at night? Probably Oscar or Gabe. The two of them always took their stunts too far.

As she rolled the stranger onto his back again, she took in his face for the first time. Until now, she'd been too focused on saving the guy's life, but as the familiar lines of his profile clicked into place in her mind, her heart picked up its pace once more.

Enrique Martinez.

Since she'd learned about the mission and its objectives, Aria had understood where she was headed. She was going to the Colony—the same place she has seen on the streams for years. She even looked like a Colonist. But seeing Enrique before her, so close she could touch him, made her brain short circuit as reality crashed down around her.

Dr. Withers had been right. The Colony really wasn't on Mars, it was right here on Earth.

She stretched out a trembling hand and touched her fingertips to his cheek. For four years, she watched Enrique on the streams, fantasizing about situations that could bring them together. That he was here in front of her now was almost too improbable to believe.

His eyelids fluttered, bringing her back to the reality of the situation. He couldn't see her.

She pressed herself to her feet, hissing as the searing pain ricocheted up her legs.

Enrique's eyes opened, fixing on her as he lifted his head. Aria froze until his lids drooped and he dropped back to the ground. She paused only long enough to ensure the steady rise and fall of his chest before turning and diving back into the water.

Chapter Twenty-Two

*A*ria surfaced a dozen meters away. The shore was still dark, shaded by stout pine trees that stood like silent sentinels guarding the settlement beyond.

Scanning the vicinity as she went, she crept out of the water. Her heart hammered in her chest. She just saved Enrique Martinez. She pulled him from the water, touched him. Although she'd dreamed about such a moment for years, she never thought it would happen. It was always a fantasy. Even if the Agency had selected her for the next Mars mission...

No wonder the second settlement was on the other side of the planet. It made for a good excuse about why new colonists couldn't meet up with established ones. If the second mission took people to Mars at all. It was just as likely the Agency had set up a second secret site on Earth to send people to. The only question was why.

"Aria, where are you?"

She jumped and looked back out to sea to find who'd spoken before remembering the earpiece she wore. She raised her wrist and tapped out a message on her comm. *I'm on land. Just need to get changed.* She unzipped the waist pack Reed had given her and pulled out the shirt, pants, and shoes. Before she zipped it back up, she ensured the data transfer stick, memory modifying cylinder, and rations hadn't fallen out.

"Head inland," Declan said as she finished dressing. "Stick to the shadows as much as possible, though. Accessing camera feeds is a little trickier than I thought it'd be. I don't want to tip off anyone at the Agency that we're here."

Aria tapped her ear comm once before starting up the beach. She padded over the smooth stones that gave way to a craggier landscape. Pine trees sprouted wherever the rocks were more than a few centimeters apart. Once she'd watched a documentary about the terraforming of Mars and how scientists had genetically engineered some of the heartiest trees on Earth to thrive in the Martian environment. When the Agency had built this place, had they used those genetically modified trees here, or had they cheated and used ones that grew on Earth?

As she pushed passed the needles, she did her best to bury a sense of betrayal. Why would the Agency go through so much trouble to convince the world that these people had been living on a different planet for years? She couldn't fathom what there was to gain from keeping up such a lie, and it wasn't as if Dr. Withers had been forthcoming with her theories.

But none of that was Aria's concern. She was here to get the information Withers wanted so Withers would release Alonzo. Nothing could distract her.

The trees thinned as she drew nearer to the settlement. She strained her ears for the sound of voices, footsteps—any sign someone might be around—but she heard nothing.

If her time watching The Colonists had taught her anything, it was that there wasn't much to do after dark. Some people worked overnight shifts, but those who didn't spent their after-dinner hours one of two places: at home or at the Hub, playing VR games with friends.

She crept out from the safety of the tree line and scurried to the back wall of the nearest building. It was long and featureless but for two sets of windows facing the trees. Both were dark. If anyone was working in this building tonight, they would be in a room near the front.

She lifted her wrist and typed a message. *I've reached the first building, but I don't know where I am.*

"I'm sending a schematic of the island to your wrist comm."

Her comm vibrated before Declan finished speaking. She tapped the attachment icon and a holographic map popped up in the air before her. One building blinked red.

"Based on where you should've come to shore, I'm guessing you're here. It's an emergency bunker with rafts and other supplies in case they ever need to evacuate the island." Declan chuckled to himself. "Based on historic movements of Colonists at this time of day, I'm outlining the safest path for you to take."

Yellow dashes slashed their way through the map, hugging the edges of pine groves behind buildings. The lines led all the way to the supply depot, highlighted in green.

Aria tapped her comm to let him know she understood. She snuck to her left along the back of the bunker and peeked around the edge to be sure the coast was clear before dashing to the building beside it.

"I'm going to sign off for a bit while I try to hack into the stream feeds," Declan said as Aria scrambled from the bunker to the next building. "It's safer to keep intermittent contact so no one notices an open channel and gets curious."

Aria tapped her earpiece. A soft tone beeped in her ear, letting her know Declan had broken their connection.

She was alone.

She slunk around the back of two more buildings before cutting toward the main road that looped around the outer edge of the Colony.

A cluster of buildings across the street backed up to another outcropping of pines. If she could pick her way from wooded area to wooded area, she could keep to the shadows. The trick would come when she left this grouping of trees because there wasn't another for a long stretch.

She sank her teeth into her lower lip before streaking from the trees to the nearest building. Pain ricocheted up her shins with every step, but she didn't slow her pace until she was out of sight.

A group of adults turned onto the nearest footpath and Aria pressed herself against the wall, keeping to the shadows as much as possible. As soon as they turned onto another path, she scurried to the next building. Now came the tricky part. Declan's map led her through the intersection of paths to reach the next grove of trees. She sucked in a breath before leaving the safety of her hiding place.

She was a few steps beyond the intersection when the door of the building she had been hiding behind swung open. A man laughed as he turned to the person following him out the door.

Aria's mind spun. She was too far out to go back the way she came, but she wouldn't be fast enough to reach the tree grove without being seen. As soon as the man turned forward, she was done for. She needed a place to hide, now.

With precious milliseconds ticking away, Aria limped as quickly as possible toward the nearest building. The front windows were dark. Whatever staff worked there during the day was probably long gone.

Not risking a glance over her shoulder, she pulled open the door and slid inside.

Aria pressed the door closed behind her and released a breath. Her heart hammered in her chest as she counted the seconds. Three seconds. If they'd seen her, would they follow? Five seconds. She should slip into a room so if they came in after her, they wouldn't see her right away. Ten seconds. If they found her, how could she explain herself without endangering the mission? She considered checking the first few doors to see if a room was open for her to hide in, but there was no way of knowing what waited behind them.

As moment after moment elapsed and no one entered after her, Aria relaxed. They hadn't seen her, or if they had, they hadn't thought anything of her presence. She would wait another minute to be sure they were gone, then she could continue on her way.

She rested her hand on the door handle, planning out her next move. If the coast was clear, she would dart across the road to the next bank of trees. After that, she should have a straight, uninterrupted shot to the supply depot.

"Zora?"

She froze, the word sending a chill down her spine. The voice was familiar, but she couldn't place it. She swallowed and considered her options. She could fling open the door and make a run for it, but there was a chance the man would give chase. But if she stayed, how could she explain her presence?

"What are you doing here?"

She pressed her lips together. It was too late. Her split second of indecision was enough to make the choice for her. As she spun to face him, she told herself it would be okay. She could think of a way out of this. Everything would be fine.

But as her eyes landed on the man who spoke, all of her encouraging thoughts fizzled out. She struggled to swallow as she came face to face with Rashid Korbel, Zora's father.

Chapter Twenty-Three

*R*ashid took long strides forward, concern creasing his brow. "Zora, what are you doing here? Is something wrong at home?"

Aria stared up at him. Her lips twitched, but no explanation came to her. Not that an idea would do her any good—it wasn't as if she could speak.

"Your mother's supposed to ping me if..." His words faded as he glanced at the device on his wrist. "Oh." He ran a hand through his hair, displacing the thick black strands. "I'm sorry, honey. I must have missed the message while I was working on..." He shook his head and stretched a smile across his face. "It doesn't matter. Let's get you home, shall we?"

Panic flooded Aria. The last place she could go was the Korbels' house. As soon as she arrived and Rashid saw his daughter was already there, her cover would be blown. The mission would be over. What would happen to Alonzo then?

But if she ran, Zora's father would give chase. In her present condition, it was unlikely she could outrun him. And talking her way out of the situation was obviously impossible.

Rashid skirted around her and opened the door. As she stepped out into the night air, Aria wondered if she could send a quick message to Declan for help. But when Rashid closed the door, he fell into step beside her and placed a protective arm around her shoulders. There was no way to send a ping without him noticing. Besides, she wasn't sure Declan would receive it since he had turned off their audio link.

"Don't get me wrong, Zora. I'm glad you wanted to get out of the house. But it's been so long, it would make your mother and me feel better if you took us with you." He squeezed her shoulder. "I'm sorry I missed your mother's ping. Things should settle down soon. Once the baby's born, she won't be on call all the time." His pace slowed as he removed his hand. "Dear, why are you wet?"

Aria forced a smile and Rashid sighed and started walking again. "Maybe tomorrow we can get up early for a walk at sunrise. How does that sound?"

Aria didn't even try to respond, but Rashid didn't seem to expect an answer. While she was grateful he didn't find her behavior odd, she couldn't figure out why.

Dread coiled in the pit of her stomach as the Korbels' house came into view. If she started coughing once they were inside, maybe Rashid would go to the kitchen to get her some water. If he was distracted long enough, she could run out the back door. When he went looking for her, he would find the real Zora in her room. The plan wasn't without its flaws, but it was the best she could come up with.

Aria allowed Rashid to lead her into the house. Although the Colonists stream rarely showed the Korbels outside of work, she already knew what to expect inside. Simplicity of design meant that each of the houses was laid out in the same way. Zora's bedroom door would be in the back corner of the house where it couldn't be seen from the kitchen.

Rashid had barely closed the door behind them when Aria began coughing. The sound was quiet and strained, but Zora's father took note. "Let me get you some water. Then straight to your room."

Aria nodded as Rashid stepped into the kitchen area. She waited for his attention to turn to his task, but his eyes didn't leave her. He pulled a glass from the open shelf and placed it under the tap, watching her the whole time. "I'm not sure how late your mother will be. All she said is Samara is having contractions. I don't know if she's in labor, but she could be."

Aria sucked in a breath. Samara. The baby. Outside this dome, everyone on Earth was waiting with anticipation for the birth of the first human on Mars. If only they knew the truth.

Rashid cut off the tap and strode to Aria. "We'll talk about this tomorrow."

Aria accepted the glass and took a few sips of water. She tried handing it back, hoping Rashid would turn his back long enough to permit her escape, but he wouldn't accept it.

"Take it to your room." He applied gentle pressure to her shoulder and led her toward a door. "I'm sure it doesn't seem fair to you, but remember your mom and I are looking out for your best interests. If you're feeling better—if you're ready to venture back out into Colony life... Well, that's a conversation we should have before you wander out alone."

She nodded, even though she wasn't entirely sure what Rashid was talking about. They stopped beside the door, and she just stared at it. This was it. Her mission was over. When she walked in, when Zora saw her, she couldn't imagine the reaction she was in for. She fingered the zipper on her waist pouch. She could use the memory disrupter. Rashid didn't need to know she was ever here.

Before she could unzip the pouch, Rashid reached for the door. Panicking, Aria pushed forward, knocking him out of the way. If he saw the real Zora inside, everything was ruined. But if she could slip in without him noticing anything was wrong, maybe—*maybe*—she could figure a way out of this

If her actions confused him, his reaction didn't show it. Sighing, he turned back toward the common room.

Aria opened the door only a crack before slipping in. The room was dark, but a soft glow filtered in through the window. The room was unremarkable save for a lumpy figure on the bed. A relieved sigh escaped her lips. Zora was asleep. She didn't risk turning on the light for fear of waking her. Tiptoeing across the room, she aimed for the window on the back wall.

Aria was less than a meter from the window when her foot came down on something uneven. Her impaired legs were too slow to correct her balance and she pitched forward, hands in front of her to brace her fall. On instinct, she gripped the side of the bed, jostling it as the full weight of her body collided with the side.

She froze, eyes locked on the figure on the mattress. She waited for Zora to stir, to see her, to scream—but the form remained motionless. Aria narrowed her eyes and leaned over the bed. Something wasn't right. The room was too still. She couldn't hear Zora breathing.

Because Zora wasn't in the bed. Upon closer inspection, Aria found the mass she had taken for Zora's sleeping form was nothing more than blankets folded and draped to look like a person.

But if Zora wasn't here, where was she?

Chapter Twenty-Four

*E*nrique's eyes fluttered open. Something was wrong. A sharp object poked him in the back to the left of his spine. Had he fallen asleep with his tablet in the bed again? And where was his blanket?

He blinked again. He wasn't in his room at all. As a breeze rustled through the pines, it all came back to him. The raft. The water. He was going under, tethered to the craft. But then she had saved him.

He sat up, coughing as water trickled down his throat, his eyes searching the area for any sign of Zora Korbel.

No, that was crazy. Zora barely left her house anymore. He must have hallucinated.

Nothing made sense. He wondered how long he'd been out. Based on the stars overhead and the dampness of his clothes, he reckoned it hadn't been too long.

The hair on the back of his neck stood up. "Hello? Is someone there?"

No one answered, but someone moved behind the pine trees near the path that led back to the settlement.

His muscles coiled, ready to spring. He stood and crept forward, keeping his eyes locked on the hidden figure. Probably one of his friends—Ravi or Oscar. Those two always tried to spook others for the laugh factor, but he didn't know why they would bother now, with the streams shut down. Why waste their time slinking around in the darkness for a joke if there weren't millions of people watching?

"Hello?"

For the first month after they landed, Enrique had expected monsters around every corner. Although his father assured him they were the only living beings on the planet, Enrique was convinced that there was some kind of alien life no one had yet discovered. But as time passed, he'd outgrown those flights of fancy. He knew every centimeter of their settlement. He had explored every pine grove. The odd rustle of boughs didn't bother him anymore.

But something about this person standing out of sight, watching him, made goosebumps rise on his skin.

"Okay, you got me. You can come out now."

The figure shifted but didn't draw nearer. Enrique took another step and froze when a low sound floated through the night air. The hum sent a tingle down his spine, and when the noise morphed into a high wail, his stomach clenched.

The sound cut off just as he identified it. A voice. When it started again, the *ooh* morphed into a higher *ah*. He jogged forward but stopped short when she came into view.

Zora Korbel.

They'd met at mission training, but she'd spent most of her time with the girls in their age group. And once they'd arrived on Mars, she'd spent less and less time out in public until she withdrew completely. For the first couple of years, she'd become something of an obsession for many of his friends. Ravi once tried to convince her to come out of her house after her parents had gone to bed. She responded to the pebbles he tossed against her window by pelting them with handfuls of berries.

Because of her isolation, some guys in the settlement saw her as the ultimate challenge. To many, romantic relationships were little more than fodder for better ratings. On more than one occasion, Enrique had overheard Noam and Louis plotting how they might woo Zora. Enrique never took part in these discussions. In fact, he often went for long stretches forgetting she existed.

But now that she stood in front of him, Enrique wasn't sure how she ever strayed from his mind. It was hard not to notice her good looks during training, in the days when he and the other teen boys had in-depth discussions about which girl from their limited pool they wanted to stake a long-term claim on. But in the years since he'd last seen her, Zora had grown into a young woman so beautiful it was almost unnerving. Her luminous hazel eyes seemed unnaturally large as she peered at him.

She paused in her song and tipped her head, squinting as she studied him. She looked as surprised to see him here as he was to see her.

"Hey, Zora." He took a step toward her. Although she didn't move away, concern creased her brow. "Remember me? Enrique Martinez?" He offered her his hand, but she didn't even glance at it. After a few moments, he let it drop to his side. "What are you doing out here?"

Her gaze shifted past him and she lifted her hand to point out over the water.

He waited for her to speak, but as the seconds ticked by it became clear she wasn't going to. "You saved me."

Her eyebrows drew together as she dropped her hand. She held his gaze with an expression so intense he couldn't look away. When she opened her mouth, he leaned forward with anticipation.

A melodic staccato of *ahs* floated from her lips and she lifted her arms above her head, spinning like a dancer. Switching to *oohs*, she leapt like a deer onto the path and twirled her way back into the settlement.

He followed her progress with his eyes until she

disappeared from sight. When she was gone, he shook his head to anchor himself back to reality.

No wonder Zora's parents kept her at home. She was crazy.

However, she'd also saved him from drowning when his raft sank. He supposed someone didn't need to be sane to be a hero. Whatever her reason for coming out tonight, he was thankful.

He ran his palms over his pants. They were only slightly damp. With any luck, they'd look normal by the time he got home. He wasn't sure how he'd explain to his father and stepmother why they were wet otherwise.

It wasn't until he was halfway home that he realized Zora had been completely dry.

Chapter Twenty-Five

"I've got good news and bad news."

Aria tapped on her comm to let Declan know she heard him.

Since leaving Zora's house, she hadn't run into anyone. She had been lucky with Rashid. Luckier still that Zora hadn't been in her bedroom. But that luck would run out if Rashid went to check on his daughter soon. Aria had no way to know where the real Zora had gone or when she would be back. If Rashid noticed she was missing and put out an alert to the rest of the colony, everyone might come searching. And then she'd be back to where she was before—in danger of discovery.

She didn't want to think about what would happen to Alonzo if she failed.

"Which do you want first?" Declan continued.

Aria rolled her eyes. She always hated that question.

What did it matter which part of the news she heard first if half was bad?

"Was that an eye roll?"

Are you looked around, but saw no sign of a camera. She lifted her wrist. *You can see me?*

"That's the good news." Declan sounded pleased with himself. "Now the bad news. I can't get all the cameras online at once without raising red flags. I'll have to switch them on as you enter different zones. It's not ideal, but at least I won't be entirely blind."

"Is she there yet?" Reed's voice was clear, despite sounding farther away.

"I already told you no. But she's close, aren't you, Aria?"

She nodded, hoping he could see her. As she continued toward her destination, she typed another message. *Are there still limits to how long we can be in contact? Will you have to turn off your camera feeds, or can you watch me the whole time?*

"That would be the other piece of bad news."

Aria sighed. She supposed it was good that Declan could at least watch her at intervals, though she didn't like that she would be on her own for long stretches of time. But she had gotten out of her last tight spot on her own. And she was nearly to her destination. As long as she didn't run into any more trouble, she could get to the transport, fly to the spaceship, and get the data within the next half hour. By the time she finished, most of the colony would be asleep and she could make it back to the water without any problems. She would get Withers her information and she and Alonzo would be home before dinner tomorrow.

"The supply depot is at the end of this road," Declan said. "Everything looks clear where you are. Let me switch feeds and... Oh."

Aria froze, straining her ears for any hint of noise that would indicate someone was approaching. The only sound that greeted her was that of the breeze whispering through the pine boughs. She typed a message on her wrist comm. *What's wrong?*

"What? Nothing. You're not in any danger—at least not that I can see. But that's the problem. I can't find a stream feed covering the depot. It's about time for me to cut comms anyway. Lie low in those trees to your right until I make contact again."

Aria bristled at the order. She was so close and now Declan wanted her to hide until he could yammer in her ear some more?

"You heard him, Ayers," Reed snapped. "Move to the trees."

She scowled in the general direction of where she guessed the camera to be before complying. She took slow, exaggerated footsteps toward the trees, hoping to show the full measure of her annoyance. But since her movements were already slower and more exaggerated on account of the appearance-modifying chip, she might not have hit the mark.

"Okay, then. I'll check in again in about fifteen to

twenty-five minutes. Keep your head down until then." One long, low beep indicated Declan had severed their connection.

Aria studied the tangle of tree limbs. There was no good way to get through here without getting scratched by needles or covered in sap. The night air was growing colder by the minute and the thin fabric of her long-sleeve shirt offered little protection.

Scanning the tree line, she searched for a good way to enter the grove. She found one spot that looked like it might get her a meter or so in, but before she tried, she stopped herself. What was she doing? The last thing she wanted was to sit around for half an hour until Declan reestablished their link. No one was out now. The coast was clear. If she waited, there was no guarantee things would stay that way. And it wasn't as if he would provide any help. He'd already admitted he couldn't see the supply depot. It was possible he wouldn't find it during their communication hiatus—and then what? She'd have to go in blind anyway.

Every minute she wasted was a minute Alonzo had to spend in a cold, gray cell. She wished she'd been able to speak to him before shipping off on the mission. There was no way of knowing if he had any clue what was going on. Was he worried about her, or was he upset she hadn't come to him yet?

Declan and Reed were here only because Withers had ordered them to come. And even then, they weren't here with Aria—they were outside the Colony.

If Aria failed, their boss would reprimand them, but it wasn't as if Withers would send their loved ones, or them, away to an aberration camp.

Aria stepped back onto the road. She didn't care what Declan and Reed ordered her to do—she would get to that shuttle and get the data she'd come for.

She jogged along the road as quickly as she could while not making too much noise. The sandy footpath gave her little trouble and she slowed only in the most shadowy areas to be sure there was nothing to trip over. There were no houses out this way and no staffed structures. Unless someone was out for a late night stroll around the settlement or coming from the depot itself, Aria doubted she'd come across another living soul.

When the depot came into view, Aria sighed with relief. Withers had said the shuttle was in the building's center courtyard. The entire structure was dark except for a floodlight posted over the main entrance. Aria peered over her shoulder, but the night was still as ever. She wasn't keen on stepping into the light. If anyone happened by, there would be no hiding. But no one was out and it wouldn't take long to slip inside.

She put on as much speed as she could, steeling herself against the pain still ricocheting through her legs. Two more meters. A low drone emanated from the building. One meter left.

She closed her hand over the door handle and twisted, but it didn't move.

Locked? That didn't make sense. Owing to its

closed citizenry and the fact there were cameras streaming every corner every moment of every sol, locked doors weren't a priority when planning the colony.

A nine-digit panel glinted beside the door. Aria's fingers hovered above it, but she had no way of guessing what the code was. Entering the wrong digits could trigger an alert.

If she'd waited until Declan reestablished their comm link, he could have hacked into the system and found the code. If he'd known there was a lock on the door, he should have told her. She wouldn't have come if she'd known she couldn't enter.

She could already hear Reed's disapproving voice berating her for not staying put. There was still enough time to make her way back to the pine grove, but the idea of walking there on her sore legs only to retrace her steps made her want to cry. All she knew for sure was she couldn't stand here in the glare of the floodlight.

Keeping one hand pressed to the side of the building, she skulked into the darkness. The further she moved along the octagonal exterior, the louder the droning hum became.

Finally she came to the source of the sound—a rectangular metal box. They had a similar climate control module at the restaurant.

Aria took a step back to study the scene. The unit was about a meter high and positioned below a window with a wide sill. With her current limitations, she wasn't sure she could climb onto the roof, but she was willing to try.

She mounted the climate control module easily. The difficulty came when trying to pull herself up on the roof. It took three tries to grip the edge and three more to pull herself upward. By the time she reached the roof, a thin sheen of sweat beaded her brow.

She allowed herself a brief rest before navigating the space between the solar panels. In the darkness, they looked like rectangular pools of blackness as she crept along to avoid losing her balance and falling on one.

With each step, satisfaction blossomed in her chest. She was almost there, and she'd done it on her own. She would be swimming back to Declan and Reed in no time, and soon she would be with Alonzo again and everything would be back to normal.

She reached the inner edge of the roof and peered down into the courtyard.

It was empty.

She blinked and scoured the area again. The shuttle wasn't there.

Chapter Twenty-Six

A looming sense of dread clung to the air around Enrique. It was only a matter of time before the truth came out.

Three short tones rang out through the crisp morning air to signal the mid-morning break, and he sighed as he wiped a sweat-dampened lock of hair off his forehead. Although the dew had yet to evaporate off the ground, he felt as if he'd put in a whole day's work already. That was always the case during his farming rotation. He typically enjoyed these two weeks as they were a reprieve from more indoor-based tasks like meal prep or apprenticeship lessons, but today it was as if everything about the outside world mocked him for his failed attempt at exploration. The sun shone brighter than usual, its light glistening off the expanse of ocean surrounding the island, taunting him.

He turned his back on the sea and kept his head

down as he resumed his task. He'd arrived early to avoid pre-work small talk. While he hadn't been foolish enough to tell any of his friends about his plan to venture to across the sea, he worried they'd be able to sense the failure clinging to him like a flight suit. The combination of an early start and a location in a distraction-free corner of the garden meant he was nearly done with his job for the day. If he kept his head down, he could finish soon and head home before lunch for some much needed rest.

"Enrique, what're you waiting for, man?"

"Phobos," Enrique muttered before forcing a smile and turning to face Ravi as his friend jogged to close the distance between them. "I was just going to finish up here. Go on. I'll catch up." He did his best not to flinch at the lie, hoping Ravi would forget about him until the break was over.

Ravi stopped when he was still a few meters away. "You won't want to miss this. We're setting up at the tables to discuss the stunt."

Enrique stiffened. "The... stunt?" He cleared his throat when the words came out higher than usual. If someone had seen his nautical disaster, he'd never hear the end of it.

Ravi's eyebrows furrowed. "For when the streams start up again. Come on." He motioned for Enrique to follow him and started up the path.

Relief swelled in Enrique's chest. News of his failure wasn't common knowledge. With a sigh, he set his garden fork down beside the basket of carrots he had already harvested and followed his friend.

By the time they arrived at the break tables, everyone else from the rotation was accounted for. The girls—Jade, Maria, Tanis, and Shira—clustered at one table, while Gabe and Oscar sat at the one beside it. Enrique slid into the seat across from Ravi.

"I don't know why we need to plan a stunt," Jade said, combing a lock of hair behind her ear with her fingers. "All the streams will be focused on Samara and Ren. Once the baby's here, we can rotate in. Hold the baby while Samara takes a nap. Change a few diapers. Easy."

"That's what I was planning, too," said Tanis. "But right before comms with Earth went dark, I overheard my parents talking about one of the last things they read on the newswire."

Enrique perked up.

"The Agency is choosing people for a new colony," Tanis said.

Everyone sat up straighter.

"This is good news, right?" Oscar asked. "More people, different dynamics."

Maria rolled her eyes. "What part of *new* colony are you missing? They're not coming here."

"They might get their own stream," Tanis said. "It's possible they'll stream these newbies before they even get here. What we need is a stunt that gets the attention back."

As the others talked over each other to suggest ideas, Enrique tuned them out. New people were coming to the planet and all his friends could think about was ratings. Would it be so bad if their lives weren't broadcast every moment of every sol?

"You guys aren't thinking big enough," Tanis insisted, her voice cutting above the others. "It needs to be something really special."

Everyone at the tables fell silent, but Shira leaned forward. "As usual, you're all ignoring our ace in the hole." She waited, eyebrows raised, for someone to come to the conclusion she seemed to think was so obvious. But after several seconds ticked by, she let out an exasperated sigh. "Zora Korbel."

The hair on the back of Enrique's neck stood up as a murmur rose around the tables. It wasn't the first time someone floated Zora's name at one of these stunt-planning meetings, but it was the first time her name elicited any kind of reaction from him. Zora was a recluse, and he learned years ago not to ask questions about her—like why she didn't take part in work rotations or attend the mandatory Colony-wide meetings. Before last night, he couldn't remember the last time she crossed his mind. Now, he leaned in despite himself.

Oscar cracked his knuckles. "I agree with Shira. Like I said, more people, different dynamics. Zora's the closest thing to bringing in an outsider."

"When's the last time anyone even saw her?" Jade asked.

"At the baby shower," Ravi said, perking up. "Just for a second. She didn't even come in. She showed up with Dr. Eliza and left with her dad."

"So the first time she comes out of her house in as long as anyone can remember, she's got a parental escort?" Gabe shook his head. "Doesn't sound promising."

Enrique gripped the edge of his chair under the table. When he saw Zora last night, her parents were nowhere around. She couldn't be on too short a tether if she'd jumped into the sea and swum out to save him.

As the conversation veered in another direction, Enrique found himself wanting to stop it, to spend more time discussing Zora. He wanted to know every detail about her. Plans spun in his head. Labor and delivery of Samara's baby would occupy Dr. Eliza for hours. If a group staged a stunt near the Korbel house, it might draw out Rashid, then Enrique could...

Could what? Break into her house? Try to draw her out? Force his company on her despite the fact that she had chosen a reclusive life? He shook himself. Was he so desperate for a deviation from the norm that he was fantasizing about someone who was clearly unbalanced? Even if he were to spend time with Zora, there was no reason to think she would be more lucid than she had been last night.

And yet she had the presence of mind to dive into the sea and save him. There was no doubt in his mind he would be dead now if it wasn't for her intervention.

The tones to recall them to work rang through the air and Enrique sprang to his feet. Ravi shot him a concerned look, but he ignored it. Let the others take their time getting back to their stations. Enrique wanted to finish up his task for the day and get home without being pulled into any more scheming for more stream time.

As he trudged back toward his plot of carrots, he tried to convince himself it was because he was above it, because gaining popularity back on Earth wasn't something he strived for.

But a voice in the back of his head whispered the truth: He didn't want to let slip any details about his encounter with Zora because he didn't want to fan the flame of fascination. He didn't want to get his hopes up that he would see her again only to have them dashed.

If he saw Zora again, it wouldn't be part of any stunt.

Chapter Twenty-Seven

*A*fter a night spent curled into a tight ball at the base of a tree, Aria's body protested each step she took as she trudged through the woods in the direction Declan had told her to go, but she pressed on through the pain. The meal pod she'd eaten before making her way to the ground had taken the edge off her hunger, but it didn't give her the same sense of satiety as a normal breakfast.

It didn't matter. The sooner she found the shuttle and retrieved the information from the spaceship, the sooner she could get home and have a real meal. According to the countdown timer Declan had set up on her comm, there were ten hours left until the streams came back on. Whether she accomplished her task or not, she needed to be gone by then.

Aria tried to convince herself that was plenty of time. But she didn't know how long it would take to track down the shuttle. This mission was no longer as straightforward as she expected.

After giving her directions when she woke this morning, Declan had signed off, promising to come back online when she reached her destination.

Enrique Martinez's house.

Aria tempered her excitement as she drew closer to the residence. When Declan scoured the stream footage, he glimpsed something odd. Two years earlier, Oscar, Noam, and Gabe tried to take a joyride in the shuttle. They didn't get far before some adults stopped them and forced them to land on the side of the volcano. But before Phoebe Tomlin, Enrique's stepmom and the island's chief of security, flew the shuttle back to the supply depot, the cameras in that area went dark. The next time Declan located her on archived footage, she held what appeared to be an ignition chip. If there was any chance of finding the shuttle, Aria needed to retrieve that chip and upload its data to Declan.

It made sense that Phoebe would move the shuttle to a secret location. It wasn't unheard of for the Colony's teens to attempt a stunt a second time if someone thwarted the first go. As the security chief, Phoebe was the natural choice to keep the chip safe.

But Aria's skin tingled as she drew nearer to her destination. It felt like fate. After saving Enrique's life last night, she was sure she would never see him again, but now she was going to his house.

Where he wouldn't be, she reminded herself. Declan already assured her that the Tomlin-Martinez residence was empty. She needed to focus on the mission, not fantasize about running into Enrique again. She was lucky he had been unconscious last night, otherwise how could she have explained herself?

When the pines thinned, Aria checked the time on her wrist comm. The whole trip had taken about ten minutes. Her throbbing feet and aching legs made it feel like so much longer.

Declan wasn't due to check in for at least another five minutes. The thought of standing around for that long was enticing. The pain didn't go completely away when she stood still, but its throbbing discomfort faded into the background after a time. But as welcome as a reprieve would be, it would make it that much harder to move again when it was time. The best thing would be to keep going. The sooner she did this, the sooner the pain would stop.

Sucking in a breath, she surged forward through the last of the pine boughs. The street beyond the house was quiet—almost unsettlingly so. She hadn't noticed while stepping through the snapping under-brush on her way through the woods, but out here in the open, the silence was remarkable. No birds sang, no small animals skittered around.

Shaking off a shiver, she lumbered as quietly as she could manage toward the back of the house. According to Declan, the back door existed for safety regulations rather than function. In all her hours watching the streams, she couldn't recall ever seeing anyone use the rear entrance of any home. Still, the door glided on its track as if it had been installed only yesterday. Aria held her breath until she slid it closed behind her.

The silence within was comforting, but only because it meant she was alone.

Slinking toward the common room, Aria kept as close as she could to the walls that separated the bedrooms from the rest of the house. She trained her eyes on the window straight ahead, straining for any sign of movement beyond. Not that it would matter if a parade trooped past at this point: While from this angle the glass was transparent, the solar-storing glaze on the outside made it opaque to those looking in.

Still, she couldn't help glancing out the window at intervals as she approached the wall desk. It was stowed to allow for ample space in the room around it, and it took three tries to unclasp the latch at the top before it swung down on its hinge. A screen flickered to life, but Aria ignored it, undoing a second latch and lifting the desktop to reveal a series of resizable compartments stuffed with an overwhelming number of data chips.

Aria tapped her wrist comm and pulled up the holographic schematic of the chip Declan had sent to help her identify the correct one. When he sent it, she teased him about how he thought she needed it. Now she vowed not to tell him it was coming in handy.

She poked through the chips in the first compartment, but nothing matched the image Declan sent. Moving on to the second, then the third, Aria fixed her focus on the task at hand.

A series of thuds echoed through the house and Aria leapt backward, bumping into the two-person seat behind her. When the familiar drone of a fan filled the room, she blew out a breath. She needed to get a hold of herself. Closing the distance to the desk, she resumed her search.

Adrenaline was ebbing from her system when a familiar chime sounded in her ear. "Where are you? I can't get a visual."

Declan's voice was laced with worry and a twinge of guilt spiked through Aria's gut. Maybe she should have waited for him to reestablish comms before she entered the house. She lifted her wrist to type an apology.

"I hope you're still in the woods," Declan continued. "If you're anywhere near the Martinez house, you need to take cover. We've got incoming."

Aria's finger froze, suspended above her wrist comm. Incoming? From where? She glanced out the front window, but the scene outside was as still as ever. There was no movement on the left side of the house.

But the door on the right side slid open to reveal Enrique Martinez. The clouded expression on his face morphed into one of confusion. Not breaking eye contact, he slid the door closed behind him. "What are you doing in my house?"

Aria stared at him, her mind blank. Even if she could speak, words would have eluded her.

"You're inside, aren't you?" Declan's voice was tight with panic. "Are you by the back door? Can you make a break for it?"

Aria glanced toward the back of the house. She was about as far from the door as Enrique was from her, but if he chased her, there was no way she could outrun him. He would overtake her in seconds.

"What are you doing here?" Enrique took a step forward but stopped like he thought better of moving any closer. His eyes flicked to the corners of the room as if expecting someone else to pop out and let him in on the prank. When his gaze strayed to the desk behind her, his brows pulled together.

Aria's fingers twitched with the desire to type out a message to Declan, but there was no way to pull off the maneuver without Enrique asking who she was pinging.

"Aria, can you hear me?" Declan asked. "Abort. Get out of there. Now."

"No."

Reed's voice in Aria's ear made her flinch.

Enrique tilted his head and took another small step forward. "Are you following me? I haven't seen you in years, and now I've seen you twice in less than a sol. Not that I'm not thankful you were at the water last night, but... Why are you in my house?"

"Whatever you do, don't run away," Reed said through the comm.

Aria stifled a snort. It was hard enough to walk. The thought of running made her faint.

"If you want to salvage this mission, do what I tell you."

Enrique moved toward her until there were less than two meters separating them. "Why are you rummaging through the desk? What are you looking for?"

Aria fought the urge to tug her shirt down over the pouch at her waist as his eyes flitted over her. She kept as still as possible as Reed murmured a plan in her ear.

"You can tell me, or I can ping one of your parents —or my stepmom—and wait until they get here." Enrique lifted his left wrist to display his comm.

"Now," Reed hissed.

Aria pointed to her throat.

Enrique dropped his arm to his side. "There's something wrong with your neck?"

She shook her head.

"You have a sore throat? We don't have medicine here. You should know that—your mom's the head doctor."

She gritted her teeth. It was so much easier pantomiming with Alonzo—he always figured out what she meant on the first try. She tapped her throat again before touching her lips and shaking her head.

Seconds ticked by before the scrunched expression

on Enrique's face softened. "You... can't talk?" He studied her again, but this time the attention didn't make her uneasy. "But last night..." He pressed his lips together, cutting himself off. "Is that why you never come out of your house?"

She nodded, playing the role Reed had cast her in.

Enrique closed the distance to the desk and ran his fingers over the various chips crammed into cramped compartments. "That doesn't explain what you're doing here."

Aria tugged on her earlobe, using the gesture to cover a surreptitious tap on the comm in her ear.

"I hear you, I hear you," Declan muttered. "Believe it or not, what Calix wants me to do is harder than just... Oh, got it."

Aria's lips twisted into a smile, but she schooled her features when Enrique looked up. She held up her wrist. When the motion elicited only furrowed eyebrows, she reached out and tapped his comm.

Sparks radiated up her arm from where her fingers brushed the device and she fixed her attention on her own, hoping Enrique couldn't detect the flush in her cheeks. They were close now—as close as they had been the night before. Her fingers itched with the desire to touch his hand, his cheek—to test the softness of his hair.

"Why aren't you typing?" Declan asked. "Is there something wrong? I had to patch a couple connections to make your comm interface with his without it showing up on the system's mainframe…"

Aria shook herself and tapped the flashing circle on the screen of her device. Now wasn't the time for silly fantasies. Enrique watched as she typed out the story Reed fed her.

Mars is messing with my biochemistry. My mom explained it. Something in the atmosphere here is hurting me. As long as I'm here, I'll keep getting worse.

She sent the message to Enrique and watched his mouth twitch as he read it.

"Is there something your mom can do?" His brow knit as if the question hadn't come out right.

Aria tapped out a second message. *She's tried everything she can think of. Even the teams back on Earth agree there's nothing more they can do. My dad keeps telling me the Agency is making plans to bring me back to Earth, but there haven't been any updates. And now that they're bringing over new colonists, I'm afraid they've put me at the bottom of the priority list.*

He read his response and sighed. "I'm sorry." He rubbed his forehead like he was attempting to process her story. "Why are you being affected? The atmosphere here isn't bothering anyone else." He tilted his head, studying her. "You're not an aberration, are you?"

Aria froze, her stomach hardening like a rock. His tone was nonchalant, almost dismissive. As if he was sure he knew the answer already. Surely the girl before him couldn't be one of *those* people. She couldn't imagine his reaction if he learned the truth.

Enrique shook his head as if to answer his own question. "Maybe new colonists coming is a good thing. They could send more doctors. New people, new ideas." He stared at an indistinct spot over Aria's shoulder and she recognized the look in his eyes as one she'd seen on Enrique countless times—the desire for more, for adventure—a longing for things beyond the ordinary.

Enrique closed his eyes and gave himself a shake. "Or maybe the second wave of colonists will bring—"

Aria was already typing a new message. *What good will they be on the other side of the planet?*

The longing in his expression evaporated and he focused on Aria with an intensity his eyes hadn't held before. "If you can't wait for the next wave, then what…" He turned back to the chips strewn over the desktop. "The ship. You want the ignition chip to the shuttle so you can get to the ship."

She nodded. Blood rushed in her ears.

The corners of his mouth twitched. "You're going back to Earth." He ran both hands through his hair. "Do you even know how to fly?"

Aria bit her lower lip, not sure how to respond and for once wishing to hear Reed's voice in her ear.

After a beat, Enrique shrugged. "Who knows? Maybe you do." He turned to the desk she'd been riffling through. "The ignition chip won't be in here.

These are all for my dad's work. Nothing but data about planting times and harvest schedules and nutrient densities. Phoebe keeps all her things in their bedroom."

Aria held her breath as Enrique dropped the desktop and latched it closed before folding the whole thing back to the wall. Her body lurched toward the bedroom door, but she caught herself before she took a step.

Enrique's lips twisted into a smile. "What are you waiting for? Let's go find that chip."

Chapter Twenty-Eight

*E*nrique couldn't take his eyes off Zora as she took careful steps into his dad's bedroom. He still couldn't believe she was here, but her presence only begged more questions.

His empty threat about contacting Phoebe or her parents had the hoped-for effect of making her talk, but even her answer clarified little. Sickness explained her seclusion from the Colonists, but not why the reason would be kept from everyone. If the planet was disrupting her biochemistry, such an issue couldn't be contagious.

As he crossed the threshold, a shiver coursed down his spine. He wasn't allowed in this room. Phoebe called it a "private space." Enrique had tried to use the phrase on her regarding his own bedroom, but that made her quote the Colony's charter about how individuals who arrived as minors could move into housing of their own on their twenty-first birthday or when they got married, whichever event occurred first. Since he wasn't interested in marrying any of the girls on the Colony—even as a stunt to get his own house—he had three years to wait to be out from under Phoebe's thumb.

He didn't know what his stepmother had to be so protective of. The room was a mirror image of his, with a small closet along the left side, a bed along the far wall, and a pull-down desk on the wall to his right.

He glanced above the door to double check the red recording light was off. Bedrooms were streamed for only a few minutes a day—always in daylight—and the red light showed the stream was active. But no one would look in on them today. They were cut off from Earth for at least the rest of the sol.

Zora followed his gaze. He offered a smile. "It's weird knowing nobody's watching, isn't it?"

But instead of smiling or nodding, Zora dropped her gaze and turned to the closet.

Enrique's stomach clenched. What a stupid thing to say. He swallowed and rubbed the back of his neck. "But I guess you don't think much about the streams, do you?"

She glanced over her shoulder and her mouth quirked like she was trying to smile, but it came off more like a grimace.

Enrique's own smile faltered. What was his problem? Were his social skills that rusty after talking with the same group of people for the last several years? It took a moment to identify the sensation swirling in his stomach. He was nervous.

Zora reached for a matte silver box on the shelf above the hanging clothes, but her fingers couldn't gain purchase on the sides. Enrique strode to her side and reached over her head to snag the box for her. It wasn't until a jolt of electricity zipped up his arms where his skin brushed hers that he realized he should have asked if she wanted his help and given her time to step aside. But even as he set the box on the floor and watched her crouch beside it, he didn't step away.

Enrique's father often attributed major events in his life to fate. Meeting Enrique's mother, Ximena, in a transport on a day he was running late to work had been fate. Meeting Phoebe three years after Ximena died from the maculosus flu—again in a transport when he was running late to work—made their relationship fated as well. Phoebe being selected as mission commander for the Martian colony on the first anniversary of their wedding? Fate.

Enrique did his best not to scoff when his father made these assertions, even though he had always thought the whole idea of fate and things happening for a reason was silly. But now, he couldn't help wondering if his father had been on to something. Enrique hadn't seen Zora in years, only to have her show up just in time to save his life. Now here she was again, only this time, it was her life that needed saving.

If that wasn't fate, Enrique didn't know what was.

As Zora shifted through the contents of the box—a few loose memory chips, an old photo screen, and a handful of trinkets, Enrique crossed the room to the pull-down desk. Like the one in the other room, this one housed a compartment beneath the surface full of various chips. A familiar navy blue one caught his attention and he avoided touching it as he searched the surrounding chips.

As he worked, his eyes were drawn to Zora. Where her hair had looked black as space last night, today he detected a slight red tint. He wondered if it was as soft and silky as it appeared.

He shook himself and turned back to the desk. His goal was to help Zora. Staring wasn't helpful.

Still, before a full minute passed, his gaze drifted to her again. Zora sat on her knees, pressing something against her wrist comm. A look of pure relief relaxed her features.

"Did you find it?" he asked.

Zora turned and opened her mouth like she wanted to answer aloud, but a spasm crossed her face. Her eyes wide, she struggled to get her feet under her without the use of her hands.

He surged to her side and gripped her arms, but she gestured wildly toward the main room. He tugged her to her feet before glancing out the bedroom door.

"Phobos. What's she doing home?"

Panic flooded Enrique as he watched Phoebe

nearing the front door. He didn't know how he could explain riffling through her belongings, let alone Zora's presence.

Instinct took over. "I'm sorry about this," Enrique murmured before taking Zora by the shoulders and shuffling her into the closet. Her eyes went round as she stumbled backward, but he ignored the terrified look. He could apologize a million times later. Now he needed to hide and hope Phoebe wasn't staying long.

Zora shoved the hanging clothes aside as she folded herself into the closet. But when her foot caught on his father's spare shoes, she slipped and her hands shot out to catch her fall.

The ignition chip glinted as it spiraled through the air and landed in the middle of the bedroom.

They were out of time.

Enrique closed Zora within the closet before spinning on his heel and scooping up the fallen chip. He was still two steps away from the bedroom door when Phoebe entered the house.

She froze when she caught sight of him. "What are you doing home? And why are you in my room?"

Enrique bristled. It was his father's room as much as it was hers, but now wasn't the time to pick a fight over semantics. He needed a lie. One she would believe. "I, um…"

Her shrewd eyes narrowed as she crossed the room toward him. "What's in your hand?"

Enrique's fingers curled around the chip as a

shadowy plan took form in the back of his mind. "Don't be mad. I can explain."

A muffled thud came from the closet and Enrique's throat went dry. It took all his willpower not to turn toward the sound.

Phoebe's attention didn't waver. "Really? You can explain rummaging through my room for—"

"For the memory chip my mom recorded before she died." Enrique dipped his head, hoping to affect a somber posture. Guilt twanged at his insides, but he did his best to ignore it, telling himself his mother would understand the need for the lie. "After all these years, I still haven't watched it. But it's time."

Phoebe took a half step backward. "The memory chip?" She pointed at the device in his hand. "That's not what that is."

"Oh." He held his palm up, pretending to inspect it closer. "I thought I remembered it looking like this, but I haven't seen it in years. I guess I remembered wrong."

His heart pounded in his ears as Phoebe studied him. He arranged his expression in what he hoped to be a neutral one.

It felt like an hour before Phoebe spoke. "That memory chip is yours. Why not just ask for it instead of sneaking around?"

Enrique's lips twitched as he considered how to word the next part. "You know how Dad gets if I bring her up. And I didn't want to ask you because I didn't want to make you feel like... like you're not a good enough mom."

Phoebe's stance softened and she reached forward, resting a hand on Enrique's shoulder. He did his best to remain relaxed, although he couldn't remember the last motherly touch she had attempted. While she was occasionally physically affectionate toward his father in Enrique's presence, she was more reserved toward Enrique, like they were roommates forced to live together by circumstance.

"That's sweet, but you don't have to worry about my feelings. I know I'll never take your mother's place, and that's okay." Phoebe dropped her arm and crossed the bedroom to the still-open desktop. After sifting through the cubbies contents for a few moments, she pulled out the navy blue chip and held it up. "Here it is. Don't worry about returning it. Your dad always intended for you to keep it when you were ready."

Enrique raised his left hand, but Phoebe withheld the device. "Forgetting something?"

The fingers of his right hand twitched. "I can put it back."

"I'll take care of it. I'm sure you want to have some time with the chip before you head back to the farm station."

Scenarios spun through Enrique's head. If he tried too hard to hold onto the ignition chip, she would see though his lie. If she got too curious, she would find Zora. While he wasn't sure that would be a disaster, it could be. Zora's parents probably didn't know she was here. How would they react if they learned what Zora was trying to do? Would they take more drastic steps to lock her away?

Enrique held out his right hand, the ignition chip resting on his upturned palm. Phoebe took it and replaced it with the navy chip. Her lip curled as she turned toward the closet. "Now to put this one away."

Enrique's heart thudded as she moved across the room. One step. Two steps. Three steps. Her hand stretched toward the sliding door.

A buzz hummed, as loud as a crack of thunder in Enrique's ears. Phoebe stopped short of the closet and retracted her arm, turning her wrist to glance at her comm. "Phobos," she murmured, pulling a metal wallet out of her pocket and clicking the chip into place along with several others. "There's an alert that needs my attention. Promise you'll stay out of trouble."

Enrique forced what he hoped was a natural smile. "Always."

Before the word left his mouth, Phoebe was on her way out of the room. Enrique stood still as a statue, scarcely breathing until she closed the front door behind her.

He crossed to the closet and pulled the door open. "That was close." He shoved a lock of hair off his forehead. "I thought for sure she would find you."

Zora nodded, her ashen complexion indicating she feared the same thing. With effort, she used the walls of the closet to push herself into an upright position before taking a step out and lifting her wrist comm. Her finger flew over the screen as she typed out a message.

That was quick thinking about the memory chip.

A muscle in Enrique's jaw jumped as he read the words. "I saw it when I was searching." Contrary to what he said to his stepmother, he hadn't forgotten what the chip looked like. His father had tried to give it to him several times after his mother died, and each time, Enrique had refused to take it. Now the device sat cold against his palm, feeling weightier than it should. "I knew I couldn't tell her what we were after and that seemed like the most obvious alternative."

Zora's face tightened and Enrique's heart sank. They lost the ignition chip, and it was his fault. If he'd thought faster, he could have pocketed the chip before Phoebe saw it.

"We can get it back." The words tumbled out before he could work out how to make good on the promise. "Phoebe always has that wallet on her, but maybe I could get her to set it down somehow. Or—or maybe we don't need the chip. I've always done pretty well on mech rotation. I might be able to wire the shuttle to fly without the chip. We'll go to the supply depot and—"

Zora touched his wrist, sending another current of sparks zipping along his arm. The contact ended almost as soon as it began, leaving Enrique's skin tingling as she typed something on her wrist comm.

It's not there. I downloaded data from chip and might be able to locate it.

Relief swept through Enrique. He hadn't screwed up Zora's chances.

She typed out another message. *Thanks for your help. I'm sure you have to get back to your rotation.*

He grinned. "No, actually. Done for the day."

But instead of looking relieved, Zora's brow creased. She sent another message. *You promised your stepmom you'd stay out of trouble.*

He chuckled. "I appreciate that you're trying to look out for me, but I can handle my stepmom." Pocketing the memory chip, he strode out of the bedroom and veered right toward the seldom-used back door. His fingers curled around the handle before he realized Zora still hovered in the bedroom's threshold. "What are you waiting for?"

She offered her upturned palms, her eyebrows drawn together.

Excitement bubbled up, just as it had last night before he climbed into the raft. That adventure had failed, but this one couldn't. "Let's go find that shuttle."

Chapter Twenty-Nine

*D*eclan blinked, his eyelids gritty with salty air and lack of sleep. The world around him shifted into focus, bringing with it a spike of panic. How long had he been out of it? Were the streams back online?

He pressed his fingertips to the invisible dome once more and connected with the electrical impulses beyond. Coded information flooded his brain. Ones and zeroes strung together in a line that his mind assembled into pictures, sounds, and other bytes of information. Video feeds were still offline and there had been no transmissions sent or received by the Colony since his last check. He heaved a sigh of relief. He hadn't missed anything.

"This is taking too long. Where is it?" Calix took a seat on the bench at the port side of the boat. His right cheek bore the imprint of a crease of fabric from the sleeve of his shirt and his eyes still drooped in a way that suggested he'd woken from a nap too soon.

At least he'd been able to sleep. Declan had caught about an hour on the atmo-shuttle ride here from the selection center, but he'd been awake since they hit the ocean.

"Find it?" Declan echoed as he tapped his miniscreen. He cradled the back of the tablet and pushed some of the information spinning in his head to the device. Images blinked to life for a half second at a time as he cycled through the Colony's camera feeds, prioritizing them based on Aria's last location. Calix had been extra frosty toward Aria since Withers implanted the tech that changed her appearance, but referring to her as "it" seemed extreme. "Should take a minute or so to sift through the feeds."

Calix's face scrunched. "The feeds? I thought you told me there was no sign of the shuttle on the feeds?"

The image on Declan's screen—a wide angle shot of the road leading to the Hub—stuttered before blinking away to blackness. Calix hadn't been asking about Aria. The data Aria transferred before losing the ignition chip had been enough to triangulate a general location, but he had hoped to narrow it down so Aria wouldn't have to search the entire hundred-meter radius. But the parts covered by camera feeds were dotted with caves. So much for ultimate surveillance. "I meant scan to locate Aria. Make sure she's doing okay. It's time for a check-in, right?"

Calix sprang to his feet. "Are you telling me you haven't contacted her since her run-in with Phoebe? It's been almost an hour."

Declan swallowed around the lump in his throat. "I got…distracted. I must've…"

Calix didn't wait to hear the rest of Declan's stammered explanation. He strode toward the craft's stern before disappearing below deck. Declan stared at the spot where he receded from view for a moment before squeezing his eyes shut and shaking his head. He couldn't worry about what Calix was doing. If Aria had been on her own for an hour, Declan needed to make contact as soon as possible. She was probably worried —scared, even. He hoped she'd found somewhere secluded to hide out. The last thing she needed was to run into any more colonists. It was a miracle no one had figured out Aria didn't belong there, and there was no telling how long her luck would last.

An hour had passed since she was at the Martinez house. As much as he wanted to ping her comm, he couldn't until he narrowed down her current location. To conceal his digital footprint, he fed their communications through the most direct route possible. Sending a general ping increased the chances someone on the Colony would figure out something strange was going on.

Declan increased the speed on the camera scroll, keeping the body and facial recognition data for Zora Korbel in the forefront of his mind as each image flashed. But as twenty feeds, then forty, then sixty provided no matches, Declan's stomach clenched. Had someone caught her? There was no prison on the island, but there were a handful of places to detain a person should the need arise. If someone figured out she wasn't Zora...

"Give me your arm."

Declan jumped, nearly dropping his miniscreen at the sound of Calix's voice. He regained his grip on the device and turned toward Calix, keeping his left hand pressed against the dome. "I'm a little busy."

Calix sneered. "Fine. The hard way it is."

Before Declan to could ask what he meant, Calix grabbed his right wrist and turned it upward as he pulled the arm straight. With his other hand, he pressed a silver cylinder to Declan's inner forearm. The coolness of the metal was almost instantly replaced by the sting of a needle prick.

Declan's heart galloped in his chest and fire raced through his veins. Beads of sweat swelled onto his forehead and his limbs trembled with energy he couldn't name. "What did you do?"

Calix made sure Declan had a firm grip on the screen before releasing his wrist. "It's to keep you awake. I hoped Aria would be back by now and I wouldn't have to use it, but she's been gone too long and I can't risk you dozing off again."

Thoughts, data, and images raced through Declan's mind so quickly he couldn't make sense of any of them. He tried to steady his breathing to order his thoughts, but the swirling increased.

"Just give it a minute." Calix checked the pulse at Declan's wrist and nodded as if confirming a hypothesis.

Declan squeezed his eyes closed. "And then what? Are things going to slow down?"

"No. The rest of you should catch up."

Before Declan could ask what he meant, the world seemed to freeze. Every spinning bit of information swooped into order. It was as if he stood in the center of converging streams. He could feel the pulse of each one, sense the ones and zeros as natural extensions of his body. He thought of Aria not as she truly existed but in her altered state—a lead-footed Zora Korbel who couldn't speak. Images from security footage shifted around until a handful of still photos filled his mind's eye. Aria entering the woods behind the Martinez home. Walking down a deserted road at the far edge of the settlement. Entering a grove of pines overlooking the sea. And each time accompanied by the person Reed had instructed her to ditch.

Declan blinked and the images dissipated. Calix watched him, his head listing to the side. "You find her?"

"She's within the search radius. But so is Enrique."

Chapter Thirty

*A*ria stood on the rocky beach, shielding her eyes from the sun's glare with a hand cupped over her brow. She spun in a slow semicircle, surveying the water's edge and the pine forest, peering between branches and studying treetops.

"There's no sign," Enrique said, finishing his own inspection. "Are you sure we're in the right place?"

Aria chewed her lower lip. This was the location Declan sent before he broke off comms. When Enrique asked how she got the information, her vague response about an algorithm satisfied his curiosity, but she didn't know how long that explanation would hold.

She hadn't heard from Declan at all since he told her about the false alarm he sent to Phoebe's comm to get her out of the house. He was supposed to scour the feeds for a view of the search area to help narrow it down, but she had no way of knowing whether he had been successful. He was way overdue for his check-in, and it took everything in her not to let her nerves show.

She typed a message to Enrique. *It could be anywhere in a hundred-meter radius.*

He glanced at his wrist comm. "Probably not *anywhere*." He raised his chin toward the water. "There's nowhere to park it out that way." Grinning, he bumped her shoulder with his. "There you go—I cut our search grid in half."

Heat rushed into Aria's cheeks at the casual contact. It was the kind of thing Alonzo would do all the time, but it felt different coming from Enrique. With Alonzo, the touch was borne out of familiarity, of kinship. But she just met Enrique, so there had to be a different reason for the gentle nudge.

She stopped before her thoughts spiraled further. She couldn't allow herself to get distracted from her mission. The streams went back online in less than nine hours. Alonzo was counting on her.

Another flood of tingles rushed through her body when she turned to Enrique to find him staring at her. "I'd ask if you want to split up, but I think I already know the answer. Want to head straight inland and swing south?"

Without waiting for a response, Enrique started toward the trees, keeping his pace slow enough for Aria to keep up. Her cheeks burned again. Was her crush on him that obvious? Here she thought she was acting normal. She gulped down her embarrassment.

Enrique held a pine bough back to allow Aria enough space to pass by. "How long has it been?"

She swallowed, mind spinning as she tried to figure out a plausible story to tell. When could Zora have developed feelings for him?

"Was it the first hint something was wrong?" he continued. "Trouble walking?"

Aria's lumbered steps almost faltered as Enrique pushed aside another branch. She caught herself, sighing with relief. He wasn't calling her out for having a crush—he was concerned about her physical struggles.

Just when she thought she couldn't like him more.

She shook the thought away. She could save her fantasies for when she and Alonzo were safe at home.

Except at home, Enrique wouldn't be beside her, close enough to touch. He wouldn't be millions of kilometers away on another planet, either, but he may as well be. Once she left the Colony, he would be as out of reach as if he were in a different universe.

The beep in her right ear told Aria that Declan had reestablished comms.

"Any luck yet?" Declan asked, his words tumbling out faster than usual. "There are limited stream feeds in your area, and I can't get eyes on you."

Aria fell a step behind Enrique and typed a quick message. *No sign.* She wanted to ask what took him so long to make contact, but Enrique glanced back to check on her progress too frequently.

"Declan says you've got company," Reed said.

Aria gritted her teeth, trying to come up with a suitable explanation—one she could communicate in a word or two.

"I get it," Reed continued.

Aria's stomach twisted while she waited, helpless, for whatever mocking comment was coming her way.

"It's a smart move."

She stumbled, grabbing a nearby branch to keep herself upright. Enrique cast a concerned glance over his shoulder.

"I've seen you limping around. Declan says that chip makes it hard for you to walk. Enlisting Martinez to do all the searching for you is good thinking."

She sent up a quick thanks to the cosmos for ensuring there were no camera feeds covering her location.

"Once you find it," Reed went on, "you can mind wipe him and send him on his way."

When Aria's step faltered this time, there were no nearby boughs to catch her fall. She crashed to the ground, bracing for impact with her hands. Pine needles dug into her palms.

Enrique was at her side in an instant. "You all right?" He crouched beside her and took her hands in his, inspecting her palms and brushing away the dirt and plant matter with the pads of his thumbs.

Aria's breath caught as the warmth from Enrique's touch radiated through her. Reed's words echoed in her mind. Dr. Withers had given her the memory modification device as a last resort. She wouldn't have to use it on Enrique, would she?

"Maybe I should scope things out on my own," Enrique said, still swiping her palms, sending sparks shooting up her arms. "You can rest up, and I'll come get you when I find the shuttle."

She chanced a glance at his face. Concern furrowed Enrique's brow, but there was a measure of hope sparkling in his brown eyes.

He pursed his lips. "I've been thinking. Let's say we find the shuttle and get you to the ship. The navigation system should plot the course back to Earth itself, but even on the way here when most us were in sus-sleep, there were always two people awake as a safety precaution."

Aria stared at his thumbs as they crossed the flesh of her palms, mesmerized by the motion. She tried to burn the sensation into her mind. The pain in her legs receded with each passing moment as his rhythmic touch drew her focus.

But then the movement ceased and he squeezed her hands like he feared a rogue wave would sweep her away. "Take me with you. Back to Earth. I know you said it's the Mars atmosphere messing with your biochemistry, but what if something goes wrong when you're in space? Even if you're in contact with the Agency, they'll be too far away if your legs give out—or worse. I can help." The corners of his mouth quirked into a smile. "I want to come with you."

Aria's mind spun. The gentle pressure of Enrique's hands, the hopeful glint in his eyes, the earthy scent of him, the warmth radiating off his body—it was all too much for her to process. Too many times to count, she had imagined scenarios where Enrique Martinez would look at her this way, like they were the only people on the planet. The only people in the universe. Her heart hammered against her chest, but everything else seemed to slow down, as if time itself revolved around this moment.

Enrique brought his right hand up to stroke her cheek with a touch so light she feared she was imagining it. "What do you say, Zora?"

Just like that, the illusion crashed around her. Time sped up and the silence of the surrounding trees pressed in like a weight threatening to crush her. Even with Enrique right in front of her, she was still engaging in fantasy. He wasn't speaking to her, Aria Ayers, aberration. Enrique was sharing this moment with Zora Korbel, the Colony's recluse. Nothing about this was real.

Aria's stomach lurched and she pressed a hand to her mouth to combat anything that might threaten to rise. Acrid bile stung the back of her throat.

Enrique sprang backward, putting space between them. His eyes were wide with confusion. "I'm sorry. I didn't…" He shook his head as he stood up. "I'll keep looking for the shuttle."

As Enrique headed deeper into the woods, Aria watched, unable to move. Maybe she should have tried harder to convince Enrique to let her search for the shuttle alone. How was she going to explain her behavior to him? Her finger hovered over her wrist comm, but nothing came to her.

"You okay?"

Declan's voice in her ear made Aria jump. Her cheeks burned as she realized he must have heard the whole exchange with Enrique. Her only comfort was he hadn't seen what a fool she'd made of herself.

Not sure how to answer, she tapped the ear comm twice.

"Stop coddling her," Reed snapped. "Ayers, you gotta get out of there. You've got incoming."

Ignoring the pain, Aria got her feet under her and pressed herself to standing. Her gaze drifted in the direction Enrique had disappeared. She needed to get him.

"It's Phoebe," Declan said. "The sensor malfunction didn't distract her as long as I hoped it would. I guess Enrique was acting too squirrelly at their house. She checked on his location through the family link software on their wrist comms. She's heading right for you."

If Phoebe was tracking Enrique, going to him was the last thing Aria should do.

Chapter Thirty-One

*E*nrique kicked at a loose pile of soil as he trudged farther up the gentle slope of the mountain. He'd crossed a line with Zora. What was he thinking? While it was true they weren't strangers, they might as well be after zero contact for so many years. When she fell, helping her up was the most natural thing to do. But when he touched her hands, he didn't want to let go. He was waiting for the perfect moment to suggest he come with her back to Earth, and that had seemed like it.

But he took it too far. Why had he felt the need to touch her face? Now things were awkward. And while he stood by his assessment that Zora shouldn't undertake the journey to their home world alone, Zora would have every right to say she didn't want to spend months upon months trapped on a spaceship with him.

He shook the thoughts from his head. That was a

concern for another time. It didn't matter whether she would let him come with her if they never found the shuttle that would take them to the ship.

The crunching of feet on dried pine needles drifted toward him and a grin stretched across his face. He'd told Zora to wait where she was, but maybe she had time to process what happened—or almost happened.

But even as the thought occurred to him, he dismissed it. Whoever was coming through the trees moved much faster than Zora could.

Then who could be approaching?

Panic flooded him as he recalled stories his mom used to read to him about big, bad wolves lurking in forests—until he remembered where he was. There were no wolves on Mars. The only thing large enough to be making those sounds was another human—one of the two hundred he had lived with for the last four years.

"Enrique?"

Something akin to dread jolted through his stomach at the sound of his stepmother's voice. He glanced at his wrist comm and cursed. In all the time they'd been on Mars, he couldn't remember his dad or Phoebe tracking him down using the family link. That Phoebe was doing it now couldn't be good.

A voice in the back of his head urged him to hide, and he scanned the vicinity for cover, but it would be useless. Phoebe was tracking his comm, so she could find him anywhere on the island. He may as well stand his ground and deal with what was coming.

"I'm over here." Enrique winced at the sound of his voice. It was higher than usual, like that of a child trying to convince an authority figure he hadn't broken any rules even when all evidence was to the contrary.

He cleared his throat as his stepmother came into view.

Phoebe pressed a hand to her heart before crossing to him and squeezed his upper arm. "What are you doing all the way out here?"

Enrique stared at the spot she touched, not sure how to react to the contact. "I, um…" He rubbed his palms against the thighs of his pants and felt something in his right pocket. His mother's memory chip. "I needed to take a walk to clear my head after…" He met Phoebe's eyes, ignoring the twinge of guilt at the lie. "I guess I wasn't as ready as I thought for that memory chip."

Phoebe tilted her head. "Are you sure that's what this is about?"

Enrique's throat went dry. He tried to keep his face impassive as he strained to swallow. "What else would it be about?"

She frowned. "I can count on one hand how many code yellow alerts I've gotten since we've been here. And when I got to the supply depot and found out the sensor had malfunctioned, it seemed a little too coincidental." She crossed her arms over her chest. "That wasn't just any chip you mistook for your mother's memory chip. But you knew that already."

Enrique took a step backward. "I don't know what you're talking about."

Phoebe sighed. It was the same sound he had heard from his father a thousand times before. The you're-not-as-smart-as-you-think-you-are sigh. The I-know-exactly-what-you're-trying-to-hide sigh. "There's a raft missing from the emergency supply shed."

Enrique froze. Last night seemed so long ago. In his confusion of waking up on the beach and Zora's reappearance, he hadn't given much thought to the fact that someone would notice it was gone.

"If it was any other day, I would check in with Gabe or Oscar or Irina, but today is different. The streams are down, so why would they pull a stunt now? You, on the other hand." She pressed her hands to her hips as she surveyed him. "You think I haven't noticed that look in your eyes. I know you better than you realize, Enrique. When I married your father, I vowed not to try to take your mother's place. But I'm afraid because of that, sometimes it might seem like I'm not trying to be part of your life. I don't think I ever struck the right balance. But I do care for you, and I want what's best for you."

Enrique stared at her, not sure how to respond. This was the most open she had ever been with him—about anything. He couldn't repay that honesty with a lie. "You're right. It was me. I was going to sail out to the closest island and explore. Then I was going to come right back, I promise. But I didn't get very far before the raft took on water. It sank—I couldn't…"

Phoebe pressed a hand to her chest, her eyes full of concern. "But you're okay. That's all that matters." She pursed her lips. "It might be a good thing you attempted your adventure. I'll have a team check the remaining rafts to see if any others are damaged. It's no good to have a them stored up for an emergency only to sink if we ever try to use them."

Enrique tilted his head. "You're not mad?"

"I'm thankful you're okay." She crossed to him and squeezed his arm again. "And I understand."

He snorted. "You do?"

She nodded. "You're eighteen. If we were on Earth, you'd have the whole world to go explore. Here, you have an island. But I am a little concerned you planned to go on your grand adventure alone. What if something went wrong while you were away? Did you think about that?"

Enrique shifted, his stomach twisting as he recalled his last interaction with Zora. Hadn't he been making the same argument to her?

Phoebe tilted her head, squinting. "You were alone, weren't you?" She sighed, shaking her head. "Never mind. I already know the answer. I know there was someone hiding in my closet."

Enrique's eyebrows hiked up his forehead. "You do"

His stepmother's smile answered for her. She hadn't *known*, she'd *suspected*. And his response was confirmation.

"Who were you planning to take with you? Ravi? Oscar?"

His nose wrinkled. Oscar could be fun to spend time with, but Enrique couldn't imagine being cooped up on a spaceship with him for months on end. Oscar was the kind of person who would pull pranks even if there were no cameras watching.

Phoebe tilted her head. "If not one of them, then who?" She offered a small smile. "No one will get in trouble. I'm just curious."

Enrique sighed. He knew his stepmother well enough to be sure she wouldn't drop the subject without an answer. His father often said Phoebe's tenacity made her such a good security chief for the mission because she wouldn't rest until she had all the facts about a situation. "Zora Korbel."

Her eyes widened. "Zora? How in the galaxy..." She paused, her brow knitting. "She's not well, Enrique."

"I know." The words came out sharper than he anticipated and he exhaled before continuing. "That's why I was helping her." He stopped himself from saying more, although he was sure there was nothing about Zora's condition that Phoebe didn't already know.

But her confused expression lingered. "Zora was at our house earlier? Is she out here with you now?"

He nodded. "I told her to rest while I searched."

Phoebe drew back her shoulders. "Take me to her."

Enrique sighed. "Follow me."

But when he arrived at the spot where he'd left Zora, she wasn't there. A quick search of the vicinity turned up nothing.

Concern creased Phoebe's brow. "We should check her house."

Enrique's stomach clenched. "I don't want to get her in trouble."

"I want to make sure she's safe." Without allowing for further discussion, Phoebe led the way back to the heart of their settlement.

Enrique knew the way to the Korbels' house, even if he'd never had occasion to visit. Although it was in a different grouping than his own home, he passed by frequently. But never had his stomach writhed as he approached.

Phoebe marched to the door and knocked, while Enrique hovered behind her, unsure what to expect.

The door slid open to reveal Dr. Eliza, a stylus tucked behind her ear and a concerned look on her face. She checked her wrist comm as if afraid she missed a ping. "Phoebe. Is something wrong? Is Samara—"

Phoebe cut her off with a shake of her head. "No,

we're not here about Samara or the baby. I'd like to speak to you about Zora."

The groove between Dr. Eliza's eyebrows deepened. She stepped backward and swept her hand toward the sitting area in the house's common room. "Please, come in."

As Enrique followed his stepmother into the house, he couldn't help scanning for a sign of Zora. But the kitchen and common area were empty. The doctor's tablet lay abandoned on the couch. She picked it up and tucked it away in the fold-down desk on the wall.

"Can I get you something to drink? Tea?" The doctor crossed toward the kitchen, looking to Phoebe.

"Yes, please." Phoebe followed Dr. Eliza's trajectory, taking a seat at the counter separating the kitchen from the common room. "Tell me, Eliza," Phoebe began as the other woman turned on the tap. "Has Zora been out and about today?"

The doctor spun, droplets of water spraying across the floor. "What? You know as well as anyone, Zora stays at home."

Phoebe didn't blink as she wiped a bead of water off the back of her hand. "I saw her at the Hub during the baby shower. I thought maybe she was improving."

Zora's mother held Phoebe's gaze. "She isn't."

Enrique bit the inside of his lip. Besides her difficulty walking and inability to speak, Zora had seemed healthy enough. Indeed, she was strong enough to save him from drowning last night. Would sharing that information with the doctor give her hope or upset her?

Dr. Eliza turned back to the sink to continue filling the kettle. "Usually Rashid and I can work out our schedules so they don't overlap, but things have been so unpredictable this close to the end of the pregnancy. He had to be at the Hub before I could leave, so he brought Zora along with him."

"He couldn't just leave her here by herself?" Enrique asked.

Phoebe raised an eyebrow as if questioning who he thought he was by interjecting into their conversation. But Enrique was curious. Zora was around his age, so it wasn't as if she required constant attention or guard. Why wouldn't her parents leave her alone?

The doctor busied herself preparing the tea, ignoring his question.

"So, Zora's been here all day?" Phoebe asked as if Enrique hadn't spoken.

"Of course." Dr. Eliza didn't turn around. "We had breakfast together. She's been in her room ever since."

Enrique glanced toward the back corner of the house. He couldn't see the door to the home's smaller bedroom, but he knew it was there. Had Zora snuck out and back in without his mother noticing?

"May I use your bathroom?"

The words tumbled out of Enrique's mouth so fast he almost missed the doctor's perfunctory nod of permission. He tried to be casual as he walked toward the bathroom door, watching Phoebe out of his peripheral vision to make sure she wasn't paying too much attention to him. As soon as he was out of sight, he darted past the bathroom door. Sucking in a breath, he pulled open Zora's door and stepped in, sliding it closed behind him.

It wasn't until he was inside that he realized he might be walking in on Zora changing or something else not meant for his eyes. He held his hands over his face like a child counting to twenty before going to seek hiding friends. "Sorry to barge in. Knock twice if I shouldn't uncover my eyes."

He waited a few seconds, but when no knocks reverberated through the air, he lowered his hands.

At first, he couldn't make sense of what he was seeing. Every bedroom he'd stepped foot in on the Colony had looked the same: a square room with minimal furniture. Sometimes the bed or desk had been repositioned, but they were always present. A few people were lucky enough to have a small rug for a pop of color, but even those rooms had the same stark white walls.

But Zora's walls were marked with dark red splotches and symbols. Along the wall where her desk was hung were row after row of thin, straight twigs about the length of his hand. Her floor was spattered with droplets of what looked like dried blood.

Enrique shook himself. No. Blood dried brown, and these drops were maroon.

Zora stood facing the back wall, her arm moving back and forth furiously, showing no sign she noticed Enrique's presence.

He stepped toward her, taking care not to tread on any of the dark smudges on the floor as he tried to make sense of the scribbles on the wall. Markings seemed to be grouped into areas—some the size of his hand, others larger than four tablets put together. Some of the squiggles and lines were neat and tidy where others appeared to have been scrawled quickly. Nothing resembled letters or numbers, yet no part assembled itself into any kind of image, either.

"Zora?" Enrique kept his voice low. "My stepmom found me. She's out there talking to your mom now." He ran a hand through his hair. "Phoebe knows you were at my house—but I didn't tell her you snuck in. And I didn't tell her about what happened in the water last night, either."

Zora's arm stilled. She turned, her brow furrowed as she scanned his face. After a few seconds, a look of recognition washed over her features and she smiled, pointing at the wall where she'd been working.

Enrique glanced at the spot she indicated, but it was full of the same nonsensical symbols as the other parts of her room. "That's great," he said, not sure how else to respond. "But we've got a problem. Phoebe knows we were looking for the shuttle. I don't think she realized where we planned to take it, but still. I doubt we'll be able to get near the shuttle again soon. And, knowing her, she'll move it somewhere else before we can go find it. I'm sorry."

She watched him, head tilted, until he finished speaking. Slowly, she lifted her left hand until it was level with his face. Extending her pointer finger, she touched the tip of his nose before turning back to the wall.

Frustration flared in Enrique's gut as Zora added more inscrutable marks to those already written. He gripped her shoulder and spun her to face him. "Why are you acting like this?"

She reached up to tap his nose again and he encircled his fingers around her wrist to keep her hand down.

His nose wrinkled. "Where's your comm?"

Zora blinked. Enrique stared into her eyes, but they looked different than they had in the woods—all brown without a hint of blue around the pupils. And her dark hair held none of the red tint that had sparkled so brightly in the sunlight.

"What's going on, Zora? You can tell me."

She pressed her lips together, inhaling through her nose. Her arms went slack and she opened her mouth and tipped back her head. A series of *ohs* and *ahs* floated up into the air as she exhaled a complicated melody, her voice growing louder with each note.

Enrique dropped her wrist and stepped backward. "Zora?"

The bedroom door slid open, banging in its track.

"What are you doing in here?" his stepmother demanded.

Dr. Eliza pushed past her, crossing toward Zora. "It's fine, Phoebe." She reached for her daughter, but her fingers didn't quite make contact as Zora spun in place, throwing open her arms as she continued to sing.

Enrique shook his head. "I... I don't understand."

"She's not well," the doctor said, her voice sad. "Something happened to her on the flight here. Since we got to Mars, she's... deteriorated. I've coordinated with scientists back on Earth, we've run every test we can think of, but... You can't fix something when you don't know what's wrong."

Zora's song faded to a hum and she turned back to the wall to continue her scrawling.

Enrique watched her for a moment. "She can talk?"

Dr. Eliza shrugged. "For the last year, the most we've gotten out of her is what you just heard. She sings like that when the mood strikes, but never words."

Enrique's mind spun. The Zora in front of him now bared little resemblance to the one he spent the day with. What could have changed in half an hour? Was she putting on a show for her mother, or was there something deeper going on?

And if she was acting this way around her mother for some logical reason, why wouldn't she let Enrique in on it?

His heart twisted in his chest. Perhaps his impression of her last night hadn't missed the mark. Zora was delusional, and she'd pulled him into her crazy fantasies along with her.

He turned to Dr. Eliza. "I'm sorry. I didn't know." He sighed and looked at his stepmother. "I'm ready to go home."

Chapter Thirty-Two

*A*ria floated in place twenty meters offshore. The weak faux-Martian sunlight had already dispersed to nearly nothing despite the fact she wasn't deep. The odd water flowed over her gills, leaving a metallic aftertaste in the back of her throat.

She lifted her wrist and checked the time. Almost ten minutes had passed since she jumped into the sea to avoid being seen by Phoebe Tomlin. She hadn't heard anything from Declan since he warned her to take cover, so she typed a message into her comm, checking twice to make sure she set it to go to Declan before hitting send. *Is the coast clear?*

A full thirty seconds passed before Reed's voice flowed into her ear. "Yeah, Tomlin and Martinez are out of the area. You should be good to get out of the water and continue the search."

Aria continued to tread water. *What's going on with Enrique? Is he in trouble?*

"Tomlin didn't haul him off in handcuffs or anything," Reed said. "He'll be fine. And the stepmom did you a favor. Now we don't have to figure out a way for you to ditch him after you find the shuttle."

She stopped kicking her legs, allowing herself to drift toward the ocean floor. That was it, then. Enrique was gone. Would he come looking for her once he got away from his stepmother? She shook her head as her foot brushed a tendril of seaweed. No, Reed was right. She would have had to part ways with Enrique anyway.

She only wished she had the chance to say goodbye.

Seaweed twisted up to her knees, but she didn't kick to get away. Part of her wanted to sink into the vegetation and never come back up. If Alonzo were here, he would mock her for being so dramatic.

Alonzo.

Aria pounded her legs against the water, remembering the reason she was here. Alonzo needed her. She couldn't fail him.

"W-wait. Stop."

Declan's voice made Aria freeze. It wasn't the words as much as how he said them. He sounded lethargic, like his tongue was too large for his mouth.

"Relax, Perth," Reed said, his tone verging on kindness. "I can keep watch while she—"

"No." The word came out like a gush of air. "I'm

getting something. The… The shuttle. Search radius narrowing."

"You think the shuttle is in the water?" Reed asked, giving voice to the question swirling in Aria's mind.

At first blush, the idea was preposterous. But if the vessel was an atmo-shuttle, it would be water tight. And what better place to hide something than somewhere the average person couldn't access?

"South," Declan said. "Twenty meters. Can't get a read on how deep."

She struck off in the direction he indicated, not bothering to remind him she was built for searches like this.

She kept her gaze trained on the sea floor as she swam. At first, only unremarkable stretches of seaweed waved back at her, but then a steep drop-off took her deeper into the blackness. She tapped on her wrist comm to turn on the flashlight, training the beam to shine out over her fingertips.

"Anything?" Reed asked.

Aria gritted her teeth, unsure how he expected her to answer. Ignoring him, she swam on.

"Ayers, do you copy?"

She brought her hand up to tap on her earpiece, but as she did, the beam of the flashlight caught a shape too sleek and angular to be natural. She refocused the light, a grin spreading across her face when the shuttle came into view.

Aria darted through the water and looped her arm

through one of the shuttle's grab bars before typing a message. *Found it.*

"Yeow!" Declan shouted.

Aria pressed her hand to her ear, even though she could do nothing to block out the sound. When Declan said nothing else, she typed another message. *What's going on?*

"Everything's fine," Reed said, but he sounded distracted. "Just give him a second."

Aria held her breath, a sense of foreboding creeping down her spine.

Declan made another incoherent noise. "Yikes. That was rough, but I'm back in business."

Before Aria could even lift her wrist to ask what Declan meant, he was speaking again.

"I need you to find the upper access hatch. Engineers designed this model of atmo-shuttle to complete low-orbit resupply missions, so there's an airlock where you can get in. I need you to hold your comm up to the access panel so I can tweak some settings."

Words tumbled out of Declan's mouth so quickly it was difficult for Aria to keep up, but she did as he instructed. She wished she knew what was happening with him. His sudden switch from lethargic to supercharged worried her.

But as she held her wrist to the side of the shuttle, waiting for Declan to do his thing, she shook herself. Why should she care what was going on with Declan? He lied to her when they met, pretending to be part of the selection so he could gain intel on her. He worked for Withers and whatever shadow-Agency she headed. All that mattered right now was that Declan could help her accomplish her mission.

A light blinked to life, first red and then green. A heavy *thunk* echoed through the water, followed by a metallic groaning. Aria held tight to a grab bar to keep from being sucked in with the inrush as the airlock door opened.

Once the pressure equalized, she released the handle and swam into the cramped capsule, closing the door behind her and twisting the wheel-shaped lock closed. *I'm in.*

"Just a minute, and…"

A hum filled the small space as the water drained. Aria's skin tingled as adrenaline rushed through her system. It was happening. It had taken longer than they expected for her to reach the shuttle, but now she was here. She would get to the spaceship, plug in the thumb drive, and download the information that would set Alonzo free.

Pain jolted up Aria's legs as the diminishing water level forced her to bear her own weight again. She found her footing on the lower rungs of the stainless steel ladder that led between the doors. Her hands clutched the upper rungs tighter than necessary to alleviate pressure on her legs.

A panel on the door below flicked to life. The light flashed green and a beep pierced the small space.

"Ready?" Declan asked.

Aria tapped her earpiece.

"Door opening in three... two... one."

The lower hatch slid open in a blink. Aria gritted her teeth as she started down the ladder. Her legs trembled with each step downward, her bones blazing as if on fire.

She missed a rung and her hands, still wet from the sea, lost their grip. Aria crashed to the shuttle's main level, crumpling into a pile at the bottom of the ladder.

"What was that?"

Aria sucked in a breath, wincing. She tried to take stock of herself, but the pain in her legs was so intense she couldn't tell if she'd gotten hurt in the fall.

"Aria?" Panic laced Declan's tone. "Aria?"

She brought up her wrist to type a response but stopped short, her fingers hovering over the comm. She scrutinized her skin in the dim glow of the emergency lights. The familiar constellation of freckles that had been obscured by Zora's flesh dotted her arm. They were faint, but visible. She wasn't herself, but she wasn't Zora anymore, either.

"Respond, Aria. Let me know what's going on."

"Ayers," Reed snapped. "You still with us?"

She cleared her throat. "The chip," she said in a voice not quite her own. "It's malfunctioning."

"Aria, is that you?" Declan asked at the same moment Reed muttered, "Phobos."

"It's me." Aria's voice was gravelly, but whether

from disuse or an effect of the chip, she wasn't sure. She tried to stand, but her shaky legs wouldn't handle her weight. She did her best to swallow the yelp of pain that clawed its way up her throat. "Tell me you can hack the ignition."

"Already done," Declan said.

She sighed with relief. "Good. Now tell me you can fly this thing."

"Of course I can," he scoffed. "Except I can't. At least, not right now."

"What's that supposed to mean?" She tapped on the screen of her wrist comm to pull up the countdown. Seven hours. "I'm here. What's the problem?"

"Kelp harvest," Declan said. "I caught it on the security feeds. When I thought the shuttle was in the woods, I figured you'd be so far away from where they're working they wouldn't notice the takeoff or the shuttle flying up the side of the volcano. But based on your location in the water, there's no way they'll miss you. For now, you have to hang tight."

Aria struggled to arrange herself in a seated position, her back pressing against the cool steel wall beside the ladder. "For how long?"

"Until they're done."

Aria cursed under her breath. She couldn't believe she had gotten so close only to be stuck waiting.

Chapter Thirty-Three

*E*nrique pushed his zucchini spirals around on his plate with no intention of eating them. His stomach had been in knots since he and Phoebe left the Korbel residence. He couldn't reconcile the Zora he spent the sol with—lucid, driven, empathetic Zora—with the girl singing and twirling around her room, painting nonsense symbols on her walls.

Dr. Eliza might have been able to shed light on the differences, but he couldn't bring himself to ask her. The strain in her face was obvious when they spoke of her daughter, and he didn't want to add to it.

Enrique didn't notice the conversation at the table until it stopped. Silence rang in his ears and he dragged his gaze up to meet his father's. "What?"

His dad tilted his head, sending waves of brown hair spilling over his forehead until they threatened to cover his eye. He needed a haircut, but he would never get one until Phoebe put her foot down about him looking like a wild man. "Are you all right? You seem… upset."

Enrique took in a breath, but no words formed. He didn't want to talk about Zora, about how he had started to plan the first things they would do once they got back to Earth while he searched for the shuttle. But her face loomed so large in his thoughts that he couldn't come up with another reason for his behavior.

Phoebe reached across the table and rested her hand on his father's wrist. "Santiago, Enrique and I had a talk today and he said he was ready to watch Ximena's memory chip. I knew where you kept it, and I knew you wanted him to have it when he was ready."

His father sucked in a breath and squared his shoulders. "Enrique." He reached out and squeezed his son's upper arm. "I'm glad you're ready. And I'm here to talk, if you need to. It's good to remember those we've lost."

Not sure what to say, Enrique nodded. As soon as his father turned back to his meal, Enrique glanced at Phoebe, who offered a small smile.

She just lied for him. She had the opportunity to tell his father everything—or force the conversation to make Enrique reveal it all—but she covered over the day's events. Gratefulness welled up in his chest, along with something like affection for Phoebe. It was among the few motherly things she had ever done for him.

Phoebe carried the conversation for the rest of the

meal, but Enrique didn't pay attention. He managed a few mouthfuls of food, knowing his father—who was in charge of nutrition for the Colony—wouldn't let him get away without eating something. He was about to excuse himself to his room when his father stood and cleared everyone's plates. "I have to go back to work for an hour or so. The kelp harvest should be over now, and I've got to make sure everything is stored properly." He held Enrique's gaze, and Enrique did his best not to blink. Even without words, his father's promise to talk was clear.

Enrique swallowed the knot of guilt in his throat.

"I'll walk with you," Phoebe said, standing. "I have a few more things to take care of before the streams start up again."

Enrique watched as his father and stepmom walked out of the house together, and he followed their progress down the street until he could no longer see them through the front window.

Part of him was glad to have the house to himself. While he was thankful for Phoebe's quick thinking, he didn't like the expectant look on his father's face. Despite having had his mother's memory chip in his pocket all day, Enrique had no desire to watch it. If he played it now, it would only be to distract him from everything that happened with Zora, and he couldn't bear to use his mother's last words for him in that way.

He stood and crossed to the common room to the couch. He lay down on it, propping his feet up in a way that would make Phoebe purse her lips if she were here to witness it. How could everything have changed so completely in the last sol? This time yesterday, he was giddy with excitement about going on his first real adventure. But the raft sank, and Zora saved him. Now, the girl he'd spent almost no time thinking about for the last four years was the only person on his mind. Zora had told him there was something in the atmosphere messing with her physiology, but Dr. Eliza claimed it was the sus-sleep cycles on the journey here that had caused Zora's troubles.

He sighed. It didn't matter. Zora was unwell—that much was clear. He couldn't spend the rest of his life preoccupied with her. He didn't know what could help her, but assisting her to get back to Earth was out of the question.

Maybe there was no helping her. There was just moving on.

Enrique's wrist comm buzzed and for the briefest moment, he allowed himself to imagine the ping was from Zora. But before he looked at the device, he pushed the fantasy from his mind.

The ping was from Phoebe. Intrigued, he sat up as he read it.

Meet me at the shore behind the emergency supply bunker. I have a surprise.

Enrique reread the message three times to make sure it said what he thought it did. He couldn't remember ever receiving a surprise from his stepmother, but if today had taught him anything, it was that Phoebe Tomlin might not be the person he thought she was. Today, more than at any other point since he'd met her, she had behaved like a mother would. Maybe now that they shared a secret, a wall between them had broken.

Enrique didn't know what kind of person to expect on the other side.

Chapter Thirty-Four

The shuttle's control panels blazed to life, and Aria adjusted her grip on the ladder rung to her right. "Are you sure about this?"

"You're joking, right?" Declan scoffed. "Do I question you about breathing underwater? No. So don't question my skills at interfacing with tech."

"I guess you're right," Aria murmured, but despite Declan's argument, she squealed as the shuttle jolted upward.

Although she would give anything to be in control of the shuttle, she had to admit that even if she had a clue how to fly this thing, she wouldn't be able to focus enough to keep from being seen and avoid crashing. The pain in her legs was increasing exponentially, and she wasn't even putting pressure on them. She could only hope Reed's plan would buy her enough time to make it to the ship's bridge and back.

Aria caught glimpses of green and blue out of the shuttle's front window, but she closed her eyes when the ruddy brown top of the volcano came into view. "Don't hit it. Don't hit it. Don't hit it," she mumbled under her breath.

"I can hear that," Declan grumbled. "Your confidence in me is good for my ego."

Her stomach swooped as the shuttle sank downward, and a firm jolt told her when the craft touched down. She opened her eyes and let out the breath she hadn't realized she'd been holding.

"See. Told you I knew what I was doing," Declan said, sounding pleased with himself.

"Are you ready?" Reed asked.

His question sent a shiver down her spine. Aria looked at the injector she held in her right hand. While she was waiting for the kelp harvest to wrap up, she had noticed a first aid kit hanging on the wall. After much effort and a fair bit of cursing, she made her way to it despite the pain in her legs. Most of its contents weren't helpful—bandages, antiseptic, anti-nausea pills—but there were a handful of vials with names she didn't recognize that Reed decoded. One of those vials was a local anesthesia. According to Reed, the dose would give her relief long enough to make it to the bridge and back.

"You remember how to dial in the dosage?"

Aria tried not to let the question offend her. Reed

had talked her through the steps several times in the three hours she'd been waiting. "I've got it."

"Because you only get one shot at this," he continued. "If you inject all of it in one leg—"

"I know." She huffed, checking the dosage indicator one last time before pressing the device to the side of her leg above her knee. A sensation like fire swept through her leg, followed by one like ice. A shocked cry escaped her lips and she clenched her teeth until the sensation died down to a gentle tingling. She blew out a breath before injecting the rest of the anesthesia into her left leg. This time, when the fire and ice came, she was ready for them.

When the tingling subsided from both legs, she tried to stand up. It took three tries to get her feet under her. "This is weird. It's like I'm walking on stilts or something."

"Opening the main door now," Declan said. "The passage to the bridge should be on your left."

Aria's steps were slow and labored, but at least she wasn't in pain. Reed checked in with her three times before she traversed the thirty-meter path to the bridge.

"Okay, what am I looking for?" The controls looked much like those in the shuttle, only scaled up. Where there had been four panels in the shuttle, there were four times that on the ship. Some had buttons and flip switches while others were blank screens, waiting to be powered on.

"The primary panel should be in the center of the

control area." His words came out slowly, each one slurring more than the one before. "It's a tower that stands separate from the others."

She bit her lower lip. "Declan? You okay?"

"Yeah, 'm *fine*."

Although Aria was sure he wasn't being truthful, she shoved her concern aside and scanned the controls. She identified the primary panel and crossed to it. There was a slot under the screen that seemed the perfect size for her transfer chip. She fished it out of her waist pouch and slid it into the hole.

A screen blazed to life on top of the podium. "Okay, it turned on. Now what do I do?"

"Now comes the easy part," Declan said, his words slow and distinct. "The system should prompt you to enter a command."

Aria glanced at the screen. "Yes. What do I type?"

Silence stretched out for two seconds. Five. Fifteen. Aria tapped her earpiece. "Declan? You still there?"

"What?" Declan cleared his throat. "Oh, yeah. Um, where were we?"

"I need to enter the command." She bit her lower lip. "You're not inspiring confidence right now. I thought you said you knew all the tech things."

"I *do* know all the tech things," he insisted, his words slurred. "Type *action zulu-six-eight-niner*."

Her finger hovered over the screen. "Type what?"

"Action," he said slowly, "zee-six-eight-nine."

She blew out a breath and typed the word and sequence. "Now what? Declan?"

The silence on the other end of the comm was deafening. She stared at the screen, hoping it would indicate she had entered the right information. But the cursor continued to blink and nothing changed.

"Declan?"

She heard something indistinct on the comm and pressed the earpiece as if doing so could clarify the noise. "Declan?"

"Phobos," Reed spat. "Phobos *and* Deimos and Mars for good measure."

"What's going on?" Panic swelled in Aria's stomach. She wished she had a visual link to what was happening on the boat, not just audio.

"Tell me the data transfer started already," Reed said.

Aria blinked. "The data… But what's going on with Declan?"

"Is the data transferring?" he snapped.

"No. No! I don't think so. Declan gave me an order to type in and then he stopped responding. What's wrong with him?"

"Did you press enter?"

"What?" Aria stared at the screen, trying to remember. "No. He didn't say hit enter, so I—"

"Hit enter now," Reed said, his tone calming. "With any luck, the stars will align and the data will download. Otherwise…"

Aria didn't want to think of what "otherwise" might entail. Holding her breath, she tapped *enter*. The screen went blank and her stomach dropped, but a split second later, a long empty rectangle appeared, along with a readout. One percent.

"It's working," she said, her words coming out in a rush.

"Glory," Reed murmured.

"And Declan?"

A beat passed before Reed answered. "Exhaustion. The amount of data he's been processing since you entered the Colony… Well, let's just say it's taken a lot out of him. Withers expected it could happen and she gave me a drug to keep him lucid, but it's taking a toll on him. I… I've got another dose, but I don't think he can handle it. It could send him into cardiac arrest."

Aria wrapped her hair around her hands. She was used to Calix Reed sounding in control—arrogant, even. The doubt in his voice scared her. "What are you going to do?"

"Give him a quarter dose. That should wake him up enough to keep you from being detected. But beyond that, you'll be on your own."

She swallowed. "Comms?"

"We'll still have comms. And you'll still have me to talk to."

A laugh bubbled out of her. "Lucky me."

Reed chuckled too. "You haven't even heard the best part."

Aria unwound her hands from her hair. "Don't leave me in suspense."

"Just got word from Withers. The solar storm wasn't as bad as advertised."

She froze. All the mirth in Reed's voice moments before had vanished.

"The show's producers will start the streams again ahead of schedule. You're down to two hours."

"Phobos," Aria murmured. This mission was supposed to be easy. How foolish she had been to think she would be home by lunch time!

She sucked in a breath. The end was in sight. Once the data downloaded, she could leave.

The bar on the screen shimmered and the number ticked upward.

Three percent down. Ninety-seven to go.

"That data better download fast," Reed said. "The swim in took you about an hour. That doesn't leave you much time."

Aria shivered. According to Declan, even though there were no cameras in the maintenance tunnels, the entrance and exit were surveilled. If she didn't get back to the boat by the time the streams were back online, it wouldn't matter if she retrieved the information. The Agency would know she was here and Alonzo would be doomed.

Chapter Thirty-Five

A sense of déjà vu swept over Enrique as he stood on the shore, staring out over the darkening horizon. Not twenty-four hours ago, he stood in nearly the same spot, preparing to venture off across the sea. He couldn't wrap his head around just how much different he felt today.

"Ah, there you are."

Enrique jumped at his stepmother's voice as she approached from an alcove to the south. Composing himself, he turned to face her. "I've never been one to pass up a surprise." He tried to smile, but his mouth wouldn't cooperate.

She beckoned for him to follow and retraced her steps. "I've been doing a lot of thinking today," she said as they stepped from rock to rock onto a thin strip of land that jutted out into the water. "I remember how excited you were when you found out they picked our

293

family to come here. For weeks, all you talked about was Mars. You studied maps. You memorized facts. Every person we passed knew we'd been chosen. I suppose I never considered that this place wasn't what you imagined."

Phoebe disappeared around an outcropping of trees. Enrique watched his footing as he stepped on the large, worn stones that littered the shore. But as he rounded the edge of the last pine, something else snared his attention. Sitting on the shore in the center of the secluded alcove was a raft, inflated and tethered to a stake that had been pounded further up on the beach.

"What is this?" Enrique asked, approaching the craft. It was identical to the one he had used the night before.

Phoebe crossed to it, lifting the rope connecting the raft to the stake. "Isn't it obvious? I want you to have your adventure, Enrique."

He gaped, unsure how to respond. Not long after they arrived on the Colony, Phoebe had grounded him for four weeks because he took an extra treat ration. Every night during that time, she impressed on him how important it was to follow every rule to ensure the safety and survival of everyone on the Colony. He couldn't reconcile that memory with the woman standing behind him, looking at him expectantly.

"As security chief, I'm the last one who should encourage this. In fact, if I caught one of your friends trying this, I'd stop them without question. But I know you, Enrique. I know how careful and responsible you are. And after today, I know what this adventure means to you."

Enrique stepped toward the raft as if in a trance. He couldn't believe this was happening. But after everything that had occurred in the last sol, it almost didn't surprise him. Not everything was as it seemed. Zora Korbel wasn't a girl in need of saving—she was ill and confused. And Phoebe wasn't cold and distant—she was a stepmother who cared for him more than he ever realized.

"I've already figured out what I'll tell your dad. I'm sure he'll worry, but if he's mad, I'll take the blame." Phoebe motioned toward a satchel in the raft. "I packed provisions and extra water. Also an emergency beacon in case things go wrong. And promise to be back within two sols, or I'll send out a search party. Stay close."

He swallowed around a lump in his throat as he nodded. "Of course. I wasn't planning to go far to begin with. I…" He studied his stepmother's face. Her pale blue eyes were wide and filled with an emotion he couldn't place. Pride? Hope?

Love?

"I can't tell you how much this means," Enrique whispered.

"You're welcome." She smiled, holding her arms out. "I know we don't hug, but…"

Enrique chuckled as he leaned in to embrace her. She wrapped her arms around his back and he relaxed against her. He couldn't remember the last time someone had held him like this. His father occasionally slung an arm over his shoulder, and Ravi and Oscar punched him in the arm every other sol. This was different. "I promise I'll come back."

Phoebe shifted and something cool and circular pressed against the side of Enrique's neck. He barely had time to register the sensation before the sting of an injection replaced it.

His vision blurred and his muscles went slack. He lost control over his body as Phoebe lowered him over the edge of the raft.

"No, you won't," his stepmother said as Enrique's vision faded to black.

Chapter Thirty-Six

*A*ria tapped her fingers against the edge of the console as she watched the bar creep toward the hundred percent mark.

She shifted her weight from leg to leg, feeling a twinge in her shins each time she pressed down into the heel of one of her feet. The anesthesia was wearing off, but it didn't matter. She would be back in the water soon.

Ninety-eight.

Just under eighty minutes remained on her countdown clock. It would take at least an hour to swim back to the exit hatch. That left less than twenty minutes to finish downloading the information and pilot the shuttle back to the sea. A weight settled in the pit of Aria's stomach. She wasn't sure she had enough time.

Ninety-nine.

She went over the exit strategy in her head. It

wouldn't take long to return the shuttle. Once she was in the water, she would head straight for the hatch, and she could put this place behind her forever.

One hundred.

Aria cheered as the screen flashed the words *transfer complete*. She pulled the data stick out of the console and tucked it back into her waist pouch. Before she zipped it back up, she thought to grab a ration so she would have the energy to swim the ten kilometers back to the exit hatch.

As she felt around in the pouch, her fingers brushed against a cool metallic cylinder. The memory disrupter. A twinge of guilt twisted her stomach. She had no way of knowing what kind of mess she was leaving for Enrique to work through. What would happen if he tried to talk to the real Zora about what happened today? She should have modified his memories and sent him on his way back at his house.

She shook away the thought as her fingers grasped one of the ration pods. It was too late to change things now. She had a mission to complete.

"Is it all done?" Reed asked as Aria popped the ration into her mouth.

"Yep," she said as she zipped the pouch and started back toward the hangar bay. With the drug wearing off, she moved down the passage faster than she had when she arrived. The pain was tolerable—less intense than it had been while she trekked over the island. She didn't want to think of what it would be like when the anesthesia wore off completely.

"Perth is still pretty out of it. Conscious, but barely. He's still interfacing with the Colony's systems."

Aria struggled to swallow the ration pod. "Well, that's good, right?" She winced. Labeling this situation "good" felt cold, but if the alternative was being discovered before she could get out—or not being able to get through the exit hatch—she would have to accept Declan's current state.

"What I'm saying is he won't be able to fly you back to where the shuttle was hiding," Reed said. "The good news is these things are pretty easy to fly. I can talk you through it."

Aria entered the hangar bay. The shuttle sat with its main hatch open, just as she left it. She limped inside and closed the opening before taking a seat in the pilot's chair. She blew out a breath. "I'm here."

Her fingers trembled as she followed the steps Reed laid out. She'd never piloted anything more complicated than a DuoCraft, but with just over seventy minutes left before the streams came back online, she was willing to try anything. She needed to get the data back to Withers so Alonzo could go free.

"Last thing before you get this bird in the air," Reed said. "Turn on the HUD."

Aria stared at the controls in front of her. "The…"

Reed sighed. "HUD. Head-up display. It puts information on the front window so you don't have to look down. When you start the engine, say, 'enable HUD.'"

"Easy enough," Aria muttered as she pressed the green ignition button. When the engine started without protest, she sighed with relief. Whatever hack Declan did to override the need for the ignition chip was still active. "Enable HUD."

Data readouts flashed on the front window.

"All right, Reed. What's next?"

"Remove the docking clamps and put your hand on the control stick. Once you're in the air, you'll fly out of the hangar bay and out of the caldera."

Aria struggled to swallow as she followed Reed's directions. Declan had taken care of all this remotely on the way in and she couldn't help wishing he were conscious enough to do it again now.

Her stomach swooped as the transport dipped when the clamps released. She hesitated before nudging the control stick forward. When the whole transport jerked, she yelped and released the lever.

"Ayers, what's going on?"

She gulped. "I don't know if I can do this. It's not like driving a Duo."

"You've got to," Reed said.

"I know, I know," she sighed. "Withers wants this data."

"Well, yeah, but that's not the reason. If you stay there, eventually you'll starve and die. I've learned people can find the strength to do most anything when the other option is death."

Aria flinched at the stark reality of the situation, but Reed was right. She closed her fingers around the control stick again. "All right. Tell me what to do."

She tried not to watch the countdown on her comm as she followed Reed's instructions. After easing out of the ship's hangar, she engaged the thrusters to boost herself up over the caldera's wall. She hovered there for a moment, staring out over the landscape below. Daylight was fading, and the dusk sky, though simulated by Agency tech, was lovely. A handful of lights dotted the settlement on the north side of the island. She wondered where Enrique was now.

"Are you out of the caldera?" Reed asked, jolting her back to reality.

"Yeah. Yeah, I'm ready for the descent."

"Now's the easy part. It's like a slide. Just go down, keeping yourself as low as you can without hitting the trees."

She snorted. Sure, easy. But since the alternative was hovering above the caldera forever, she gritted her teeth and eased the shuttle forward, slowly at first. By the time she traveled a few dozen meters, the transport seemed to have developed a mind of its own.

"I'm going to crash!" Aria gritted her teeth, gripping the control stick hard enough to turn her knuckles white with effort.

"You won't crash," Reed said. "At least, I don't think so."

The HUD displayed the craft's altitude, and Aria tried to focus on the numbers instead of the proximity of the tree tops as the shuttle zipped by. The sea loomed dark and foreboding in the waning daylight.

"You need to adjust course. Two degrees to your left."

Aria nudged the stick to the left and held her breath. She was sure the HUD blazed the information somewhere, but she didn't trust her piloting ability enough to even search for it. "Am I good now?"

"Close enough," Reed muttered.

Aria swallowed. The shuttle streaked toward the shoreline and she fixed her gaze on a spot in the water. Was that thirty meters out? It was difficult to tell this high up.

"Ease back on your speed," Reed said. "Don't want you flying past the coordinates."

Aria did as Reed instructed, her stomach jolting as the craft slowed to a crawl.

"Seriously, Ayers? A little faster than that."

She adjusted the speed again and corrected her altitude to follow the slope of the volcano. The initial adrenaline of flying ebbed from her system and she exhaled. Maybe this wasn't so unlike piloting a DuoCraft after all.

"Almost to the water," Reed murmured.

Aria snorted. As if she couldn't see that for herself. "Thanks for—"

The rest of her words were lost as a shockwave of pain rushed through her legs and settled into a swirling knot in the pit of her stomach. Her arm jerked sideways, tugging on the control stick and sending the shuttle veering off course.

"What happened? Pull up, Ayers! Pull up!"

Reed's words barely registered, but his panic forced Aria's eyes open. She pulled up on the stick to avoid crashing into a towering pine, but she was sure she heard the scrape of its boughs against the underside of the vessel.

"You're off course. Circle right. What's going on?"

Aria swallowed back a howl as she turned the shuttle around. The searing pain in her legs didn't ebb. She tore her eyes from the HUD for a quick glance down to assure herself her legs weren't on fire.

"Still with me, Ayers?"

"Yeah," she grunted. "Where am I aiming?"

As if it had been waiting for her to ask, the HUD changed, displaying two green lines on the left and right side of the screen that converged on a point in the distance. Aria adjusted course to keep the target in the middle of her screen.

"You've got to turn… Oh, wait. You're good. You're on course now."

She was sure he had questions, but all her effort went to keeping on target. She feared if she broke concentration to speak, the pain would overtake her again.

As she glided over the water, she slowed the shuttle. The target on screen grew larger and larger as she neared it until the circle glowed green with a white X in the center. She hovered in place, not sure what to do. "I'm here."

Reed released a shaky chuckle before leading her through landing procedures.

Aria held her breath as the water crept higher and higher over the HUD, enveloping her in darkness lit only by a handful of instruments in the shuttle.

The craft sank lower and lower until it jolted against the sea floor.

Aria cried out as the vibrations rolled through her body, intensifying the throbbing in her legs.

"Ayers? You're making me nervous."

She gritted her teeth. "Pain block is wearing off."

"Deimos," he muttered. "I thought that would buy you more time."

Aria snorted. "You and me both."

"Can you get into the airlock? You've got about seventy minutes to make it back. It took you an hour to swim from the edge of the dome to shore on your way in, and you're coming at it from a different angle this time."

She swiveled her chair around and tried to stand, but putting weight on her feet brought tears to her eyes. The answer was no, she couldn't make it into the airlock. Her legs were worse than useless; they were an active liability.

Aria closed her fingers around the pouch at her waist. Staying here wasn't an option—not within the boundaries of the Colony and certainly not in this shuttle.

"Yeah, I can make it."

She attempted to brace herself on the wall to get her feet under her, but bearing weight elicited a scream she couldn't swallow. Reed didn't comment, for which she was thankful.

Steeling herself, she slid out of the chair and smashed onto the floor below. Crawling on her elbows and forearms, she crept forward, centimeter by centimeter, until she reached the ladder. She sat and reached for the highest rungs her fingers could close around. With all her strength, she heaved her body upward. Her muscles ached and burned as she reached for another rung, and another, until her legs dangled below her. But there was still so far to go.

She stretched for another rung, but her grip faltered, leaving her dangling by one hand. A fall from this height wouldn't be dangerous, but she didn't know if she could recover from it.

"I don't think I can do this."

"You've got to, Ayers."

Tears leaked down Aria's face. "It's too far."

"No, it's not," Reed said.

"You don't know!" she snapped. Her grip on the

rung loosened, the fingers of her left hand rubbing against the metal. "You're sitting in a boat. I'm the one in here, alone, with a piece of abandoned tech in my head."

"Think about his face," Reed said, his voice even. "Your brother. Alonzo, isn't it? How far would you go to save him?"

Aria's grip slipped again, but she swung her right hand up to help bear her weight. How far would she go to save Alonzo? Around the world. To the moon. To Mars.

In a way, she had already made it to Mars. Now she had to make her way back.

With a scream that echoed off the shuttle walls, she pressed her right foot onto a rung and pushed herself upward. Her shin and femur felt like they were shattering into a million pieces, but she didn't stop. She reached for the next set of rungs with her hands while propelling herself upward on her left foot.

Blackness encroached on her periphery and a wave of nausea threatened to flip her insides out, but she pushed forward again. And again. And again.

No sooner was the airlock door closed beneath her than she collapsed onto it with a thud. Sweat beaded her brow and her stomach roiled, but she had made it.

Using the rungs for support, she pulled herself onto her knees and released the airlock on the other side. She sighed with relief as the icy water rushed in, soothing against her skin.

She typed a message into her wrist comm as the water surged around her. *On my way.*

Kicking to propel herself through the water still sent shockwaves through Aria's body, but they were only mild irritations compared to the agony of bearing her body's weight.

"I sent the coordinates of the escape hatch to your comm," Reed said. "Follow the path and you'll be there before you know it."

Aria glanced at the device on her wrist. An arrow blazed across the screen, pointing her home.

"I have to cut comms now. We've already been on too long and there's no telling when the Agency will start monitoring the Colony again. I'll check in with you again in half an hour."

A beep sounded in her ear as Reed shut down the link. She turned her comm's flashlight on its lowest setting to dispel a degree of darkness surrounding her. The weak glow made her feel as if she were swimming along in her own bubble galaxy amid an infinite universe of black.

Except she wasn't alone.

A droning buzz reverberated through the water, so familiar she was convinced she was imagining it. There were no motored boats on the Colony, but the hum was unmistakable.

The sound only got louder as she swam. Whatever it was, she was drawing nearer to it.

Her muscles tensed. Although Aria was several

meters under water, if someone were on the surface above, they might see the glow of her light.

She was about to switch it off when the sound stopped. She paused, floating in place. Ten seconds passed before the drone started up again, the pitch higher, as if suddenly unencumbered.

Aria exhaled as the sound drifted farther and farther away. Whatever it had been, it was gone now.

She shook herself. The threat had passed and she was wasting time. She checked her wrist comm to reorient herself, but before she could continue, a splash near the surface drew her attention. Her first thought was a bird diving for a fish, except it was much too large a sound for any bird she'd ever seen, and there were no birds here.

The object kept falling.

Aria glanced at the timer on her wrist comm. Sixty-eight minutes. She needed to get going. But something wasn't right here—she could feel it in her bones.

She turned up her flashlight's intensity and caught sight of a figure dropping through the water. It was sinking fast, as though tethered to an anchor.

Not *it*. *Him*.

Aria would have recognized the outline of his body even if she hadn't just spent all day by his side.

Enrique.

She had no idea what was happening or why—all she knew was, without her help, Enrique Martinez would die. The weight he was tethered to continued to drag him down. She knew what Reed would say—that she had to get out, no matter what. She couldn't be discovered once the streams came back online.

But she couldn't leave Enrique like this.

Without giving herself a moment to change her mind, she dove for him. She aimed for his legs and grabbed hold of the rope, halting the downward progress of the weight.

The loop around his ankle was loose and she tried to pull it off him, but it caught around his shoe. Using her teeth to pull the knot out of the laces, she loosened the shoe and wrenched it off his foot. After the second try, she eased the rope over his heel and released it, allowing the anchor to continue its descent.

Enrique bobbed in the water above her. Kicking her legs brought a new stab of pain through her, but she ignored it, shouldering Enrique's body and propelling him toward the surface.

The scene above the water line was like a memory. The raft drifting several meters away lost pressure, slipping by degrees into the sea.

She shook her head. It was no use trying to figure out what was happening here. All she knew was she needed to get Enrique back to shore.

The island loomed dark and mysterious ahead, the outline of the volcano silhouetted by the last rays of sunlight. Aria focused on her breathing to distract herself from the constant stinging throb in her legs.

She clawed her way up the sand bar to the shore,

dragging Enrique behind her. "Just a little farther," she murmured.

The world tilted around her. Every inch of her body felt like it was on fire. Her muscles stopped responding and she splashed backward into the water.

As her body convulsed, one word cut through the night.

"Zora?"

Chapter Thirty-Seven

*A*ria rocked back and forth, bobbing along on the surface of the ocean. The sun warmed every inch of her body as she relaxed on the deck of her DuoCraft.

Someone splashed water on her face, and she tried to summon irritation to lob at Alonzo for getting her wet.

Except Alonzo wasn't here. And she wasn't dry on her Duo, she was wet, still half submerged in strange water. The heat she mistook for sunlight ebbed, leaving her shivering. And the name that echoed again and again wasn't her own.

"Zora? What... I don't... What?"

Aria pried her eyelids open, blinking when darkness greeted her. She turned to Enrique, who eyed her with distrust. With fear.

"Who are you? *What* are you?"

Aria's hands moved to cup her neck, but she froze when the wan light from her comm washed over her arms. *Her* arms, not Zora's. The freckle pattern that had been barely visible back in the shuttle was clear against her pale skin.

"I can explain," she said, although what she would say remained elusive.

Enrique sprang backward, splashing at the water's edge as he put space between them. "You can talk? I thought you couldn't—except for the singing."

"Singing?" Aria shook her head. She wasn't sure what he meant, but there wasn't time to ask, so she continued. "Enrique, I'm sorry. I'm not who you think I am."

The truth tumbled out before she could stop it, and once she spoke it, she realized she didn't want it to stop. She knew the risk—not only to the mission, but to herself, to Alonzo. But she didn't want to lie to Enrique. She had already done enough of that.

He crouched a meter from the shore, water ebbing and flowing around his ankles. "Who else could you be? Where did you come from?"

"My name is Aria Ayers, and I came from out there." She pointed toward the invisible edge of the dome.

Enrique tilted his head. "Mars?"

"No. Earth." She sighed. "You're still on Earth."

His mouth opened, a thousand questions spinning behind his eyes.

She held up a hand. "I don't have all the answers. Someone sent me here to complete a mission—to get information off the spaceship. These people—they have my brother. And unless I do what they say, he'll die." Closing her eyes, she exhaled. "I'm sorry I lied to you. I wasn't supposed to interact with anyone, but I couldn't let you drown. Either time."

Enrique ran a hand through his damp hair, eyes round as he processed her words. "It was like you were two people because you *were* two people. *You* saved me last night, which is why Zora was dry when I saw her."

She shrugged off his realizations, not sure what he was going on about. There were more important things to address now. "Why were you out on the water again tonight?"

Enrique blinked, the confused look in his eyes replaced in an instant with one of anger. "Phoebe."

"Your stepmom?"

He stood, staring toward the shore. "She said she wanted me to have my adventure. But then she injected me with something."

"And she tied an anchor around your ankle." Aria's mind spun, but one explanation floated to the surface. "She knows." She pressed her hands to her forehead. "Of course she does. She was the mission commander, now she's in charge of security—in charge of keeping everyone here on the island. After your friends tried to take a joyride in the shuttle, she hid it underwater to make sure no one else could try because if they got too far, they'd figure out you're not where you think you are." She covered her mouth. "This is because of me. She thought you were trying to leave. Maybe she even figured out I wasn't Zora."

"She tried to kill me."

The weight of Enrique's words pressed on Aria's shoulders like a slab of concrete rubble. There was no other explanation for what she had intervened on. "I'm so sorry. I never should've let you help me."

"What am I supposed to do? I can't go home like nothing happened. I can't sit around waiting for her to try to kill me again." He paced back and forth in the surf, hands cupping the back of his head, muttering under his breath.

Aria followed his progress with her eyes. He was right. Even if he went straight home to tell his father what happened, there was no guarantee Santiago would believe him. With the cameras offline, he couldn't prove his version of events, so it would be his word against Phoebe's. Even if his father believed him and the rest of the Colony agreed to hold Phoebe accountable for her actions, there was no way of knowing whether Phoebe was the only one who knew the Colony's secret. If she had a partner, Enrique couldn't trust anyone. He would never be safe.

There was only one solution. "Come with me."

Enrique stopped, dropping his arms to his sides. "What?"

Aria shifted in the water to get her legs under her.

She braced for searing pain when she put weight on them, but it didn't come. Her muscles were weak and shaky, but it was a welcome reprieve after what she had been enduring. Declan had guessed the leg pain was because Zora was taller than she was. Now that Aria was back to looking like herself, the pain was gone.

"You're not safe here anymore," she said. "Come with me."

He threw up his hands. "Where? Back to Earth?"

"Aren't you listening? We're *on* Earth." She pointed out over the water. "The world you thought you left behind is ten kilometers that way. Let me take you there."

Enrique stared out toward the indigo horizon, jaw set as he considered the offer. He closed his eyes and exhaled before fixing his gaze on Aria. "Let's go."

She glanced at the countdown on her wrist comm. Sixty-three minutes. "We don't have much time before the streams come back online. Can you find something small that floats. I don't want you getting exhausted on the way."

He nodded. "I'm sure there's something in the emergency bunker. I'll be right back."

Aria watched Enrique's retreating back until he disappeared into the trees. She couldn't believe what was happening. Enrique was coming with her. Never, not even in her most intricate fantasies, had she ever considered Enrique being part of her everyday life. All her daydreams revolved around her making her way to

Mars, of them exploring the alien terrain and taming the new planet.

She rubbed absently at her ear comm. It was a good thing Reed wasn't listening in at the moment. She could only imagine what his reaction would be. But what did he expect her to do? She couldn't leave Enrique here.

Withers wouldn't be pleased either, but it didn't matter. Aria completed the mission. She got the data the doctor wanted. Withers would have to hold up her end of the bargain and release Alonzo.

Aria's mind whirled with lists. Enrique would need some kind of disguise before he could go out in public. He had one of the most recognizable faces on Earth. Aria could take Enrique to New LA and dip into her savings to afford some modifications to change his appearance just enough to keep people from stopping him in the street to tell him he looked just like Enrique from the Colonists.

A twig snapped amid the pines, drawing Aria's attention. She smiled when Enrique appeared between branches, but her relief was short lived.

Phoebe stood behind him, one hand gripping the back of his shirt, the other pressing a stunning device to the back of his neck.

Panic flooded Aria. Her first instinct was to dive into the water, but she couldn't leave Enrique alone. And even if she could reactivate the tech in her neck, it was too late. Phoebe could already see her true form.

A cruel smile twisted Phoebe's lips as she forced Enrique forward. "You're the girl who's been masquerading as Zora Korbel, I presume."

"Let him go." Aria tried to swallow, but her throat went dry. She wasn't sure what the device Phoebe held would do, but she was positive its effect wouldn't be good.

"I don't know how you got here or who you're working for, but I can't let you leave," Phoebe said.

A shiver ran down Aria's back. She couldn't let Aria leave, but she couldn't let her stay, either.

"You tried to kill me," Enrique said, his voice tight as he took forced steps forward. "Then, what? You were just going to go home to my dad like nothing happened? How could you do that?"

Phoebe adjusted her grip on Enrique's shirt. "It's my responsibility to make sure no one finds out the truth. My loyalty is to the Agency. It always has been. You and your father? You were means to an end. The standards set by the international council for the first group of colonists meant that if I was going to come, I needed a husband and child. Your father had the right skillset, and he's easy to manipulate." She nudged him forward. "Like father, like son."

"Let him go." Aria held her hands up in surrender. "You don't have to hurt either of us. Let us leave. You can still say Enrique died trying to explore another island or whatever cover story you were going to tell the others. And we'll both be gone."

Phoebe chuckled. "I'm not a fool, child. There's no way you're working alone. You came here for a reason, and I can't let you leave with any evidence this colony isn't what everyone believes it to be."

Aria's heart hammered against her chest. Her fingers twitched as she considered her options. She could dive into the water and swim to freedom. But if she brought the information back to Withers and saved Alonzo, how could she live with herself knowing the fate she left Enrique to? But then, if she gave up the data stick, she might save Enrique, but Alonzo would still be in danger.

Phoebe shoved Enrique another step closer, and his foot caught on one of the rocks littering the beach, making him stumble. His stepmother kept a firm grasp on him as his knees collided with the ground, yanking him backward so he looked like a prisoner awaiting execution.

Aria held one hand out toward Phoebe while the other grasped the zipper on her pouch. There was only one option.

"I'll give it to you," Aria shouted. "Don't hurt him. Let him come with me, and I'll give you the data stick."

Phoebe eyed her with mistrust. "How can I be sure you don't have more than one copy?"

Aria reached into the pouch and felt around for the device. "Search me if you want. But you and I both know time is running out before the streams start up again. Have you thought about how you'll explain me being here?" Her fingers brushed against a cool cylinder and she folded it into her palm.

The older woman's face pinched as she weighed her options.

Aria pulled the device from the pouch and held her fist out to Phoebe. "Do we have a deal?" She fit her thumb against the button on the back of the cylinder and pressed it as she took a step forward.

A smile curved Phoebe's lips. "Fine. But you hand it over first. Then I'll let the boy go."

Enrique caught Aria's eye as she took another step forward. "What are you doing? What about your brother?"

"I'll figure that out," Aria said. "Don't worry."

She swallowed as she took another step toward Phoebe. The device in her hand vibrated and she relaxed her thumb against the smooth depression in its back.

"Tuck it into my shirt pocket," Phoebe said.

Aria nodded. Her whole body trembled, but with fear or anticipation, she wasn't sure. Another step brought her so close to Enrique she could feel the heat radiating off his body. But most importantly, it brought her close enough to Phoebe.

Holding the device level with Phoebe's eyes, Aria pressed the button in back and a blue flash lit up the older woman's face. Her expression contorted into a mask of rage, but only for a second. By the time the light shut off, Phoebe's mouth was slack, her eyes glassy.

Both arms went limp, and she dropped the stunner to the ground.

Enrique sprang to his feet, putting distance between himself and his stepmother. "What did you do?"

Aria didn't answer Enrique's question. She crouched down to pick up the stunner and pressed it back into Phoebe's hand. "Put this back where you found it. Today was normal. Like all the days before it. And now you're tired, so you're going to go home and go to sleep."

Phoebe nodded before turning and making her way up the beach toward the bunker.

Enrique gaped. "What did you do? What is that thing?"

"It doesn't matter. There's no time." Aria didn't have to look at the countdown on her wrist comm to know she had to leave now if there was any chance of getting back before the streams turned on. She would have to swim at top speed—or as fast as was possible with her muscles feeling like jelly.

He drew closer, brushing his knuckles along her upper arm. "By my count, that's three times you've save my life in less than a sol. I'd say I hope I can return the favor, but to be honest, I'd rather not be in any more life-or-death situations anytime soon."

She did her best to force a smile, to meet his eyes, but she couldn't.

He took another step, standing so close his presence

seemed to fill the whole world. "I don't know how to thank you, Aria."

The sound of her name on his lips broke something loose within her. She wished she could stop time and live in this moment forever, but such an act was beyond her.

She dragged her gaze up to meet his and her breath caught when she saw the intensity in his eyes. He looked at her like so few ever had—like he didn't just acknowledge her presence, but he truly *saw* her.

The clock ticking in the back of her mind stilled and she abandoned herself to the moment, allowing herself to live in that look, in the way it made her feel. Her skin sparked and tingled with anticipation as Enrique moved closer still. A constellation of fireworks exploded where his fingertips grazed her jaw.

She closed her eyes as his soft lips pressed against hers, tender but urgent. Her left hand came to rest on the back of his neck while her right one continued to clutch the cylinder—each point connected to a different reality she must choose between.

Enrique broke the kiss and took a half step backward, his mouth twisting like he was trying to smile. "Sorry. I… I really wanted to do that."

Aria exhaled, shoulders slumping as tears stung her eyes. She had imagined this moment countless times. Now she was here with Enrique before her, *seeing* her, wanting to leave his life behind. It was everything she had ever dreamed.

"At least one of us will remember it."

The cylinder vibrated and she lifted it until it was level with Enrique's eyes. She pressed the button and the blue light illuminated his bewildered face.

Gulping, she stowed the device and zipped her pouch before splashing into she sea and diving below the surface, leaving Enrique alone on the beach, none the wiser she existed.

Chapter Thirty-Eight

*C*alix Reed's stomach knotted with apprehension as he waited for the comm link with Aria to initiate. There were only ten minutes before the streams were back online, and based on their last conversation, she should be at the hatch waiting for the unlock code.

With Declan out of commission, Calix hadn't been able to rely on his skills to check for the code, so he had spent the time since he broke contact with Aria combing through data. The process was so tedious he had been tempted to give Declan another mini dose of the drug, but his earlier assessment still stood. He wasn't sure how much more Declan's body could handle. And while he wasn't fond of his companion, he didn't share Dr. Withers' opinion about individuals being inherently disposable.

A tone chimed from the invisible wall against which Declan's right hand remained pressed, and Calix sighed with relief. "Ayers, you with me? Are you at the door?"

He tapped the side of the tablet on his lap, drumming out a beat with his fingertips. Five seconds passed. Ten. A list of problems ordered itself in Calix's head, along with possible solutions.

Fifteen seconds.

It had been too risky sending Aria in alone. She wasn't trained. She was just a kid whose aberration matched what Withers needed. And while his boss believed fear as motivation was adequate to accomplish most tasks, Calix didn't underestimate the importance of understanding and discipline.

Twenty seconds.

"Ayers?"

The sound of splashing water filtered through the speaker. "I'm here."

Relief flooded Calix, followed by a wave of concern. While she was on the shuttle, the agony Aria was experiencing had been clear in her voice, but now there was a different quality lacing her tone. Exhaustion. "What's wrong?"

"It's just… It's getting hard to swim. This water… It's different from what I'm used to. It's wearing me out."

Calix set his tablet on the starboard bench and leaned against the side of the boat, squinting off into the darkness where the entrance point to the Colony should be. While he hadn't been part of the team who worked on modifying the tech now attached to Aria's brainstem, he had overheard plenty of talk from those assigned to the project. "Ayers, listen—this is important. Are you feeling tired, or are you feeling like you can't control your body?"

"What's the difference?"

He sighed. The difference was whether or not she got out of the Colony alive, but he didn't say it. "Just... keep swimming. You've got to be close now."

"Heading... Heading back underwater."

Calix banged his palm against the side of the boat. Withers had assured him the team had fixed whatever part of the chip's programming was causing people to seize and become unresponsive. And maybe she believed they had. As far as he knew, Aria held the record for longest use of the chip. Still, he itched to remove it as quickly as possible. He was glad he had insisted on having the appropriate equipment on board. Even if the ETA for the atmo-shuttle to pick them up was within thirty minutes, he didn't know if Aria could wait that long.

His wrist comm buzzed with a ping from Aria. *Code?*

He exhaled with relief. This was it—the home stretch. The mission was almost over. "Try seven-nine-eight-four-two."

Calix counted the seconds until he heard a metallic thud and the groan of a hinge resisting opening. Several more seconds elapsed before his wrist comm vibrated again. *In.*

He stared off into the blackness, imagining he could pick out her location within the shielded dome. She would make it. Withers would have the information she needed and her plan could move forward. And although the mission hadn't been without its difficulties, Ayers was on her way out. For her sake, he wished the chip had held out until she'd returned to the boat, but part of him was glad she was back to looking like herself.

The mechanical hum of the pumps pushing the water out of the airlock ceased, pulling Calix from his thoughts. "Ayers?"

"Yeah, yeah," she muttered.

More mechanical clunks echoed through the speaker and Calix assumed Aria was opening the inside door. "At least the walk through this time should be easier on you, right?" He checked the countdown on his comm. Seven minutes until the streams were back online. He gritted his teeth. He'd hoped they would've already been on their way back to the mainland by now, but at this moment he would take a win however they could get it. "You remember the way out? Ayers?"

Aria yelped and sounds of a crash echoed through the air. Calix cursed under his breath. He would give anything to have a feed on her, but Declan had reported on her way in that there were no cameras in the maintenance structure.

"What's going on?" His muscles coiled, but there was nothing for him to do besides stand here and wait.

"I... I can't feel my legs. Reed... I can't... I can't move them."

Calix cursed again, pacing the width of the ship. "How close are you to the outside hatch? Can you crawl?"

"I'm trying."

His stomach jolted at the desperation in her tone. When he reached the starboard side of the boat, he plunged his right arm into the water up to the elbow, testing the strength of the power lingering within him. He had been holding on so long already, he wasn't sure how much time he had. It wouldn't do either of them any good if he drowned trying to help her.

"Just a little farther, Ayers." He pulled his hand from the ocean and shook his arm to dispel most of the water. "You can do it. You got the information, and your brother's going to be fine. You just have to get out of there."

"I'm to the door," Aria reported, sounding breathless. "Code?"

Calix checked his tablet screen. "One-seven-six-five-nine."

Aria grunted on her side of the line and Calix clenched his fists, imagining the strength of his will was enough to get her into the airlock and through to the other side.

His wrist comm beeped. Four-minute warning.

The hum of pumps pushing water into the airlock rumbled through the speaker. "How much longer until it's filled?"

The hum droned on, but Aria didn't speak. Calix glanced at his comm, but no ping came through.

"Ayers? Tap your comm if you can hear me."

He held his breath as he waited for the hollow knock he'd grown accustomed to when she couldn't talk, but it didn't come.

"Ayers?"

His comm beeped again. Three minutes.

"Deimos," Calix muttered, kicking of his shoes as he pulled up the location of the maintenance hatch on his comm. "Phobos and Deimos." He placed one foot on the gunwale like Aria had done a day earlier. Sucking in a breath, he dove into the water.

The warmer surface water turned icy less than a meter in. Calix held his breath as he kicked his legs to propel himself deeper. The hatch was fifty meters below the surface, but his lungs burned less than a fifth of the way down.

Pain seared each side of his neck as the borrowed aberration took hold of his body. As he continued downward, he released the last of his pent-up breath and inhaled the briny seawater. Instead of choking on it, the liquid filtered through the newly-sprouted gills behind his ears.

He consulted the arrow on his comm and altered his course until a pale blue light shone through the black gloom of the water. When he was near enough, he grabbed hold of the handle to the right of the keypad and punched in the same sequence he recited to Aria. A hollow thunk thudded through the water as the door unlocked.

He pulled open the door to reveal the airlock, bathed in white light. Aria floated motionless near the top of the space. Calix gripped her wrists and pulled her out before forcing the door closed again.

Looping one arm beneath both of hers, he kicked against the side of the maintenance ring and dragged her toward the surface.

They were only halfway up when Calix's neck began to burn. It was what he had feared. Aria's aberration was ebbing from his system. But he had enough left to get them to the surface.

He had to.

He took in one last gulp of water before the gills disappeared and kicked with all his might toward the surface. He had to be almost there. Just one more stroke. Maybe two. He could do a third, surely.

Calix gasped as he broke the water's surface. He sucked in several lungfuls before turning his attention to Aria. The gills on the sides of her neck fluttered in the night air, useless. But the steady rise and fall of her chest indicated they had done their job when they were needed.

He adjusted his grip on Aria and swiped his wrist comm until he located a familiar contact.

Uma Withers answered his ping before the second tone ended. "Yes?"

"It's done," Calix sighed. "Have the team come get us."

Chapter Thirty-Nine

*P*ersistent beeping pierced through the fog in Aria's brain. How many times had she told Alonzo not to set an alarm if he wasn't going to turn it off?

Alonzo.

Aria's arms jerked, but they didn't move far. Something held them down. She tried several times to open her eyes before her eyelids obliged, scraping like sandpaper as they split apart.

The ceiling overhead was awash in a soft white glow. A screen to her left flashed numbers that didn't make sense while a machine on her right continued its intermittent beeps.

"She's up," called a familiar voice she couldn't place.

Aria tried to sit up but she was strapped down to a

narrow gurney. She shifted beneath it as if doing so might loosen the ties.

"Calm down." Calix Reed came into view, a look of mild irritation tightening his features.

Something clicked in Aria's mind. *He's the one who spoke earlier.* "Were you watching me?"

He shrugged as he set to work undoing the straps across her shoulders and waist. "Drew the short straw. Declan's in the room next door. They're getting his electrolytes back in balance, but he should be fine in a few hours."

She turned her head to look in the direction he indicated, but a dull ache in the back of her neck stopped her. She touched the spot only to find a tender raised ridge below her hairline.

"No complaints about how that scar looks." Reed crossed his arms over his chest. "You were in no condition to wait on the team on the atmo-shuttle to take that chip out, so you were stuck with me doing it."

Aria shook her head, the fog clearing enough for her to remember the last moments of the mission. She'd crawled into the final airlock but blacked out before the water filled the compartment. "Did you save me?"

Reed shrugged. "I couldn't leave you floating in the airlock. No one was supposed to know we were there."

Before she could thank him, he sprang away from the gurney as someone else entered the room. The door hissed closed.

Dr. Withers studied Aria, causing a wave of dread to crest in Aria's stomach. It didn't dissipate when Withers' lips twisted into a smile. "I'll admit, Miss Ayers, you had more trouble completing the mission than I anticipated."

Aria's throat went dry. She struggled to swallow, but Withers didn't seem to require a response.

"However, you were also more resourceful than I would have imagined." Withers circled around the foot of the gurney and approached the screen on the back wall. "Not only did you bring back the information, everything on the Colony seems normal."

Withers tapped the screen and the image changed from medical readouts to a set of familiar faces. Ravi Patel, Jade Osborn, Shira Maddox, and Gabe Tremblay tipped their heads back in laughter as they sat around a table at the farm station.

Aria's breath caught as the angle switched to show Enrique. A smile stretched itself across his face as he tossed a corner of his roll at Ravi.

Withers turned off the stream. "As if you were never there. Exactly as I instructed."

Aria tore her eyes from the blank screen. After what happened with Phoebe, Aria should be happy Enrique was alive, but thinking of him opened a gaping hole in the center of her chest. He didn't remember her. Although she knew it was for the best, the fact hollowed her out. "And Alonzo?"

Withers smiled again. "I was wondering when you'd

ask." She lifted her chin and Reed handed her a miniscreen from his belt holster.

The familiar ping tone sounded three times before it connected. Alonzo's face filled the screen, his expression pinched with worry that didn't fade when the comms linked.

"Aria? Are you okay?"

Her stomach twisted at the fear in his voice. "I'm fine. I'm…" She stopped short of telling him she was safe. While no longer in immediate danger as she'd been on the Colony, sitting in this featureless room with Dr. Withers standing over her made her feel trapped. "Where are you?"

Alonzo swiveled the screen to show off pieces of a room she knew as well as her own. "Some guy with perfect hair brought me home early this morning."

Aria glanced at Reed, who didn't meet her eyes. "What about Dad? What did you tell him."

A muscle in Alonzo's jaw jumped. "I told him what they instructed me to." The words came out like a growl. "Admitted to him we went to the selection center and that I got cut but you're still there."

She sighed. It would be weeks before her father let her hear the end of it for disobeying him. She vowed never to let him know he had been partially right about the centers. At least when the organizers learned about what she was, they hadn't added her name to a registry —or worse.

"Are you satisfied that your brother's safe?" asked Dr. Withers.

Aria blinked. "Am I…"

Withers turned to Reed. "That's enough."

Reed snatched the miniscreen from Aria's hand before she could react. Alonzo called out, but his voice was silenced in the middle of his word. As he attached the screen to its holster, Reed kept his gaze trained on the floor.

"What are you doing?" Aria demanded.

"Holding up my end of the deal," Withers said. "You got the information without ruining the illusion of the Colony. I let your brother go."

Aria rubbed at the tender spot on the back of her neck. "Thanks for making sure I healed up after having that tech in my head, but if you don't mind, I think I'll be going now." She stood, but Withers didn't back away. Gritting her teeth, Aria brushed past the doctor, but when she approached the door, it didn't slide open. She pressed her thumb to the panel, but the sensor buzzed and the light above it remained red. "Let me out of here."

Withers tilted her head, eyes squinting like she couldn't quite understand Aria's words. "My dear, our deal was for your brother's freedom, not yours. As I said, you've proven yourself more resourceful than I gave you credit for. That makes you useful."

Aria's skin prickled. "What's she talking about?"

She looked at Reed, but he only stared at a fixed spot in the corner of the room.

"You're not going home, Aria," Withers said. "Your skills and cunning make you far too valuable for me to allow you to squander your life waiting tables or salvaging old wrecks."

Aria's blood ran cold. Had Withers been researching her while she was on the Colony? "But I want to go home."

Withers chuckled. "We all want something, my dear. But sometimes the needs of the many outweigh the wants of the few." She crossed to the screen that had shown the Colony stream minutes earlier. After a few taps, a medical scan of a person from the shoulders up blinked to life. "Calix may have removed the tech that gave you Zora's appearance, but my medics put something in its place." She zoomed in on a spot in the center of the scan's neck. A small circle blazed white amid the spidery red veins and dark blue muscles. "If you try to run, we can find you."

Aria cupped the back of her own neck. "You put a tracker in me?"

The smile on Withers' lips broadened. "You're part of the rebellion now, Aria. Welcome to the Dolus Order." She crossed to the door and pressed her thumb to the sensor. It turned green and the door slid open. "From now on, you work for me."

Unfortunate Souls Series

A girl with a special ability. A secret mission. A truth that
will rock two planets to the core.

Speechless

Fearless

Hopeless

Restless

Clearwater Witches Series

Magic can be as dangerous as fire. Is dealing with witches
worth the consequences?

Crystal Magic

Wild Magic

Circle Magic

Moon Magic

Cursed Magic

Dark Magic

Christmas in Clearwater

Fate Bound Series

A werewolf's first instinct is to protect those weaker than himself. But Jack chose to protect the wrong girl.

Fate Bound

Death Marked

Soul Cursed

Destiny Sealed

The Naturals Trilogy

When only some are blessed with psychic abilities, should everyone else be forced to serve them?

Awaking

Seeking

Becoming

Shifted Series

Monsters live among us, and a select few exist to keep the world safe. Leigh Evans' life is forever shifted when she learns the truth.

Shifted

Tangled

About the Author

Madeline Freeman lives in the metro-Detroit area with her husband, her two kids, her dog, and her cats. She loves anything to do with astronomy, outer space, plate tectonics, and dinosaurs.

Connect with Madeline online
www.madelinefreeman.net

facebook.com/madelinefreemanbooks

twitter.com/writermaddie

instagram.com/madeline.freeman_author

Made in the USA
Las Vegas, NV
10 September 2021